CONNOR'S BRAIN

Connor's Brain
by Malcolm Rose

Published by Ransom Publishing Ltd.
Unit 7, Brocklands Farm, West Meon, Hampshire GU32 1JN, UK
www.ransom.co.uk

ISBN   978 178591 135 4
First published in 2016

CONNOR'S BRAIN

MALCOLM ROSE

Rans⚬m

For Kay
With thanks for her help.

I would also like to thank
Daniel L. Schacter for Searching For Memory,
Michael Paul Mason for Head Cases
and Paul Hoffman for The Man Who Loved Only Numbers.

All of the brain disorders in this book are taken from real cases but the
patients themselves are entirely fictional.

The excerpt on page 16 is from Funnybones
by Janet and Allan Ahlberg
Reprinted by permission of HarperCollins Publishers Ltd.
© Janet and Allan Ahlberg 1980

CHAPTER 1

Joy lost her childhood at the age of fourteen.

At the end of the summer term, she was tossed from a moving car like a bag of rubbish. Dazed, dumped and abused, Joy fell into the gutter under the railway bridge. She rolled onto her front, gagged and blacked out. A little blood ran from her forehead into the rainwater, making a pink puddle. The first passer-by hesitated only to take a photo of her on his mobile. The fifth passer-by hesitated, squatted down by her side and then called an ambulance.

Like other girls before her, Joy Patterson had been groomed, introduced to men, seduced by their glamorous lifestyle, fooled into thinking she was loved, passed around, paid with drink and drugs, exploited until she was soiled and spent, and finally discarded on a street in central Leeds.

Stripped of her innocence, she was second-hand, unwanted.

CHAPTER 2

Connor began his second life at the age of fifteen.

There were three people in the room. A man and a woman were holding hands on a sofa in the corner and a younger woman was sitting behind the desk. She was a funny colour. The couple looked sad and the dark woman was smiling in a serious sort of way. Connor could not recall any of them. His eyes were attracted more by the single red-topped volcano that poked out from the clutter on the desk.

The younger woman jumped up with a bright, 'Hello, Connor.' She was shorter than Connor but she seemed much more grown-up. While she ushered him to a seat at the side of her desk, she asked, 'Do you remember me?'

'Erm … '

'I saw you this morning. I'm Ranji Nawaz – the doctor looking after you from now on. You're going home today but, every other day, you'll come and spend some time here with me.'

'Oh.' Connor shuffled round on his seat to get nearer to the volcano.

The doctor leaned towards him and said in a friendly voice, 'Your mum and dad and I have been thinking about what to tell you, how much to tell you. In the end, we decided you should know everything, so I'm going to explain exactly what's happened to you. We think that's best.'

Connor drifted. He put out his hand and touched the velvety

top of the volcano. At the same time, he sniffed. 'Volcanoes smell.'

'Volcano. Yes,' Ranji said. 'We call it a *flower*, Connor. It's a nice smell and someone bought it for me because it's my birthday today.'

'Birthday.' Connor nodded uncertainly. He didn't know what she meant.

'If I'm going to tell you all about yourself, it's easiest to show you with pictures.'

She picked up a photograph and held it out so that Connor could see it. He was used to looking at pictures and trying to explain them, but this one was weird. There was no action to describe. He'd seen nothing like it before. It didn't seem to be anything – just a fantastic shape. It was all wrinkly and grey, like a partly deflated kicking ball. Finally losing interest in the volcano, Connor stared at the extraordinary image, in the same way that he would sometimes focus on clouds and find faces, animals and fierce monsters in their fragile forms.

'This,' Ranji said, 'is a normal brain. It's a sort of photograph of what's inside a head.'

'Wow,' Connor replied, suddenly enthusiastic. He stood up, put out his hand and ran his eels across the strange, wonderful picture. Then he clutched his own head. 'I've got hair and funnybone. No bottle. No see inside.'

For a moment, Ranji seemed puzzled. Then she said, 'I've got a special way of taking pictures through hair, skin and bone. I've got a really clever machine that doesn't need a window to see a brain. It can even take a picture of what's inside the brain. Like this.' She picked up a brain scan and showed it to him.

It was even weirder. Marbled grey with splashes of red and black. Even more like clouds. Storm clouds. Open-mouthed, Connor was enthralled.

'When I used the machine on you, Connor, I got a picture of what's inside your brain. Do you want to see?'

Connor nodded eagerly.

'Here it is.' She held it up next to the other picture.

When he gazed at it, Connor felt a warm shiver engulf his whole body. He had never felt anything like that before. Not that he could remember anyway. Awestruck, he placed a reverent eel on the shiny paper and traced the outline of the image, slowly and carefully. 'Mine,' he whispered. The picture enchanted and thrilled him. His hand came to rest by the black hole on one side. His brain was different. The normal one didn't have a hole. 'Mine's best,' he murmured slowly. 'Pretty shape.'

'Let me tell you as best I can what this pattern means.' Ranji took a deep breath. 'That hole means you have part of your brain missing, Connor. Your memory and most of the things you knew have gone, but you can learn quite a bit again. You know yourself you've already learned a lot. You've done really well. Come to the window.' She pointed at it and added, 'What you call a bottle.'

But Connor was still preoccupied with his brain scan. To distract him, Ranji took his hand and walked with him to the view over the city.

'Look down into the street. See? It's packed with cars. How fast do you think the cars are going? Do you know about speed?'

Now captivated by Ranji's hand, Connor exclaimed, 'You've got something on it.' He poked at the hard and shiny surface attached to her soft peel.

Ranji smiled. 'Yes. It's called a ring.'

Connor watched her take off the shiny yellow band and hold it out for him. She let it drop into his palm and he looked at it closely, turning it over and over. 'What's it for?'

'It's … a decoration really.'

'Decoration.' Connor closed his fist around it.

Behind him, the man who had not uttered a word, said, 'Give it back to Dr Nawaz now, Connor.'

Reluctantly, he held it out to her.

She said, 'Thanks,' and slid it back onto her eel. 'Look out of the window at the cars, Connor.'

They were three floors up from the road and, below them, the street was seething.

Connor muttered, 'Cars?' He had been shown photographs of cars, but he did not recognize them in the street. That was the wrong place for them. They belonged in pictures.

'Yes. They're called cars. People drive them to get from place to place.'

'What place? Where?'

'Some are going to work, some are going home, but do you know what speed they're doing?'

Connor shook his head vacantly. Again, he didn't know what she was talking about.

'They're going very slowly. Thirty miles an hour at most. But you know, people buy cars that'll go over a hundred miles an hour. A lot of those down there are very powerful. They can zoom – very fast – but here in the city they can only do thirty miles an hour.'

'Why?'

'Because of the crowds, because there's a law that says they mustn't go faster. That's the speed limit. So, they can't use all their power.' She walked him back to her desk and held up the scan of the normal brain. 'That's like a hundred-miles-an-hour brain, Connor. It's very powerful, but people with this type of brain don't use all its strength. Like cars that could go at a hundred miles an hour, they still stick to thirty. You, Connor, have a thirty-miles-an-hour brain. It won't go any faster. You have to accept that. But it means it'll work just as well as everyone else's, because they're not going at full speed. You've just got to learn how to use yours as best you can. Because it's a different sort of brain, it'll mean you'll do things in different ways. It'll take a bit of getting used to, but you'll get there.' She smiled at him again. 'What you need now is driving lessons.'

The woman was talking *to* him, not talking about him to the other people in the room as if he wasn't there at all. She spoke clearly, slowly – but not too slowly – and not too loud. She didn't treat him like an idiot. Even so, he could barely understand her words, but the picture … The picture was different. The picture of a no-zoom brain he could understand. He took it and clutched it against his chest as if it were a teddy bear. Indifferent to Ranji's word explanation, he asked, 'Why is your peel a funny colour?'

The quiet man interrupted. 'Connor, we don't … '

'It's all right,' Ranji cut in. 'It's because my family originally came from another country, a country where everyone has dark skin.'

Connor turned away from the nice woman who took pretty pictures and looked at the other two. 'Who are you?' he asked innocently.

The man's mouth opened hesitantly. 'We're your parents, Connor. Mum and Dad. You ate lunch with us a little while ago.'

Connor tilted his head to one side and gazed at them with curiosity. The man was big and his knuckles were white. His head peel was shiny with no hair, so he looked like a funnybone man. Strangely, the woman clutched a small piece of white cloth between both hands. She had bare legs, lines round her eyes and her hair was patchy – brown and grey.

'No,' Connor declared simply. 'Don't remember.'

CHAPTER 3

The holiday had everything: sun, sea, sand and suffering.

Straight after the end of the summer term, the Markham family had taken off for Barbados. It was like a fantasy. Acres of beaches and bodies. Everywhere there were bronzed bums, bared breasts, sunburn and bathing in breakers. And the herpes simplex 1 virus.

Actually, the theory was that Connor had picked up the virus back home. After all, most people carried the infection and spread it around through kissing, sneezing or coughing. Usually it was dormant inside a human body and didn't cause any harm. But overexposure to sunlight, stress and foreign food woke up the sleeping brute. When the germ erupted, the worst symptoms in most people were cold sores and the odd blister that would go away after a few days. In rare cases, though, the virus would hitch a lift to the brain in the blood stream. That's what happened with Connor. The tiny virus lodged in his left temporal lobe. Sensing the invisible invaders, Connor's body despatched white blood cells to confront, counteract and kill the infestation. But their arrival at the site of infection swelled his temporal lobe. Together, the virus and the swelling began to destroy the neurons that controlled memory and language.

Connor complained of a headache and developed a fever. His neck was stiff, sunlight burnt his eyes, his meal reappeared soon after he'd eaten it, and he got more and more drowsy and confused. When his headache shifted up several gears to unbearable, his mum and dad took him to the local hospital. There, the doctor muttered to herself, 'Encephalitis,' and suggested that they get themselves booked on a plane straightaway. 'He needs to be examined by a specialist in brain injury.'

'Is it serious?' Mrs Markham asked in a terrified voice.

'I can't say. It gives most victims a passing headache and that's all. It can be serious, though. I'm giving him something to attack the virus – acyclovir – and steroids to reduce swelling and inflammation in the brain.'

But the drug treatment was too late. Connor slipped into unconsciousness.

When he woke up in an English hospital, the breasts, bums, beaches and breakers had gone – and so had his left temporal lobe. Where it should have been, there was dead space. Nothingness. Connor's first life was reduced to sawdust. The hole left him without speech, literacy, memory, knowledge of himself and family, and without an appreciation of time. A heavy curtain fell between Connor Markham and his past.

Neither Connor's body nor modern medicine could repair that much damage. Connor's brain could not get back what it had lost. Instead, it began to cope by re-routing connections, taking a detour around the black hole. It was attempting the mother of all rewiring jobs to allow Connor to re-learn language and collect new memories. Connor's flawed and incomplete brain would struggle for the rest of his life. It would regain only limited power. But it would fight with every last neuron to manage. And it gave Connor an immense appetite for rediscovery.

Connor's mum and dad blamed themselves for this gaping emptiness in their son. After all, they'd opted for sunny Barbados. They'd persuaded Connor to go with them. They'd virtually insisted. Really, he'd wanted to stay at home so he could be with his girlfriend, Hattie. But three weeks on his own? His mum and dad feared what he'd get up to (mainly, what he'd get up to with Hattie) when he had the freedom of the house. Yet, whatever the mischief – with or without Hattie – it could never have been as serious, distressing and irreversible as the devastation inflicted on him by that vicious little virus. Between sobs, his mum muttered, 'If we hadn't forced him to go with us, we wouldn't have stirred up that bloody germ. Exotic food and heat stress!'

Unusual food and heat weren't the only sources of stress. Brad, Connor's younger and brighter brother, kept very quiet. He thought that Connor's illness could be *his* fault. He'd teased his brother about leaving Hattie. Again and again. 'Bet there's a load of sleep-overs back home. No idea who she'll be sleeping with.' 'Can't even call. The mobile charges are astronomical. Oh, I was forgetting. You lost your phone, didn't you?' It had seemed like fun to get hold of his brother's sensitive spot and squeeze it at every available opportunity. Then, when Connor had proved himself hopeless at working out Barbados dollars in a shop, Brad had also teased him about his incompetence with numbers. As far as maths was concerned, Connor had a thirty-miles-an-hour brain even in his pre-virus life. And Brad had rubbed it in. 'Just use your brain, Connor – if you can find it.' It was the last straw. Connor had let fly. There'd been an almighty row and an exchange of punches. Afterwards, the almighty virus had also let fly, knocking Connor out altogether.

The English doctor's words haunted Brad. 'You'd be surprised how little things can build up into substantial stress. And stress was probably the key.'

None of them knew that there was another reason why Connor was feeling stressed on holiday. They thought he wasn't his usual self because he'd been forced to leave Hattie behind, but he'd kept the real reason to himself.

The rest was down to bad luck. Connor could have got a mouth sore for seven to ten days, but instead he got a hole in the head for a lifetime.

CHAPTER 4

Kick-starting Connor's new life was not as simple as a slap on a baby's back.

Why were they all looking at him like that? He hadn't forgotten how to talk. Okay, the words left in his head weren't up to much, but there was no reason to look at him like that. He wasn't an idiot or anything. 'Da wals. A very lot da wals. Sprouts! A lot head sun.'

Eleanor, Connor's first speech therapist, read – no, she sang – from a book. Simple sentences spoken to the rhythm of a tapping pen. Sometimes she used the shell at the end of one of her eels to tap the table in time with her words.

> *On a dark dark hill*
> *there was a dark dark town.*
> *In the dark dark town*
> *there was a dark dark street.*
> *In the dark dark street*
> *there was a dark dark house.*
> *In the dark dark house*
> *there was a dark dark staircase.*
> *Down the dark dark staircase*
> *there was a dark dark cellar.*
> *And in the dark dark cellar …*
> *some skeletons lived.*

As she read, Connor looked at the pictures of the big skeleton, the little skeleton and the dog skeleton. He knew he was supposed to be following the words, but the pictures were much more fun. He giggled at the antics of the funnybone family. He laughed out loud. He laughed a lot. A very lot.

Five minutes after Eleanor finished and closed the book, Connor was fed up with twisting his shoestrings around his eels. He demanded, 'Funnybones!'

With infinite patience and unflagging optimism, Eleanor picked up the battered picture book and biro. She knew that Connor had already forgotten the story and the fact that she had just read it. He remembered only that he'd enjoyed it.

'More Funnybones!' He clapped his hands in excitement.

Eleanor pointed at the computer and said, 'You'll like this. Come and look.' Her patient was ready for vanishing cues training and recognition therapy, so she wanted to introduce him to computer games.

In front of the grey monitor, though, Connor yawned.

'It's like a television. It's going to show you some pictures.'

'Happy pictures?'

'Sure. It'll be fun.'

A splash of cartoon colour replaced the grey. 'Now, what have we got here?' said Eleanor, trying to entice her patient.

It was a heavy animal in a green field. It was brown and white with a serious face, a long straight back, four strong legs and a big dangling tail. Underneath it, at the bottom of the screen, the cue read *co_*. Connor stared at the animal but nothing inside him stirred. The computer let out a noise. A long dreadful noise. *Mooooo!* Connor jumped back in shock.

Eleanor smiled. 'It's a cow. Spelt c-o-w. See? I type in the last letter – w – and if it's right, the computer'll give me another picture.'

When Eleanor pressed the *enter* key, there was an explosion of bright lights and fantastic colours, and a short triumphant tune. The celebration was followed by another image.

'Sometimes, you get a completely different thing,' Eleanor told him. 'This time, it's almost the same as the last one. A black and white cow. But the clue's a bit harder. You've only got a *c*. You've got to add *o* and *w*. I'll do it this time, but watch and you'll soon get the hang of it.'

The screen erupted with another blast of colour and music when Eleanor completed the spelling.

Connor grinned when he saw the next drawing. Easy one. It was a boy. Short hair, legs apart, wearing leg things. Just like the picture on the toilet door. He looked rough and ready. Just like Connor imagined himself. The cue was *bo_*.

He knew this one. His eel hit the *y* thing to make up the word, *boy*.

The computer rewarded him with a fanfare and another splatter, as if someone had thrown multi-coloured paint against the monitor.

'Yeah!'

And he got another picture.

It was like the last one but different. This time, the cartoon person had long hair, legs together, wearing a skirt. Underneath, the cue read *gir_* . She looked sweet and innocent. Just like … No, the picture wasn't right. Wasn't happy. Connor didn't like it. He screwed up his face. Shuddering, he walked away moodily.

When he next dared to go up to the shiny screen, there was a different image. A happy one this time. A fish. A small orange funny fish with a smiley face. It wasn't just a skeleton like the fish in the funnybone zoo. It went under the water and it had got fizzes coming out of its mouth. 'Fish in fizzy drink.' Connor beamed. He liked the smiley fish. Using the letter pad, he added *t* to the cue, *fis_*, and waited for the fire colours and the fanfare. But they didn't come. The computer was unhappy with him. Stupid computer. He banged his fist on the table, stomped across the room, and shouted, 'Sprouts!'

At the bottle, he watched the white cloud shapes high in the sky and the brown leaves drifting in the wind. Eyes wide, he tried to trace the path of one particular leaf with his eel on the glass.

It was something called an audio book. Connor had to try and follow the spoken sentences in the book, but it was hard and daft. If someone was saying the story out loud, he didn't need to read it as well, did he? Instead, he sat in front of the audio thing and watched the digital time transforming one number into the next. It was much more interesting than the out-loud story.

Eleanor could not prise him away from the audio player, so she let him sit there happily, obsessively. When the first story ended, Connor called for more straightaway. She knew it wasn't the narrative that fascinated him, but she set up another anyway. When the next story began, something remarkable happened. Above the rhythmic recorded voice, Connor suddenly began to recite what he saw.

'Nought, one, two, three, four, er ... six, seven, eight, nine, nought, one, two ... '

Eleanor was amazed. Astounded. Stunned. She rose to her feet and simply stared at her patient.

'Four, fi ... , six, seven, eight, nine ... '

She'd hardly started to reintroduce him to numbers. Yet he knew them. He'd remembered! Recovering from the shock, delighted, she made an immediate note of Connor's unexpected triumph in his diary.

Glued to that digital display with figures dissolving and reforming, Connor carried on counting. 'Eight, nine, nought, one, two, three, four, fire ... '

Sitting next to Connor at the table, Eleanor pointed at the monitor and said, 'Take a look at that, Connor, and tell me what you make of it.'

Connor had shaken the bits and pieces out of a pencil case and was making yet another pretty pattern out of them. With a sigh, he stared at the picture and ran his hands over it, as if he could feel the people in it. His eels came to a stop on the left-hand side. 'There's a white ... thing.'

'A post, or wooden frame, painted white.'

'Yeah. A white thing in the ... ' His eyes flicked to the carpet as he searched for a word. 'In the floor. It's got ... ' He pointed to the curtains dangling either side of the bottle.

'Nearly. A net.'

'There's a big ball by it.'

'A football. Good.'

'There's a man by the white thing. He's standing up. He's got no … ' Connor's hand went to his jeans and yanked on the denim. 'Leg things.'

'Trousers. That's right. He's wearing shorts. Look at his top. What would you call it?'

'His head.'

'No,' Eleanor said with a smile. 'I mean, his clothes.'

His shirt blazed with colour. 'Yellow and dark and … ' Fascinated by the man's face, Connor's eel rested on the man's head. 'He's an angry man.'

'He sure is. He's got his hands on his … ?' Eleanor prompted.

Connor looked annoyed. He couldn't remember the word for hips, so he ignored Eleanor's question.

At the other side of the photograph, there was another man in no-leg-things. He was powerfully built. 'This man's running away. His arms are … ' Mimicking the man, Connor raised his arms in celebration. 'I can't see his … ' Connor looped his eel around his own face.

'Very good. His name's Liam. You know him. What do you think's happened here, Connor? What does it mean?' After a few seconds of silence, she added sympathetically, 'Can you make sense of it?'

Stupid question. Ridiculous question. Impossible question. He liked pictures but he hated that stupid question she always asked. 'What does it all mean?' Nothing. It's just a photograph. A picture of things. Nice things, bad things, colourful things, big things, little things, living things, dead things, very lots of things. That's what photographs are. Pictures of things. There was no sense in the question and there was no sense in a photograph of things. Stupid, stupid, stupid. Sprouts! Grumpily, he kicked the box of dominoes at his feet across the room. Then he shouted, 'It just is. That's all.'

'Liam's scored a goal,' Eleanor told him, ignoring Connor's tantrum. 'Look. Here's another. You're in it.'

'Me?' He looked back at the monitor.

'Yes. See? That's you, saving a penalty. It's from your team's website. This one,' Eleanor said as she tapped the keyboard, 'shows you getting an award at the end of the season. Everyone voted you the team's best player.'

Connor shook his head. He wasn't denying what he saw. The picture and the presentation simply didn't mean anything to him.

Connor had stacked one, two, three, four, five, six dominoes when Eleanor interrupted him with a question. Pointing to the tiles, she said, 'Do you remember we played dominoes today?'

'I win,' Connor replied, with the seventh domino in his hand.

Eleanor knew that Connor was merely guessing. He was giving her an answer that she wanted to hear. He didn't really remember the game, but he *had* won, so she said, 'That's right. It was a few minutes ago. What else did we do today?'

'Don't know.'

Eleanor smiled. 'Think about it.'

Showing her the domino, he said, 'I want to be an ant.'

'You can be busy again when you've answered me. What else did you play with?'

Connor sighed loudly. 'Picture shapes?'

Another guess. 'That's right,' she said again. 'A jigsaw. Well done.' It had taken them all morning to put the picture together. 'What did we do first, Connor? Jigsaw or dominoes?'

Connor shrugged.

He wasn't just distracted. He really didn't know. The sequence of games had disappeared into the black hole of his memory. 'How long did it take to do the jigsaw?' she asked.

Bored and unable to answer, he reached up and placed the domino against the soft shell of her face. He ran it down her cheek and neck and over the smooth clothes on her shoulder. Curious, he held it against her spongy breast.

Eleanor stepped back and said gently, 'No.'

'Not happy with me.'

'No. It's okay. I'm not angry or anything,' she replied. 'It's just that we don't touch there. Not you and me.'

'Why not?'

Eleanor sat down. 'That's a hard question, Connor. You see, we think of some places on the body as private. You know what I mean by private? A place we keep to ourselves or only share with the ones we love.'

'Love?' Pointing to her bust, he added, 'Why there?'

'I guess it's because they're to do with reproduction. That means having babies. You know, children. It's all about love as well.'

'How do you have babies?'

'I'm quite happy to talk about it, Connor, but I think I'd best see your mum and dad first. Perhaps they'd want to talk to you about it rather than me.'

'But I ... '

Suddenly coming back to Connor's side, Eleanor said, 'How many dominoes do you think you can stack before they all fall over?'

CHAPTER 5

Connor wasn't the only one struggling to cope.

Hattie couldn't sleep. Perhaps she'd had a bit too much to drink. Perhaps it was the shape of the sofa. Perhaps it was the sound of five other people breathing and shuffling in the unfamiliar darkness. Perhaps it was a memory. Probably it was regret.

Oliver's head fell onto her shoulder.

Hattie could tell that Oliver was awake. He had not flopped accidentally in his sleep. He was trying it on. She nudged him off.

Whispering, Oliver said, 'Come on, Hattie. What's wrong with you?'

'You know what's wrong.' She was scared that her hushed voice would boom in the quiet and arouse Alice and the others. She didn't want to share her problems with everyone in the living room.

Oliver let out an exasperated breath. 'You haven't been with Connor for ages.'

'I'm still with him – even though I'm not *with* him, if you know what I mean.'

'You can't be with someone if you're not with them.'

'He's in hospital and all. It's not easy.'

'You don't visit him much.'

'I went straightaway,' Hattie replied, finding it hard to sound really indignant and keep her voice down at the same time.

'Three times. But they said I couldn't see him. It'd be too upsetting, they said. Last time, they let me see him but ... ' She shook her head and sniffed. 'He didn't remember me. He's a bit better now, but I haven't managed to go back.'

'You can't be very ... '

Hattie put on her best withering look but it was wasted in the dark. 'It's not that,' she insisted. 'If you must know, I'm scared. I'm not sure I've got the guts to face what's happened to him. You know about Connor and me. We were ... an item. Now I'm ... I don't know. Choked, I suppose. Too choked to cope with it.' Her head drooped. 'I keep in touch, though. I talk to Brad.'

When Oliver rested a hand on her leg, she couldn't feel much through the thick sleeping bag.

In a hush, but with feeling, Oliver said, 'It's like you've got Connor standing behind you, watching you all the time. He's like a shadow – or a father. Forget him. Loosen up and get a life.'

'What?' At Hattie's cry, two of the sleeping teenagers stirred. Lowering her voice, she hissed, 'How could you? He's my boyfriend.'

'He *was*.'

'I haven't dumped him. He hasn't dumped me.'

'He's a different person now. A lost cause is what I heard. He's not Connor any more. He's a baby.'

'That's ... mean. And cruel.'

'Look,' Oliver replied quietly. 'If a footballer gets his leg chopped off in some stupid accident, you don't shove him back on the pitch and carry on as if nothing's happened, do you? You admit he's not going to play again. That's just the way it is. Tough.'

'You don't just abandon him.' Hattie wasn't yet ready to admit that there had to be a substitute.

Alice did not open her eyes. As if in a dream, she murmured, 'De-friend him, girl. He's a loser.'

Oliver nestled up closer to Hattie and put an arm round her shoulders. 'That's right,' he whispered into her ear. His hand dangled down in front of her chest.

In a sour mood, Hattie said, 'This is a sleep-over, so sleep.'

Oliver's hand didn't quite make contact with the sleeping bag or try to get inside it, but Hattie shrugged him off anyway. Her thoughts were elsewhere. She wished Connor was back to health, next to her on the settee. Back to normal. Yet that's one thing he'd never be, according to Brad. 'No chance.' She closed her eyes and saw a depressed Brad in the garden of his house, soon after the family got back from Barbados. One hand holding a bag, the other dangling heavily from the branch of a tree. 'He's damaged for ever,' Brad had told her, hardly daring to look her in the eye. 'There's no point waiting for him to get well.' Hattie wouldn't accept Brad's hasty, pessimistic verdict. Nothing was that certain, surely. Hospitals could fix all sorts. She had not lost faith in a slow recovery.

She sighed and fought back a sob.

Outside her own bedroom, there was a streetlamp. There was no light near Alice's house. The living room was so dark, it didn't matter if Hattie's eyes were open or shut, but shutting them helped to seal something in.

Anyway, even if Brad was right, she might fall for the new Connor, just like she'd fallen for the old one. Connor: big, handsome, easily distracted, hopeless at schoolwork, hardly able to keep track of a football score but unlikely to let the ball into his own goal, fun to be with, almost always kind, sometimes frustrating, open and honest. He'd be the first to admit, 'I've lost a leg so I can't play any more.' But he'd turn away and shout and scream and swear. That was the old Connor. He was a pretty good deal. All the girls said so. 'Pity he's not clever enough to do ya homework as well,' they said, 'but ya can't have everything.' At least, that's what they all said apart from Alice. Anyway, perhaps the new Connor would be a good deal as well. But Brad had shaken his head at the prospect of the new Connor having a girlfriend. 'It's more a case of minding a baby,' he'd said bluntly and emotionally. 'Each time you see him, you'd have to tell him who you are and what you did together. If you meet him again in exactly the same setting, he might remember. But he might not. If you wear something different, change your hair, look at him from a different angle, or meet him somewhere else, you're definitely back to square one.'

So, according to Brad, Hattie shouldn't wait for the old

Connor to reappear and she shouldn't expect great things from the new Connor. But what did Brad know? After all, Connor and Brad had never really hit it off. So, what *should* she do? She knew what she was doing right now. She was snuggling next to Oliver at a party. It comforted her and sickened her at the same time. How could she when Connor was still around, still in such a state? She was in danger of becoming as hard-hearted as Oliver. Hard-hearted, unfaithful and impatient. Oliver would say she had her own life to live and Connor now had a different, separate one. That was Brad's view as well. As far as Hattie understood it, Connor had a void in his brain where he once had thoughts of her. But was walking out on Connor the only option? Was their relationship really hopeless?

Hattie shook her head miserably and wiped away her silent tears. Oliver stirred restlessly. She shoved him away again with her shoulder.

One thing was suddenly clear. As soon as she could, Hattie would pluck up the courage to go back to see the new Connor. No matter how painful it would be. Then she could make up her own mind. She was scared, though. It wasn't all one-way traffic. Even if she thought he was terrific, this Connor who wouldn't recognize her might not fancy her at all. He might not want to do what the old Connor did. He might not want to go with her to parties and the youth club. He might not want to listen to the same music, share pizza and profiteroles, see the same films, make up a bowling team. He might not want to go two steps further than she thought they should. He might think she was too tall and fat. He might think that her bust was too small, her ears too prominent, her nose too turned-up, her hair too drab. She hadn't worried about such things when she had Connor hankering after her, but now …

Hattie still couldn't sleep. Maybe she *had* drunk too much. Maybe it *was* the shape of the sofa. Maybe it was the sound of the others, especially Oliver's breathing – almost snoring – so close to her ear. Maybe it *was* too dark. But it was definitely a memory that kept her awake. And it was certainly regret.

CHAPTER 6

Boys of her own age were so immature. Joy was ready for the next level.

After school, she gave Connor Markham the once over. He looked the part, but he was probably just as immature as the others. Even so, he was the gateway to being treated like a real woman. 'Hi,' she said, with a sparkle in her eye.

'Hi,' Connor replied.

'They say you can show someone like me a good time. They say you can unlock doors.'

Connor frowned. 'Maybe.'

As soon as she'd walked out of the school gates, she'd undone the top button of her blouse. Now, Joy fiddled coyly with the next one down. 'You can get me into GG's.'

'Maybe,' Connor repeated.

She'd tried to get into the nightclub before – as part of a group – but without an invitation the bouncers weren't having it. If Connor Markham had contacts on the inside, he'd get her a green light.

'This weekend's good for me. Friday or Saturday.'

'What's your name?'

'Joy.'

'Are you sure that's what you want?'

The older boys at school didn't seem older. They mucked about like kids. To be avoided at all costs. The older girls were virtually adults. Mature. Joy looked up to them, wanted to be them. In her head, she was already there. At fourteen, she knew just about everything that was worth knowing about life. She *knew*, but she hadn't experienced. Not yet. It was time for her to live life to the full. It was time to sample the important things.

'Certain,' she said.

Connor shrugged. 'All right. Where do you live?'

'Fifty-seven Springfield Road.'

Nodding, Connor replied, 'I know it. Near the football pitch – and GG's. I'll come round. Eight o'clock, Friday.'

Mum was at work as always. Her brother was away at university. Joy was at home alone. Bored.

She'd had a safe and sheltered upbringing. When Mum wasn't around, there was always Grandma to pop in and make sure she was okay. Really, they wrapped her in cotton wool. Not so with her elder brother. He'd got away with anything. Because he was a boy. He'd been allowed out with his gangly hormonal mates till the early hours. Well, now it was her turn.

For a while, she sang and danced in front of her bedroom mirror. She was Lady Gaga, Rihanna and Katie Perry rolled up into one tasty package. What else did she see in the mirror? A fresh face made her look younger than fourteen. A few curves made her look ready. She'd stun 'em all on Friday.

She wandered downstairs and out into the backyard. There, the regular robin fluttered down onto the birdfeeder. An arm's length from Joy, it seemed curious or even concerned. It was probably worried that the mealworm was nearly finished, but it looked as if it were worried for Joy.

Joy knelt by the fence and moved aside the square of rotting wood, revealing the secret hole into next door's garden. Then she whistled. Almost at once, her neighbour's neglected dog dashed excitedly through the gap and threw itself at her. The West Highland Terrier was supposed to be white, but it was always a dishevelled cream colour. Joy gathered it up in her arms and kissed the top of its head. 'Ahh. I bet you're starving again. Poor thing. Come on, I'll get you something.'

CHAPTER 7

'There is always hope, Mrs Markham.'

Connor's mum nodded. She liked the message. This was a consultant she could trust. Dr Ranji Nawaz. They hadn't all been like her.

First example. 'You have to accept that Connor's condition is beyond repair, Mrs Markham. I'm afraid you will never again have a sensible conversation with him and you should not overburden him with expectation.'

Second example. 'He's already as good as he's going to get.'

She had refused to believe these so-called experts. She'd seen Connor's eyes. They were bright like a baby's. All sorts of things were going on inside that head of his. Okay, a lot of it was weird and incomprehensible to a normal person, but something was stirring, struggling, learning. Connor's eyes told her much more than some consultant who was keen to spend his limited resources on cases that were more likely to be successful, putting him high in the consultants' league table. Connor's eyes told her he wasn't a lost cause. He wasn't a no-hoper.

Ranji Nawaz was going to be expensive, but Ranji Nawaz it was going to be. Connor was worth it.

Looking at Eleanor's notes, Ranji said, 'He gets very excited and demanding during rhythm therapy – he likes it a lot – but he gets frustrated with vanishing cues training and recognition therapy. No doubt it's because he finds them difficult and partly because he's bored by learning to read and write again. It's understandable, because it's a mammoth job.'

Connor's dad shook his head slowly and miserably. 'It'd be a lot better for him if we could get his memory for language back – his memory for anything.'

'Easier said than done, but his memory for basic numbers came back.'

His mum put in, 'We must be able to do something more for him. We can talk him through his life and show him photos of when he was smaller. Anything.'

'Yes. I'm sure you will. And you should. You should enlist the help of his friends as well. Get them to talk him through the important episodes of his life. It's all worth a try. But you've got to look at it from his point of view. Whatever you say isn't *his* memory. He'll think of it as second-hand, not true memory, because it won't ring a bell with him. He may not even trust your version of events, or anyone else's.'

'What about hypnosis? Would that bring anything back?'

'Yes,' Ranji answered. 'But it's more likely to bring daydreams than real events to the surface: fantasy girlfriends, getting abducted by aliens, having past lives – that sort of thing. In other words it'd create, not recover, memories.' She paused and then said sympathetically, 'As humans, we're very scared by memory problems, aren't we? It's because memory should be our longest lasting personal characteristic. We should take it to our graves. Memory defines who we are, doesn't it? Our understanding of ourselves depends on remembering our pasts, our life stories. I'm the person who got miserable with chickenpox at the age of four and fell off my bike and broke a tooth at eight and saw my favourite grandad die of a heart attack when I was twelve and stumbled over my marriage vows. They're *my* memories. They belong to me – and no one else has the same ones, so they make me unique. Without memory, we think we're nothing.'

Mr Markham asked, 'Does he know he's forgotten his past?'

'Yes. He knows it's out there somewhere, like the numbers.'

'Well, that's something. There's some fight in him.'

'Yes, but it's cruel as well,' Ranji responded. 'Some patients with amnesia are blissfully content. For two reasons. They don't remember all the bad things they've done, all the things they're ashamed of. And they forget they've forgotten everything, so it doesn't bother them. Connor hasn't forgotten that he's forgotten. That's hopeful *and* frightening for him. He might be so frightened by it, he won't want to know.'

'At least he hasn't done anything bad,' his mum said defensively. 'Nothing he'd be ashamed of.'

Mr Markham asked, 'It's only his memory that's gone, isn't it? Not his … you know … intelligence.'

'Eleanor measured his IQ and it's not changed significantly. The problem's very specifically memory and language.'

Needing reassurance, Mrs Markham checked for the hundredth time, 'Is he all right physically? Is he still all there?'

Dr Nawaz smiled kindly. She knew that Mrs Markham was referring to sex, a normal married life, and children. 'Rest assured, there's no physical damage at all. He can have a perfectly normal life as far as that's concerned, and any children would be perfectly healthy as well.'

'Good,' she replied. 'Because he was very popular with girls. His grandma always says, "He's a good-looking boy, is Connor. He'll break a few hearts before he settles down." All the girls love him.'

Connor's dad was not ready to think about who would want to partner Connor now. Instead, he changed tack. 'He seems to have a problem with time.'

'I'd expect that,' Ranji replied. 'You see, you and I remember more-or-less what we did in the last 24 hours, so we know a day's gone by. But if you can't remember doing anything, the time's slipped by as if it wasn't there. Do you see? His time chart's gone, so his appreciation of time is slight. I see from his record, he sometimes thinks a few seconds have passed when really it's been hours. Other times, he asks for a meal a few minutes after finishing the last one. He thinks it's been hours or even days and, of course, he's forgotten he's just eaten. He won't know days of the week and dates, either.' She smiled ruefully at them. 'I've got another patient who's lost the thread of time. He's thirty years adrift. He's got amnesia and the one and only thing he remembers is his most deep-seated, vivid and traumatic memory: fighting in the Falklands War. Without anything between then and now, he concludes it's still 1982. No matter what we tell him, his brain's convinced. He thinks he's in hospital because he's been shot in the head by an Argentinean soldier. Right now, he's waiting to be called back to the Falklands to carry on fighting.

'And there's another point,' she continued. 'The brain rules by logic even when it's damaged. I've got a sixty-year-old patient with frontal lobes damaged by a stroke, meaning his time-line's twisted. When I ask him how long he's been married, he swears it's been five months. This comes as a shock to his wife of the last thirty-five years. Anyway, to try and get through to him, I ask how many children he's got. Correctly, he tells me he's got three. Then he laughs and says, "Not bad for five months, is it?" And he gets his children's ages right. "Twenty-six, twenty-seven and thirty." When I ask him to explain how that's possible in a five-month marriage, quick as a flash, he says, "They're adopted." You see, his brain's so convinced about the brevity of his marriage that it's come up with what for him is the only rational explanation: he's adopted a grown-up family.'

Sitting between his parents, Brad murmured, 'Amazing.'

Ranji nodded. 'Certainly is. You see, Connor's brain will have its own internal logic, but we won't necessarily see it or understand it. All we'll see is his behaviour and to us that'll be illogical, perplexing and inconsistent. We'll be able to understand some of what he does, no doubt, but don't expect an easy ride.'

Mrs Markham took a deep breath. 'So, what can you do for him?'

'I can't promise anything,' Dr Nawaz said, looking at the family. 'But I want to try some games, memory triggers, see how he gets on working in a group with other memory-disorder patients.'

Interrupting, Mrs Markham said, 'You think he'll get some memory back? He might recognize us?'

'To answer that, you've got to understand something about memory. A memory's not just stored in one particular bit of the brain and when it's destroyed, the memory's gone. Full stop. It's not like that. What seems to happen is, the brain encodes memory in lots of different locations. When we remember, the brain assembles the memory from stored sights and sounds and smells rather like putting a jigsaw puzzle together. It gets the separate pieces from their different storage places and reconstructs the picture under instructions from yet another part of the brain. Connor will have lost a lot of jigsaw pieces, but he might retain a few. That's how come he suddenly retrieved his knowledge of basic numbers. That bit of the maths jigsaw was still there somewhere – an oasis of memory in a desert. More worrying, though, he's lost the index – the instructions – on how to rebuild whole jigsaws, because that's kept in the temporal lobe. When it was destroyed, he lost his assembly point for ever.'

Brad chipped in, 'A bit like deleting a computer file.'

'Is it?' Ranji queried.

Brad nodded. 'When you delete a file, a computer doesn't really wipe the disk clean. It just gets rid of all references to the file in its index. The file's still there somewhere – parts of it are scattered all over the disk – but the computer forgets where the bits are and doesn't know how to put them together again.'

'I didn't know that. In which case, you're right, Brad.' She smiled, clearly impressed with Connor's brother. 'Connor might have some memory left, but he can't access it. He's become disconnected from it.'

In pre-virus days, Brad would have felt proud and superior. He picked up on subtle ideas far quicker than his older brother. Connor would still be going, 'Uh?' when Brad had understood, worked out the implications and thought of two follow-up questions. The old Connor would not have grasped the new Connor's predicament. Now, Brad felt no pride in being several steps ahead of his brother.

'You're going to try and piece together whatever he's still got,' said Mr Markham.

Ranji nodded. 'I hope I'll be able to help him get to grips with present day life as well. In the meantime, you press on with the family and friends approach. Talk to him, show him things, let him hear familiar sounds, smell familiar smells, remind him. And be messy at home. Leave everything out. If you put something away in a drawer, it won't exist any more.'

Mrs Markham sighed loudly with the enormity of the task.

Teeming with metaphors, Ranji said, 'Look at it this way. Connor's an astronaut who's crash-landed on an alien planet. He's survived the initial impact but his life support's been completely wrecked. He faces a new life in an unknown territory without the tools to cope. It's our job to help him figure it out for himself.'

CHAPTER 8

Ranji's group was a mishmash of the ill, the bloody-minded and the old.

Stroke 1, Grumpy, Alzheimer 1, and Alzheimer 2 were playing cards. Stroke 2 and Confused were sipping tea and doing jigsaws. Stroke 2 was a mess. He never shaved the right-hand side of his face, never put his right arm inside the sleeve of his clothing, never touched the food on the right-hand side of his plate, and always got Confused to fill in the right-hand part of a jigsaw. That was because the stroke had damaged one hemisphere of his brain. For Stroke 2, half of the world didn't exist.

As always, Artist was painting pictures from his past: an unidentifiable animal in a zoo cage, two children either side of a snowman, a strict-looking teacher, a boy fishing, a new-born baby. The child-like images were the scattered fragments of his memory. He said only two words. Every now and then, he'd look over his shoulder and ask, 'Who's there?' He didn't seem to expect an answer.

Blow-To-The-Head, Brain Tumour and Alcohol Abuse were playing dominoes. Alcohol Abuse was an African-Caribbean with a wide grin and an ear-splitting laugh that belied his serious condition. Stroke 3, an old woman, sat on her own in the corner and swore a lot. She was supposed to be practising some memory exercise, but she refused to play the game. She couldn't remember the words for things brought to her on a tray but she knew every swearword under the sun – and a few more she'd made up herself. Connor liked her but, at the same time, kept his distance. His favourite was Alcohol Abuse with the enormous laugh.

Along one wall there was a big mirror or, as Connor called it, an echo. To Ranji, watching on the other side, it was a window. Secretly, she observed Connor and the others as if she had trapped them in a bottle. She was a scientist investigating the reactions she had set up carefully in her experimental test-tube.

Connor was fed up with stupid questions. People always wanted him to name things they put in his hands; wanted him to read bits from computer screens and comics and magazines and books and explain what it all meant; wanted to know everything he remembered from a time they called 'before'; wanted him to see if he recognized places from photographs and postcards and maps; wanted him to put names to people in snapshots of family and friends; wanted him to make sense of pictures. Why? They must know these things better than he did, so why ask him? He knew why really. They wanted some old Connor back. Who was he? They seemed to be far more interested in this old Connor than in him. Their endless probing irritated him. He seemed to be the only one who didn't know old Connor, the only one who didn't *want* to know old Connor.

He felt weightless and detached. And frustrated. And depressed. And powerless.

Sometimes, when he was given something that he was supposed to name, he'd throw it down. It happened usually when his rewired brain couldn't find the right connection. Once, he threw a drink thing onto the hard floor. It made a loud satisfying sound. The nurse bent down to pick it up and said, 'Oh, it's cracked.'

'Cracked?'

The nurse was trained not to disapprove of outbursts. After all, patients remembered best when they got emotional. With a shrug, she explained, 'It's broken – about to split into bits. But it doesn't matter.'

Connor was fed up with visitors as well. Always staring into his face, like they were examining him, always asking, 'How do you feel today?', 'Are you all right?', 'Do you remember … ?' Questions, questions, questions. He felt annoyed, under constant study, a curiosity. He wanted to shout, 'Don't stare at me! I'm a boy not a … , not a *thing* you stare at.' It was much more fun to listen to Stroke 3's streams of swearwords and Alcohol Abuse's outrageous laugh.

People always told Connor to talk to other people. Talk to doctors, talk to visitors, talk to patients, talk to cleaners. Talk to anyone. Talk, talk, talk. But it wasn't easy when the words wouldn't come. It was no fun at all. Besides, some of the people he was supposed to talk to looked at him as if he was from a different planet. They couldn't follow him. He didn't like a lot of talk. It was wasted effort.

And people always wanted him to say out loud numbers that they showed him. At least he liked that. He could do it. Numbers were happy. Some were bent and some were straight. Some were fat and some were thin. Most turned into different shapes upside down, some stayed the same. Some stayed the same backwards or forwards, most turned into different shapes. Nought was nothing but it was everything as well: big and fat and round. Eight was the best shape. Its top was the same as its bottom. But nine was his favourite. It turned into a six upside down and, like his brain, it had a hole on the left-hand side. He particularly liked 6690699. It didn't matter which way he looked at it. It was still 6690699. And something told him it was not just fun, but he didn't know why. Anyway, numbers were happy things. Letters? There were too many and a lot of them were ugly and unhappy anyway. Like G. That was the letter that bothered him most. Sometimes it was loopy with a flat bit that stopped its two ends joining up. A dead end letter. Sometimes, it was a hook dangling from a little round bit. Other times, it looked like a wasp: two lumpy bits joined by a line. A stupid stinging thing. No. Numbers were much more fun.

There was one visitor Connor liked. A girl. She wasn't even his visitor. She was Artist's visitor. Sometimes Artist stopped

37

painting when she talked to him. She must be a special visitor to make Artist stop his perpetual painting, but he still didn't speak. When Connor looked at Artist's visitor, she smiled at him. It was good. She was happy with him. And he was happy with her. She didn't stop and talk to him about his health. She didn't apply pressure. She didn't make any demands, didn't tell him what he should do. She just smiled on her way out.

Connor smiled back at her, but he also looked away and frowned, frustrated with himself. He couldn't remember this girl but he thought that there had once been a happy visitor, quite like her, who had stopped Artist painting. He couldn't bring a picture of her to mind, though.

One day, a girl a bit shorter than Connor was put in front of him. A man said, 'This is Hattie. She's been before. She's your friend.'

'Friend? Why is she my friend?'

The man replied, 'Because you got on well together.'

Connor looked at the girl. He'd never seen her before. She didn't look like a friend. She looked scared and soft and sad. If, instead of being real, this girl had been a photo that he'd been asked to look at and explain, he would have said that she seemed shocked and nervous. She was a strange-looking thing and she smelled like a volcano. She had long blonde hair and a round face and she was almost shaking with emotion. Still, she was his own visitor. He didn't have to share her with anyone else. She'd come to see him and him alone.

She leaned forward as if she was going to touch his face with hers, but she changed her mind and pulled back awkwardly. 'Hello, Connor,' she said quietly.

Connor nodded at her suspiciously and waited for the next question – the one they all asked.

Hattie obliged. 'How you feeling?'

Connor refused to answer. He said, 'Who are you really?'

The girl swallowed. She seemed to be struggling. 'Hattie Townsend. I'm your … Look.' She got a photograph out of her bag and showed it to him.

Now this was something he was used to. He sat down to study the picture. It was a small one. The smallest he'd seen and there was not much to it. Just two heads against a grey background. Both of the people were pulling silly faces. Happy smiley faces, though. The sides of their heads were squeezed together, peel against peel. When Connor looked up, Hattie was sitting opposite him in Eleanor's place. 'Is this me?' he asked, tapping his image in the photograph. He was not yet confident at recognizing himself.

'Yes,' Hattie replied. 'And the other one's me.'

'You?'

Hattie nodded. 'Do you see? It means you and I ... '

Connor threw the photograph towards her. 'It's just a picture! It doesn't mean anything.'

Hattie's lips clamped together. Distraught, she reached out for the photograph, looked at it briefly, downheartedly, and then slipped it back into her bag. 'Do you want to do anything while I'm here?'

'Play.'

'Play? Okay. Play what?'

'I-spy.'

'I-spy? That's what you play?' Hattie looked alarmed at the idea.

'Yes, but I get angry. I'm not happy with words.'

Strangely, water began to run down either side of the girl's face. Instead of spying with her little eye, she got up and rushed away, leaving behind only the nice smell of a volcano.

Artist had a happy visitor. It was a short, slender girl with long dark hair. She didn't have a smell but she looked right. When she got up and walked away from Artist, Connor decided to go up to her. He said, 'I've got to talk to you.'

The surprised girl glanced over her shoulder as if she wasn't sure that Connor was speaking to her. 'Me?' she said, pointing to her chest. 'Why?'

Connor shrugged. 'I've got to talk a very lot.'

'Oh, I see,' Girl replied. 'It's to help you get better, I suppose.'

Connor nodded.

'That's all right, then,' Girl said with a smile. 'You can talk to me. I've got time.' She sat in one of the armchairs and, swinging her legs, invited Connor to sit near her. 'My grandad doesn't do much talking these days, so it'll make a change.'

'Grandad?'

Girl pointed to Artist. 'He's my grandad and he's … you know … poorly. He listens to me talking, but I don't know if he takes anything in.'

'He … ' Connor imitated working with a brush.

'Yes. He paints a lot. It's good for him. Like talking's good for you, I suppose.'

In the corner of the room, Stroke 3 suddenly woke up and shouted for a cup of tea. When it didn't arrive immediately, she swore at the top of her voice.

Girl grimaced, grinned and giggled at the same time.

Connor said, 'Are you a … ?' He pointed at Ranji Nawaz.

'A doctor?' Girl looked astonished. 'Why ask that?'

'Your peel's the same colour.'

Girl thought about it for a moment, unsure. Deciding not to be offended and not to offend Connor by laughing at his question, she said, 'My dad's black – and I'm too young to be a doctor.'

Connor pointed to the little machine attached to her waist. 'What's that?'

'An iPod. You know. It plays mp3 files. Want to listen? Here,' she said, holding out some spongy things on white strings, 'you put these in your ears.'

'Ears?'

She mimicked the action on herself and Connor followed suit. Then she turned it on.

It was a very small audio book, Connor assumed. He waited for the story to start. All of a sudden, music pounded directly into his brain. Heavy drum and bass, and voices. Real voices were singing right into him. Singing, not talking. His eyes opened wide and he beamed with pleasure. 'Happy,' he shouted. While he listened, he examined the small machine in case it had got moving numbers as well, but it hadn't. Never mind. The music was fun.

When the song ended and Girl turned off the machine, he told her, 'I've got a picture.'

'Oh? Can I see?'

'Yes.' She deserved it for sharing her music. Connor showed her his best ever photo – his new brain scan.

'I've seen this sort of thing before. I've seen Grandad's. This one's your brain, isn't it? It looks good.'

'Yeah.' Connor was delighted. Girl liked his brain and he liked Girl. She didn't quiz him about his health. She didn't want to compare him with old Connor. She just liked the new Connor with the pretty brain. He pointed out his very own hole and then said, 'I spy with my little eye something beginning with B.'

'Brain?' she guessed.

'Yes! You're happy at this, better than … ' He pointed to one of the medical staff.

In frustration, Stroke 3 threw a pot plant from her memory tray, unable to put a name to it. The smashed pot with its pummelled palm came to rest a couple of metres in front of Connor and he stared at it, gasping aloud.

'It's all right,' Girl reassured him. 'It's not the first time.'

Connor's face was suddenly pale. 'But … '

Surprised by his exaggerated reaction, Girl said, 'No problem. It won't have been valuable or anything.'

'But it's … cracked.'

The soil and roots kept the broken pot together. A nurse shrugged at the young couple, smiled, and cautiously picked up the baby palm tree with its crimson leaves.

To distract Connor, Girl said, 'I'm Courtney. What's your name?'

'Me? They call me Connor.'

'I spy with my little eye two people sitting together beginning with C,' she responded with a giggle. 'Connor and Courtney.'

The abused palm was forgotten. Ancient history. Connor laughed happily. The letter C had gone up in his estimation. He decided that he liked it a lot. It was one of the few letters he could remember. It didn't have a dead end like a G. It needed only a bit of filling in to become a nought. And a downward line on the right made it into his favourite number: 9. That's how he remembered it. He was pleased that Courtney knew all about it as well.

The Institute for Memory Disorders was attached to the hospital. Courtney often called in to see her grandad on the way home from school. As she was leaving the unit, she was intercepted by Dr Nawaz who, as always, wanted to know all about her meeting with her grandad. This time, though, the doctor was even more eager to hear what she'd said to Connor Markham. Dr Nawaz encouraged Courtney to chat for a while with Connor each time she visited.

Liam Darby was feeling fidgety. He wasn't bothered about what Connor had forgotten. He was more worried about what Connor could remember – and what he might blurt out.

In the Institute, Mr Markham said to Connor, 'This is Liam. He's another friend.'

'Is he?'

'Yes, a big friend.'

Connor looked him up and down. 'He's not as big as … a house.'

Liam stood like a lemon, amazed – and relieved – at the conversation.

'He's a football friend,' Mr Markham said, as if he didn't really approve of the young man. 'You played in the same team. That's why I want you to see him.'

Connor turned to the chunky visitor. 'Football?'

'Yeah. You's a mean player. Bet you'll be just as rocking when you's outta here.'

'Football,' Connor murmured. It was plain that the word meant nothing to him.

There was no need to be nervous. Much more relaxed, Liam had already realized that Connor's brain had been wiped clean, like a wall of graffiti attacked by council workers and high-pressure hoses. Liam said, 'You and me's seen some football action, no argument.' He laughed at a memory. 'Anyhow, when they said you's brain gone funny, you semi gave me a heart attack. But you okay, man. You's still Connor.

You still look the same. Cool.' He thumped Connor playfully on the arm.

Connor nodded, pretending that he knew what this young man was talking about. Actually, he hadn't got a clue, but he liked the easy rhythm of Liam's patter.

'You and me's gonna play again. You in goal, me up front.' He kicked an imaginary football into the top corner. 'We's the mean team.'

Overwhelmed, Connor nodded again. Something told him that he would not be able to grasp the sense of Liam's rants, so he let the hypnotic words wash over him.

'You still semi-crazy over Hattie Townsend? No doubting. Anyway, I's watching out for you, man. That creep Oliver's sniffing around, but I got him in my sights.' Two eels and a thumb made a gun that jerked when Liam exploded air from his mouth. 'No problem blowing him away. I take care of you's interests.'

Connor wore a confused smile. He had trouble understanding anybody, yet with this man called Liam it didn't matter. Connor was content to soak up his comical gestures, his seductive and irresistible babble. Meaning took second place behind enthusiasm. And it didn't seem to bother Liam that Connor didn't follow him. Liam didn't demand anything in return. There were no tiresome photos to explain, no health reports to give. Yes, Connor could understand why Liam was a friend. They were the mean team.

Brad sat on a chair in the Institute, his back bent, forearms resting on his legs. He was staring thoughtfully at the floor. Eventually, he looked up at his brother who was banging all of the objects on the table in turn with a spoon, trying unsuccessfully to come up with some sort of crude tune. That childishness was what was left of Brad's older brother after the virus had taken its share of him. And Brad was at least partly responsible. Now, Brad's role was to remind Connor of past events, past arguments, that would switch on a light inside Connor's brain.

'Do you remember that time when Mum's favourite vase got broke?'

'Cracked,' Connor said absently.

'A bit more than cracked. If it'd cracked, we might have got away with a bit of glue. No. It was smashed – well and truly. Atomized. We'd both been told not to kick the ball about in the living room but … Anyway, the vase got broke. Big trouble. All hell broke loose. Remember?'

Connor's answer involved hitting everything even harder with the spoon, perhaps trying to obliterate Brad's stupid and incomprehensible question.

'I … er … I said you'd done it, but the ball came off me really. I did it but I said it was your fault. I only got docked a week's pocket-money, but you really copped it. Grounded for ages and stopped lots more pocket-money. I suppose Mum thought you should've been old enough to have more sense. Anyway, you took the stick for me.'

Mentally, Connor had taken a giant step backwards. At the same time, his illness had forced greater maturity on Brad. Japes, jaunts and pranks no longer seemed appropriate. Reclaiming Connor was a serious and prolonged business. Right now, though, Connor was more interested in the musical table-top than in his brother's confession. Hitting the half-full mug, followed by the pack of cards, the domino case, the table itself, a box of tissues and the mug again produced a very satisfying sequence.

From the other side of the room, Alcohol Abuse boomed, 'Hey. My man's got rhythm. Yeah.' He laughed at the top of his voice.

Dispirited, Brad let out a long weary breath. 'I remember the last thing I said to you before the virus. You'd gashed your finger – your eel – before we left home and you wouldn't tell us how you'd done it. Remember? A really deep cut. I said it couldn't have been your razor-sharp mind.' Brad lowered his sombre voice even more. 'You know, I blame myself for … for all this.' He nodded towards the babyish activities on the table and then waved his arm at the Memory Disorder clinic in general. 'Do you blame me for getting the virus?'

Connor stopped his amateur drumming. Face creased, he looked puzzled. He had no idea what his visitor meant.

44

Brad realized that he'd asked a question that only a healthy person would pose. Connor was not concerned with blame. To Connor, there was no blame. It was irrelevant. There was nothing leading up to that point in Connor's second life. There was only coping with the here and the now.

Recognizing that Brad grasped things quickly, Ranji invited him into her office and offered him a seat. 'How's it going?' she asked.

Brad shook his head. 'It isn't.'

'Early days, Brad. Early days. But … ' She hesitated and changed tack. 'You'll never know where you are with him, I'm afraid. He'll have good moments and bad. He certainly won't be consistent. We're only after flashes of memory.'

'It won't all come flooding back?'

Ranji was unwilling to destroy the dreams of Connor's mum and dad, but she felt able to share her concerns with Brad. She thought that Connor's younger brother was more likely to cope with her prognosis, so she decided to confide in him. 'No, I don't think so.'

'He doesn't know who I am yet.'

'It's complicated. Seeing and recognizing is only part of the picture. There's got to be an emotional response to what's seen as well. Think of it like this. You're facing a very hungry lion. You see it, you recognize it as a lion looking at you and licking its lips. That's not enough, is it? That won't save you. You've got to have an emotional response as well. Your brain's got to come up with the reaction, *Danger. Get out of here! Run!* That's automatic with a good brain like yours. Well, it's the same with faces. You've got to see a face, recognize it and then have an emotional response. With Connor, seeing's no problem, recognizing a face like yours will be hit and miss, but the reaction … He doesn't get an emotional whisper in his brain at the moment, so he doesn't know how to react. Without the feeling of warmth, he won't complete the vision process.'

'I didn't know it was so complicated.'

'People who lose that emotional input believe that their family's been replaced with look-alikes. You see, the brain admits

45

there's this woman who looks identical to mum but, because there's no emotional engagement, it concludes logically that it can't be mum. Otherwise, the brain would get a feeling of warmth. Hence the impostor theory. Even when Connor recognizes you, your parents, Hattie or me, the emotional response might not kick in, so we'll get nothing back from him – except suspicion. There's good news, though. Injured brains seem to get around this emotional brick wall with time and the impostor thing goes away.'

'But his basic problem recognizing us. That's here to stay?'

Ranji's face said one thing but her words said another. 'The brain's got a lot of spare capacity. It might learn new ways of doing things. But … '

'I shouldn't hold my breath?'

Ranji nodded. 'You can help him by throwing in as many clues as you can when you meet up with him. Speak to him straightaway. You see, he may not recognize or engage with your face, but maybe your voice will ring a bell. He might recognize someone if they speak in a characteristic way. Always wear the same clothes. If you use deodorant, keep to the same one. Smell's an incredibly powerful aid to memory.' She fingered a small bottle on her desk. 'A lot of my patients only know it's me because, before I see them, I put this perfume on. If Connor still struggles, drop your identity into the conversation. Like, "Speaking as your brother, I'd say … " If you're with Hattie, make sure she calls you Brad and you call her Hattie. That sort of thing.'

Brad sighed heavily. 'Early days, eh?'

'Yes. Early days.'

CHAPTER 9

Hattie had a dilemma: stick by Connor and be ashamed of him, or ditch him and be ashamed of herself.

Hattie was standing by the lockers outside the drama studio, surrounded and protected by a small group of friends. Devastated, she admitted, 'He plays I-spy.'

Oliver exclaimed, 'He does *what*?'

'He plays I-spy-with-my-little-eye.'

'A fifteen-year-old?' Oliver shook his head. 'I told you, Hattie. Connor's out of it. Forget him.'

Hattie burst out crying.

Alice Foley said, 'I'm sorry, but Oliver's right. What's a boyfriend for? Think about it, girl. It's got to be someone you're proud of. What's the point otherwise? You don't want someone you're embarrassed about. And you can't be proud of a boyfriend who plays I-spy.'

'But it'd be cruel to turn my back on him now. He's ill.'

Earnestly, Alice replied, 'Look, anyone who knows what's happening isn't going to call you cruel. You can't go with someone out of pity. That'd be totally cruel.'

'Yeah, yeah. I know,' Hattie said. 'You've told me, Oliver's told me, everyone's telling me it's okay to drop him – but … '

'But what?' Oliver demanded to know.

'He's sick and maybe I can make a difference. Maybe I can help him. His mum and dad, and his doctor, want me to keep trying.'

'Face it. He's screwed. His kid brother says he won't ever be right.'

'Maybe Brad's wrong. Maybe he's just feeling down about it. Even if he's right, I might be able to make it better for Connor – if only he could start to remember. I owe it to him to try.'

A group of Year 10 students sauntered towards the drama studio. Once they were out of earshot, another of Hattie's friends said, 'All this started with a germ, didn't it? You watch it, Hattie. Can you catch it if you touch him? What about kissing or … getting even more serious? You might end up like him.'

'Now you're getting carried away,' Alice exclaimed. 'Who's going to get serious with someone like Connor?'

Hattie glared at Alice for a second. 'I remember you fancied him like mad once. You told me. You backed off when Connor and me … '

Alice didn't deny it. 'He was the fittest boy around. *Was*. Past tense.'

Before the brain disease, all the girls had fancied Connor. He'd got a reputation. He could take his pick. That was part of the attraction. No one wanted to date a reject. They all wanted a boy the others wanted as well. Hattie was no different. When he picked her, Connor became her status symbol.

Now Hattie was searching in vain for someone who'd advise her to try again with Connor, but even common sense told her to let go. It was only her conscience that nagged at her. Mr and Mrs Markham and Dr Nawaz wanted her to visit him and probe his memory, but they were thinking only of Connor. They weren't considering her best interests. Her own parents hadn't been any help, either. They saw every boyfriend as a dress rehearsal for marriage and 'settling down as a family.' They couldn't get their heads around the idea that a boyfriend was just fun. And, of course, they wouldn't approve of an undress rehearsal at all. Anyway, when she'd explained Connor's predicament to them, they were sympathetic but their ruthless logic condemned him to life as a cast-off. 'How's he going to earn money, support a family, run a car and home? No, Hattie, he hasn't got any prospects.'

Hattie was certain about one thing. Connor definitely hadn't got any prospects if everyone thought like her mum and dad and her friends.

When the rest of her mates shuffled along to their next lesson, Oliver remained behind to escort Hattie. 'How about tonight, then?' he prompted, as they sauntered towards the science block.

Keeping her distance so his arm could not stray across her shoulders, she snapped, 'Maths homework.'

It was like when people died. It didn't matter how awful they were in life, as soon as they were dead, everyone said what a pity it was that they'd died, how they'd be missed, what an impact they'd had, how great they were. Alice's mum wrote the obituaries column for the local newspaper and she agreed. Post-death, it was compulsory to forget the bad things.

It was the same with post-virus Connor. It wasn't polite to speak ill of the ill, but Alice always thought Connor was retarded. Now he had the excuse of a punctured brain, everyone had to forget that he had been thick before. Everyone said he'd been a great goalkeeper but politely avoided commenting on his intelligence. But Alice didn't believe in being polite.

Okay, so new Connor couldn't recognize things. But he'd never been able to recognize some things. Like a textbook. Come to that, he'd never been able to recognize a book of any sort. Books, calculators, pens, rulers, sentences – all passed him by without bothering his brain cells. The only thing that didn't fly past him was a football.

And girls. Girls always seemed to stick to him.

Physically, of course, he was … all there. He was all there and a good bit more. On a scale of one to ten, he was an eleven. He'd always been impressive physically. He was one of the boys who'd first caught Alice's eye. In fact, he was *the* first. Maybe he'd never been bettered. On the outside, Connor could well be the best. Nice face, sexy body. But it didn't make up for what was inside. Or what wasn't inside. Alice had dropped the idea of going with him because he was not in her intellectual league. It was nothing to do with Hattie starting to go out with him. Alice was not backing off simply to avoid treading on her best friend's toes. It was because he'd always been in need of a brain transplant. In a way Alice felt as if she were attached to Connor by a spring. At a distance she'd always felt attracted to him but, when she got in close, she was repelled.

If anything, it was Alice who was first out of the blocks in the early part of the chase. Alice and Hattie had found out from Oliver that the hunky Connor was going ten-pin bowling that night, so the two girls fixed themselves up with a lane as well. Then they made sure they bumped into him. 'Oh,' Alice said in fake surprise. 'You're from school, aren't you?'

'Yeah,' he said, smiling at both of them.

'Looks like you've done this before.' Alice nodded towards the score displayed over his lane.

'Once or twice.'

Unlike most boys, he seemed to know the difference between flirting and friendliness. He waited for them to make a move.

Hattie's face was still flushed. 'Fancy taking us on, then?' she asked.

'All right.'

Pleased that two girls were coming on to him, he didn't appear to mind which one he hit it off with. His eyes lingered mostly on Alice's eye-catching figure, but he talked more with Hattie. Perhaps Hattie was closer to his level. She knew more about football.

It turned out that Alice was a class act at bowling. That was the one and only thing she shared with Connor. When she bowled, his gaze shifted quickly from her bum to the lane. 'Nice bowl,' he'd murmur genuinely each time she scattered the pins. Since that first night, she had always been able to push him all the way in a game. The two of them would have made a hot team, but they'd never got it together.

Alice didn't know about the new, diseased Connor, but she'd got the old one summed up. He was pretty well useless at everything – except games and girls. He didn't bother with anything that he didn't like and he liked only what he could do well. And when he was doing something he excelled at, he enjoyed being the centre of attention. That's why he was a goalkeeper. That's why he loved facing penalties. That's why he was so proud of his player-of-the-year award. That's why he caught Alice's eye. Despite everything, there was something attractive about his uncomplicated view of life.

Still, there had never been a need to be jealous of Hattie. No need back then and certainly no need now, because Alice didn't really fancy a boy who couldn't count beyond a football score. So there had never been a reason for falling out with Hattie over Connor. They remained best friends. No bust-up, no bitchiness. But, ever since Hattie had started going with old Connor, there had been something – a vague tension – between them.

Alice and Hattie had been mates for ever, even at junior school. They'd had the usual number of disagreements, but they'd stuck together. Alice grinned at a memory. It was years and years ago at primary school. One of the kids, a real spiteful sort, had told Hattie that her ears stuck out. 'Do they?' Hattie had cried in horror, clasping the sides of her head. Alice hadn't been quick enough to deny the playground insult. Poor Hattie had said, 'They do!' In those days of insecurity – days that never seem to come to an end – Hattie had examined her ears in a mirror and let her imagination and anxiety get the better of her. Afterwards, going into Hattie's house early one Saturday morning, Alice noticed sticky tape pinning back her friend's ears. Seeing Alice gawping at the side of her head, Hattie had yanked away the forgotten tape and confessed that every night when she went to bed she pinned her ears to her head in an effort to train them not to protrude. Of course, it hadn't done any good because her ears didn't stick out in the first place. Not much anyway. But, by then, the psychological damage had been done. In Hattie's mind, her ears jutted out like the wings of an aeroplane. That weekend, Alice had sworn not to tell a living soul about the sticky tape.

And she'd kept her word. That is, until one day when the slight tension came between her and Hattie and she'd mentioned it to Connor. 'Really?' he'd said. 'But she hasn't got big ears. Not really. Her hair … you know.'

'Well, now you know why she's got long hair,' Alice had replied.

Alice still smiled about it. Yes, they were still best mates –

Alice thought she knew what was best for Hattie and Hattie thought she knew what was best for Alice – but that didn't mean they never traded cross words. They would both claim that they stopped short of being catty, though.

CHAPTER 10

In a way, Connor would recognize his parents and brother.

As long as they were at home. There, they were in the right context. And as long as they wore their usual clothes and looked Connor full in the face and used their ordinary voices and smelled as they normally did. Then Connor was happy with them. They were clearly the people who lived with him and he'd even learned their names: Mum, Dad and Brad. The rhythm helped him to remember. Mum, Dad, Brad. But outside, or in another house, Connor could not place them at all. They were wrong. In a different setting, they were foreigners.

When his parents first took him home, one of the first things they did was to lead him up some steps into a place they called his bedroom. 'It's exactly as you left it, Connor,' his mum said. 'Quite a mess.'

It wasn't a mess. It was a busy room: an ant's nest. The walls were covered with pictures of men and women. Most of the men were wearing no-leg-things and their arms hung out of their clothes. There was usually a kicking ball in the picture as well. The women wore even less than the men. In a corner of the room, muddy shoe things with long long shoestrings were standing on a grubby newspaper. There was a clock with glowing red numbers by the bed and a pencil case and a heap of sports magazines and an echo on the wall. From the shelf, Connor picked up a model of two men trying to kick the same ball. He looked puzzled.

'It's called a trophy – or a cup,' said his dad.

'Cup.'

'Yes, a cup. You won it for being really good at football. They said you were the best in the team.'

Connor shrugged and put it down. He went to the bag that he'd brought back from the hospital and carefully extracted his favourite image of his own brain. He used the cup to prop up and show off the brain scan. Then, with a big grin, he pointed to the small machine lying on the bedside table and said, 'Mp3.'

His mum almost jumped with excitement. 'You remember!'

'It's … Number 9's. That's C.' He paused, struggling. Then he announced, 'It's Courtney's.'

'Who's Courtney, Connor?'

Connor's face crumpled with frustration as he realized that he hadn't got the words to explain.

'It's all right,' his mum put in quickly. 'It doesn't matter. But the mp3 player's all yours, I promise. Brad'll show you how to use it.'

'You like dance music,' his dad added. Eagerly grabbing any opportunity to jog his son's memory, Mr Markham added, 'Head-thumping stuff.'

Connor turned the pencil case upside down and watched everything spill out on to the floor. Then he was distracted by something outside. Below the bottle, there was a roof of glass and a small hairy animal was strolling across it.

Joining Connor at the window, Brad said, 'That's Duke – next door's cat. You used to open the window and he'd jump in from the conservatory roof.'

'Cat,' Connor murmured, trying to recall the word.

'Open the window, Brad,' his dad suggested. 'Let's see what happens.'

Sure enough, the cat stopped and looked up. As soon as Brad threw open the bottle, Duke sprang up eagerly onto the sill.

'Hold him, Connor.'

Unsure, Connor stepped towards it and held out his hands for the warm fluffy creature. As soon as the cat nestled against Connor's chest, Connor's mum began to say, 'Do you remem … '

At once, Connor dropped the cat and shouted, 'Sprouts!'

'What's wrong?' his parents cried in unison.

Connor replied, 'It ... moved.' He didn't have the vocabulary to tell them that the animal had started to vibrate like a mobile phone.

The baffled cat jumped back onto the window sill and quickly out onto the glass roof.

'Never mind.'

Then, the cat forgotten, Connor was captivated by a spider that was making a web in the corner of the bottle. He did not see his mum nudge Brad and he didn't really hear Brad saying, 'I'll take you to a match at the weekend. You used to like that.'

Ranji had encouraged the Markhams to expose Connor to the things he used to love and to allow him more freedom. She suggested that, if they were worried about him getting lost, they should write his name, address and phone number on a card and slip it into his pocket. That way, someone would always be able to get him home or contact them when he was found.

Who else did Connor recognize? There was Ranji – the dark doctor at the clinic where he went. There were two visitors as well. Courtney – the girl who really came to see Artist but who always had a chat with Connor. And there was Liam in the mean team. Connor remembered him all right. He always wore scruffy jeans and the same old sweatshirt. And he always spoke the same. Rocking, man.

At home in the hall there was a small silvery box attached to the wall by a coiled string. A banana-shaped bit was balanced on top. Connor was fascinated by it because it had rows of numbers. They were like the buttons of a computer keyboard, but there were fewer of them because all those dreary letters were missing. He pushed his favourite, 9, but nothing happened. He picked up the banana bit and held it to the side of his head like he'd just seen his mum doing. When he pressed 6690699, he smiled broadly because the numbers appeared on a grey strip and the machine made a ringing noise in his ear. Almost immediately, there was a voice. 'Double six, nine, nought, six, double nine. Yes?'

It was a man's voice, quiet and husky. Connor looked into the banana. He saw nothing but someone had definitely talked to him so he replied, 'Yes.'

The voice said, 'Don't mess with me. That's not wise. What do you want?'

Connor didn't know what to say into the talking machine. He just knew there was something about the number 6690699. He muttered, 'Six, six, nine, nought, six, nine, nine.'

'I'll give you five more seconds.'

'Erm … '

'Time's up,' the man said.

There was a click and a hum. The voice had gone.

It was chaos. Loads of boys ran up and down kicking a ball, getting muddier and muddier. Like busy ants, they didn't stop still long enough for Connor to count them all. Brad watched the football match and his brother's face alternately. 'What do you reckon?' he asked.

'I play this?' Connor replied in wonderment.

'You loved it. Don't you remember?'

'No.' Connor's memory of his favourite game had dissolved entirely.

Brad sighed sadly. Escorting his brother to a football match was not doing much for Connor's neural connections or for his own guilty conscience. 'Connor. You kept the cleanest sheet in the league last season.'

'What's that?'

'You were a keeper. You stopped the goals. Like him over there in orange. They voted you player of the year. That's why you've got a cup.'

'Oh,' he said, as he watched the yellow leaves falling to the green grass from the backdrop of brown trees.

Brad figured it was just like Ranji had told him. Even if Connor recognized a game of football, his emotional response to it had gone. He wasn't interested because his heart wasn't in it any more.

The sky began to leak. Connor held out his palm and felt the drizzle dampening his skin. He looked closely at it and then at his brother. 'It's not pink.'

'Your skin – your peel? It is.'

'No. The ... drink.'

'The rain? Pink? Why do you think it should be pink?'

Connor shrugged.

There was a break in the play. One of the kickers came up to Connor and said, 'Hey! Great to see you's here, man. We's losing. It's not like when you was between the sticks. No chance of losing, then. We was a cool team. Maybe we's gonna rock the second half, but the bets say we don't. Gotta go.'

With a blank face, Connor watched the young man retreat.

'You don't know who that was, do you?' said Brad.

'I know the ... ' He put his hand to his mouth.

Brad nodded. 'You know someone who speaks like that. Yes. But he's in different clothes, in a different place. It's your sort-of mate, Liam.'

'Liam.' Connor shook his head in disbelief. Liam was a visitor in Ranji's room.

Who else did Connor remember? There was Ranji and Courtney and ... someone like Courtney. A girl. Who was it?

While Brad talked to some of the other spectators in the second half, Connor jogged along the touchline, chasing a plastic bag that the wind had scooped up and pushed along like a balloon. Then, suddenly cast adrift of the match, Connor found himself at the corner of the field and the edge of a street. He turned left and wandered along the road. He didn't know where he was going, but he knew he was going somewhere. Number 43, number 45, number 47. Suddenly it twigged. To Connor's delight, he understood. Forty-three, no number forty-four. Then forty-five, no number forty-six. Forty-seven, no number forty-eight. The next house would have a number 49. He cheered. He was right! Numbers were rocking.

After 53 there was a real test. The next house didn't have a number. Fascinated, Connor hung over the ... tree things and stared at the door and walls, but there definitely wasn't a 55. It was a nothing house. Strange. So, would the one after the nothing house be 55 or would it be 57? It was ... 57! Connor stopped outside it. He didn't know why, but there was something about it. Number fifty-seven, the pattern of bricks, the white wood around the bottles, the beige door, the funny tree things outside. Especially the palm that sprouted long crimson leaves. He thought that he recognized it. Some impulse made him push open the swinging gate and go up to the door with 57 written on it. There was a little button to push so he pushed it. He had no idea why or what it would do.

Then he jumped back as an old woman with a curved back appeared in front of him. 'Yes?' she said, holding him with her gaze.

'I ... er ... '

Genuinely concerned, she asked, 'What's wrong?'

'I ... er ... I'm looking for ... '

'Are you lost, dear?'

'Yes. No. It's ... '

Realizing all was not well with her unexpected caller and sensing no threat in him, the woman said, 'You'd better come in while we try and get you sorted out.'

She stood to one side and Connor wandered in.

He didn't recognize anything. He knew about tables, chairs, picture boxes and clocks. He recognized them as objects, but he couldn't remember seeing those particular ones before. He knew plenty about photographs, but he didn't recognize the ones perched on every surface of the old woman's front room. He stood by the front window, staring out at the neat sculpted hedge and gushing palm. And again something sparked in his brain. A neural connection kicked in and convulsed. Suddenly, Connor heard himself saying to the woman, 'Is Joy in?'

'Joy? Who's Joy?' Then she added, 'Anyway, let's not jump the gun. I think I'd better call the police to help you out. You don't want to be roaming the streets, now, do you? That wouldn't be right.' Hand stroking her hairy chin, she turned round on the spot twice before she murmured, 'Ah,' and pointed at her landline telephone. She shuffled towards it on stiff and aching legs. Before she dialled, she turned back to her guest and asked his name and address, but the most she got out of him was Connor, and a house with volcanoes at the front and a spider inside. The small frail woman spoke into the telephone, requesting the police and saying she was Mrs Dungate living at 57 something-or-other road. She repeated his name into the phone, explained the situation and then said, 'No, I'm not calling because I'm scared. I know you hear all sorts these days – it's terrible – but Colin … Connor isn't here to hurt me. You see, I can tell these things and I'm perfectly safe. He's a good boy. I'm phoning because I'm scared for him. He's … I don't know, but you ought to come and help him get home.' She put the phone down. 'Let's go into the kitchen where we can talk while I make us a lovely pot of tea. That'll help. You need it on a day like this. It's always bitter cold and wet at the end of October. It is October, isn't it? Now, this girl … What name did you say?'

'Joy.'

'Yes. Do you think she lives here – or used to live here?'

Connor shrugged.

'Well, you might be right.' Mrs Dungate turned on the tap and filled her kettle. 'There was a family living here before me and they had a daughter about your age. I only saw her once. She looked a bit of a one to me. Maybe that was your Joy. They moved out – let me see – my memory's just awful these days – you wouldn't believe what I forget – it'd be three or four months ago or something like. When you get to my age you'll understand. Sometimes, I forget my own name and the days of the week. Anyway, I don't know why they moved away. I think they had a problem.' Shakily, she poured the boiling water into an ancient-looking teapot.

'A problem?'

'Don't ask me, Colin … I mean, Connor. Come on. Let's give it a few minutes to brew.'

'What's a … *problem*?' Connor asked.

Mrs Dungate's face creased even more. 'Oh, you poor boy. You do have a … A problem's … Well, I think something bad happened to the family and I expect they wanted a fresh start. Now, where did I put my cups?'

'Cups? Did you get them for kicking a ball?'

Mrs Dungate coughed, spluttered and laughed all at the same time. 'Me? You have got some strange ideas, Colin. But you're a dear.' She put a couple of cups on a tray and then her eyes darted around the kitchen again as she muttered to herself, 'Where's my pills?' She made a tutting noise. 'You wouldn't believe how many things I lose. I swear, they just disappear off the face of the Earth. The more valuable they are, the more they hide.' She shrugged and shook her head with a hopeless smile.

At last, she spotted her pills and shook a few into her palm. 'The doctor makes me take these for my bones,' Mrs Dungate said, before she put one on her tongue and followed it with a gulp of tea.

Connor didn't remember that he hated tea, so he accepted a cup of the stuff.

The police arrived while Mrs Dungate and Connor were still drinking. When the two constables got Connor to rummage through his pockets, he found a card on which someone had written his name and address. Before the police officers took Connor home, Mrs Dungate made them sit down and have a cup of tea as well.

Afterwards, in the police car, Connor complained, 'She called me Colin. Her memory's a very lot bad.' Then he stared up at the funny cloud shapes in the sky.

CHAPTER 11

Memories are a fragile gift: easy to make, easy to break.

Ranji was in explanatory mood again. 'You never used to hear of so many memory problems,' she said to Mr and Mrs Markham. 'Now, anyone who's getting on a bit complains about their memory. I have my theories about that. One reason could be the way we live. Once, the old were thought very wise and commanded a lot of respect because they held in their heads a huge store of history. Younger generations used to gather round and listen to their stories. Now, in the electronic age, we don't rely on the old any more. Books and online sites give us our record of history. Old human brains have less to do and, without practice, they're losing the art of remembering. It's a pity because we're devaluing the elderly. On top of that, we're all living a lot longer. We all used to die before the worst ravages hit the brain. Not any more.' She paused before adding, 'That applies to Connor as well – in a way. Years ago, the encephalitis would have killed him and we wouldn't have to deal with the consequences. Medicine saved his life, but leaves him to cope with the aftermath. Anyway, it's a good job you took my advice about his name and address. If you want to make really sure he can always be identified, sew a tag into all his clothes.'

'Is that what it's come to?' Mrs Markham cried.

'One thing I'm sure about. You've got to give him space to develop. He won't make progress if you follow your instincts and stay beside him twenty-four hours a day. Yes, there's a risk in loosening the reins, but he's got to get used to freedom and you've got to be strong and patient.' Ranji stood up and smiled. 'I've got some good news for you. It's not his memory, I'm afraid, but we've got wind of real flair.'

His mum perked up. 'Flair? What sort of flair?'

'Mental ability.'

'But … ' Mrs Markham hesitated. 'Connor had his strengths but he wasn't … that way inclined.'

'I'm not meaning overall intelligence here. No. This is quite specific.' Ranji glanced at her watch and then said, 'Let's go in and I'll show you what I mean.'

Approaching Connor in her people test-tube, Ranji said, 'It's time for the darts.'

In his eagerness, Connor ignored his mum and dad. Grinning widely, he parked himself in front of the television for the World Championships, alongside Alcohol Abuse. The sound and picture came to life just as the commentator shouted, 'One hundrerrrrd.'

Immediately, Connor copied, 'One hundred.'

It was the early stages of a quarter-final match and the next three darts all thudded into treble twenty. Beating the commentator, Connor cried, 'One hundrerrrrd and eight-teeee!'

Ranji turned to his parents and said, 'See?'

Unable to believe that his son's uncanny way with numbers had taken another unexpected leap, Mr Markham replied quietly, 'He's just learnt it parrot-fashion, hasn't he? When all three darts go in that bit, someone always shouts *one hundred and eighty*.' Even so, Mr Markham was pleased that Connor was engrossed in something mathematical. Almost immediately, though, he was saddened as well because he was clutching at straws. After all, he was feeling proud of a fifteen-year-old son merely because he was imitating something on television.

After the next throw, Connor said, 'Sixty.' His tone betrayed disappointment. That disappointment was echoed a moment later by the announcer.

'Keep watching.' Ranji whispered so she didn't break Connor's concentration.

One of the players came forward to attempt a finish of 141.

The first dart landed in treble 20 and the second, aimed at treble 19, missed and instead hit single 19. The player's eyes shifted to the right and fixed on treble 10. His dart hit the wire and slipped instead into treble 15. Immediately, Connor yelled, 'One hundred and twenty-four!' The commentator was two seconds slower to shout the same total.

Startled, Connor's mum and dad stared speechlessly at Connor and then at Ranji.

Ranji grinned and nodded. 'I think I've just convinced you. He hasn't learnt *that* parrot-fashion. Your son's becoming a mathematical athlete. Don't ask me how. The human brain's a complicated, mysterious thing.'

Mr Markham knelt down in front of Connor. 'That was brilliant. How did you work it out?'

Connor shrugged uninterestedly. Scowling, he moved his chair so that he could still see the screen and the next throw. 'One hundred and for-teeee!'

Alcohol Abuse put his hand on Connor's knee. 'My man's boss at sums!'

Ranji said, 'The brain's got one hundred billion cells and up to one hundred thousand connections to each one. Connor's brain's made some sort of new link. He can't explain how he does the maths but somehow it gets done. If you query an answer, his attitude seems to be: what else could it be? You see, it's a knack that just comes naturally to him, like a great artist who can't explain his technique but knows when a painting's right.' As rich in metaphors as ever, she added, 'If Connor was a gardener, you'd say he's got green fingers. *He'd* say he's got green eels.'

Wrapped up in the next game, Connor called, 'One hundred and thirty-four!'

They left Connor to the sports channel and talked some more in private. Downcast, Mrs Markham said, 'Don't get me wrong. What's happening is great, but it's not helping us get the old Connor back. It's been three months and he's still ... disconnected from his past, as you put it. He probably didn't even know us in there.'

'No,' Ranji admitted. 'But we keep trying. We're providing

scaffolding for his life now and trying to discover a window on his pre-virus life. You never know what'll trigger those long-term memories. Think of a family trip to a restaurant. Different people will encode the experience in different ways, so they'll need different cues to retrieve it. Dad might remember the meal best when he sees the wallpaper of the restaurant again because, at the time, he was preoccupied with redecorating the house. Mum's memory might be triggered by the taste of her main course because she was wondering if she could make food as good as that at home. The kids might have forgotten all about the meal and the restaurant, but they might be reminded if they heard the same music that was playing in the background. That's because they'd argued about the best song. You see, there are lots of different ways of remembering any one event. The trick is to find out how the brain filed it away: by taste, sight, sound, something that was said, meeting someone, or whatever. Smell's very powerful for bringing back memory.'

'What does that mean for Connor?'

'It means you carry on taking him to his favourite places, exposing him to favourite smells, playing him his favourite songs, getting him to talk to his friends, giving him freedom to rediscover things for himself. But you have to appreciate that triggers are often unpredictable. We'd never have guessed that an audio player would be a retrieval cue for numbers.'

'We're stumbling in the dark, aren't we? After all this time, we've only pulled one trigger. One isn't very good.'

'No,' Ranji replied. 'You might want to prepare yourself in case we can't retrieve any more. But,' she added quickly, 'that doesn't mean we give up. There's always hope we just haven't figured out the right cues yet.'

It was a family outing, a recreation of long-past Sundays. First stop was the railway embankment. It was a place where Mr Markham had spent hours of his life with his two young boys. To his wife, he would grumble about the waste of time, but really he regarded those hours, waiting for trains, as precious. There would be hiding games, throwing acorn competitions, bike riding, and, of course, the occasional excitement of a passing train.

Connor jumped back from the wire fence in surprise. Clearly, the train was faster, noisier, fiercer than he was expecting. Its roar obliterated his cry. 'Sprouts!'

Extracting a silvery coin from his pocket, Brad sidled up to his brother. 'Do you remember, when we were little and on our own, we clambered through the fence and put a ten-pence piece – like this one – on the rail?' He glanced at his Mum and Dad as if expecting a belated telling-off but, in the interests of Connor's memory, they kept quiet about the dangerous prank. 'When the train came it squashed the coin almost completely flat. It was so spread out, it nearly got rid of the pattern altogether.'

Connor shook his head.

'You kept it,' Brad reminded him, 'but I think you threw it out when someone at school said it was against the law to deface a coin. You thought you might get caught and put in prison.'

'Where was it going?' Connor asked.

'The coin?'

'No.' He pointed to the retreating train.

'It's on its way to London.'

'Oh.'

They all walked to the park and watched for a while a game of football, four people playing tennis, and two families feeding the ducks and swans. One toddler let out a scream and staggered back as a bold swan tried to peck the bread from his hand. Mr Markham nudged Connor. 'That happened to you when you were … I don't know … about five, I should think. You got really upset.' He took Connor to the edge of the lake and waited for a couple of expectant swans to glide across towards them. 'You'd been teasing the poor thing,' he said. 'Showing it bread and pretending to throw it but not letting go. The swan took the law into its own hands and nipped you on the leg.'

'Swan?'

Mr Markham nodded. 'That's what they're called.'

'They don't have hands!'

'No, I mean … '

Connor interrupted. 'How do they move?'

'They've got legs underneath. They paddle. After one attacked you, you wouldn't go near them again. You've never liked swans since.'

Connor looked surprised. 'They look happy.'

Mr Markham sighed. 'Come on. Let's get lunch at the café, just like we used to.'

But the traditional fish and chips followed by ice cream meant nothing to Connor. He ate them without comment, without hesitation, without a glimmer of recognition.

In the afternoon they went swimming. Connor stood at the edge of the pool and watched the people already in the water. 'They're having a … ' He imitated washing himself under the arms.

'No,' his mum said, 'they're not having a bath. They're swimming, like swans, only not as elegant.'

Connor showed no sign of recalling a swan. 'Can I do that?' he asked.

'Yes,' his mum answered. 'You were pretty good at it. Dr Nawaz says you'll know how to swim, just like you know how to walk without having to be taught all over again.'

At the side of the pool, a girl with a spectacular figure was staring at Connor. She might even have been admiring him in his swimming trunks. When Connor noticed her, she frowned, pushed off and swam away.

Brad said, 'That was Alice Foley, Hattie's friend. And yours, I suppose. Remember?'

Connor shook his head and then followed Brad to the steps into the shallow end. It was a strange feeling. The water wasn't hot, not like taking a bath, but it was just as luxurious. Connor smiled. Something told him to kick out and paddle. The next moment, he shocked himself by moving slowly through the water with a cautious breast-stroke. He didn't know what he was doing, or why, but he could do it and it was quite happy. Not as happy as watching darts, of course.

'See?' his dad said. 'You can do it. We used to come here every Sunday afternoon.'

Connor was not interested in the past. He swam another width as if he were a novice who had just realized that he could take his feet off the bottom and not drown. Enjoying himself, he splashed Brad and everyone else nearby.

'Oi!' a father shouted, protecting his young daughter from the flying drops. Buoyed by her water wings, the girl – barely more than a baby – drifted away while her father berated an exuberant Connor. The girl kicked and thrashed out, not seeing the danger ahead. Three big lads were jumping in boisterously, curling up into bombs before they hit the water. Taking no notice of the youngster in water wings, one of them took off and formed a hard ball in mid-air.

Connor pushed off from the side, grabbed the girl by her arm and dragged her out of range of the bomb, which landed instead on Connor's legs. Ignoring the pain, Connor guided the girl back to her father.

Clinging to the side and watching Connor, Mrs Markham muttered, 'It's not working, is it? He doesn't remember.'

Mr Markham paused before replying, 'Not yet.'

In their anxiety to reclaim the old Connor, neither of them recognized the new Connor's small act of kindness.

CHAPTER 12

Connor's hormones were fully functioning, even if some of his neurons weren't.

Only one thing beat darts on the … picture box thing. That girl, the one he definitely recognized, could make him forget the big scores, the doubles and trebles, the out-shots. Connor itched for Courtney to finish with Artist and come to see him instead. Her chat with the silly old man was taking a lifetime.

On the table behind Connor, Ranji was listening to another patient. Two parts of Confused's brain that were supposed to be separate had been joined by disease. She made all sorts of connections that should have had nothing to do with each other. To her, days had texture and colour. 'Monday's pale yellow and a bit lumpy – like custard,' she was saying. 'Tuesday's dark blue and it feels rough like a cheese-grater. Wednesday's really smooth and a bit soft and brown … ' Connor gave up eavesdropping. Besides, he was trying to concentrate on Courtney.

Eventually Courtney came over and took a seat next to Connor. At once, he said, 'I've got my own mp3 thing … ' He pointed to the player. 'Do you want … ? It's happy.'

'Yeah,' Courtney replied. 'I'd like to hear what you listen to.'

When she nodded her head in time to the music, Connor's eyes sparkled. He didn't know why she moved like that, but she seemed to be enjoying it. 'Yeah,' she said loudly over the music that only she could hear. 'Good.'

She listened to the end of the track and then handed the earpieces back to Connor. 'Thanks. I heard that on the net ages ago. I'd forgotten how good it was.'

'You forgot?' Connor was amazed.

'Sure. We all forget things. It's just that people like Grandad and you forget more than most.' She shrugged as if it didn't matter to her.

'I thought it was only us,' he said, meaning the Institute's patients, 'and Mrs … Treble Nineteen.'

'No, it's everyone. Didn't they tell you?'

At last Connor felt a little less detached. He wasn't so unusual after all – and it was Courtney who'd told him. Grateful to her, he reached out and touched her arm. It was something that Ranji did to him a lot.

Courtney looked down at his hand and smiled. 'The others are getting ready for a game of bingo. Are you going to join in?'

Bingo was happy. It was a number game, but it was a bit boring because some of the others took so long to work out what numbers they'd got. And one woman would yell swearwords if her numbers didn't get called out. Sometimes Connor didn't join in himself but instead helped Alcohol Abuse with his numbers.

'Are *you* playing?' asked Connor.

'No, it's not for me.'

Connor replied, 'It's not for me, then.'

Courtney watched a nurse walking towards Stroke 2 with a glass of water and whispered to Connor, 'Watch this.' The nurse popped a couple of white things into the drink, gave it a good stir and handed it to Stroke 2. Seeing Connor's perplexed face, Courtney explained, 'She's put pills in it but he won't take them. Watch.'

As soon as the nurse's back was turned, Stroke 2 got up and walked over to Artist's easel. He tipped his drink into the pot of water. When he noticed that Courtney and Connor were watching him, he tiptoed across to them and said, 'They're trying to kill me with pills, you know.' He put an eel across his lips and went back to his seat to get his bingo card.

Courtney chuckled. 'He always does that. I don't know what Grandad's painting with.' From her shoulder-bag, Courtney produced a half-drunk bottle of pop. 'Do *you* want a drink?' she asked. 'I've had enough. And it's not got anything in it. Promise.'

Connor took the plastic container and peered into it. 'Fizzy drink, no fish.'

Courtney looked puzzled. She mimicked taking a swig direct from the bottle.

Tentatively, Connor took a gulp and then wiped his mouth. 'Happy.' He held out the remains to Courtney.

She was about to take the bottle but thought better of it. 'You keep it,' she said. 'I've got to go.' She stood up.

Connor also got to his feet and, in an uncontrollable show of affection, threw his arms around her.

She clasped him briefly and then pulled away slightly as if she were reacting with embarrassment to a baby who wanted a hug. She smiled at him sympathetically.

Excited by her, he slipped his hand onto the front of her blouse.

Courtney removed his hand and backed off, saying, 'No!'

Connor was puzzled. He remembered from somewhere that he mustn't touch a girl on the chest, but he thought it would be okay with Courtney. He thought something about love made it okay.

When Mr Markham came to pick up Connor, Ranji drew him to one side and told him about the incident with a young female visitor. 'I had a chat with the girl concerned,' she said, 'and no harm's done. She understood. Connor's a boy of fifteen with all the normal curiosity and urges, but without a fifteen-year-old brain to match. That's bound to be an explosive mixture.'

'What do you want me to do?' asked Connor's dad.

'I think you'd better have a word with him about the facts of life, but it won't be easy. In some ways, he's too young for it, but his hormones say otherwise. And whatever you tell him, he'll forget most of it. Still, the time's obviously ripe.'

In Connor's bedroom, Brad was only too keen to reinforce what

Mum and Dad had been going on about most of the night. In a way, it was like having the old Connor back. Brad would have understood a piece of schoolwork and Connor would have pretended to understand. Afterwards, Brad might try to explain it to Connor if he felt like it and if his brother seemed to care. The new Connor definitely seemed to care about sex, reproduction and touching girls, and Brad relished any excuse to talk about it. Besides, he owed Connor. 'Actually,' Brad said, 'there's websites that show you lots of out-of-bounds bits, but don't tell Mum and Dad.' He took great delight in explaining it all over again with helpful illustrations.

Connor had trouble with his brother's words, but the pictures he could understand.

'Got it?' asked Brad, knowing that Connor might need it again tomorrow night. And the night after.

Connor nodded. He tried to concentrate on his brother's words and not get diverted by other pictures in his room. He now had five of his brain scans on show.

Turning away from the screen, Brad said, 'It sounds like a joke, doesn't it? Much too messy and hit-and-miss, but that's how horizontal tango works. That's biology for you.'

'That's what Mum and Dad did to make us?'

'Right. It's a bit grim to think about them having sex. Yuck! It's unlikely, I know, but I guess they must have once.'

Proud to show off his new knowledge, Connor said, 'Twice.' He smiled. He knew he was right because he was good at numbers.

Brad was still smarting after losing Connor at the previous football match. He swore that it wouldn't happen again and he kept a close eye on his brother. Most of the time. When a friend pointed out two girls who had come to support the opposition and began to discuss their merits, Brad was distracted. Only for a moment. But it only took a moment for Connor to wander away unseen from the action.

Connor couldn't remember the way, but he could follow numbers. He wanted number 57. Treble nineteen with the crimson-leaved tree thing outside. He pushed that little button yet again. The woman who answered the door looked surprised, but before she could greet her persistent caller, Connor delivered his carefully rehearsed piece. 'Everyone forgets things. It's not just you and me.' He shrugged to show that it really didn't matter. Then he wandered away to get lost some more, leaving Mrs Dungate on the doorstep with her mouth open. She shook her head, thinking to herself, 'He's a treasure, that Colin.'

At the end of the road was a building unlike all the others. It was bigger, more colourful, with signs up outside. *GG's Nightclub*.

Connor stopped and gazed at it. GG. Horrible letter. But the place also drew him in.

He pushed open the blue doors and tiptoed inside. The lights were off. Connor got the impression that the huge room should have been bright with coloured lights, bustling with party people, heady with beery fumes, and noisy with overpowering music. Right now, it was none of these things. It was dull, empty, stale and quiet.

Then, suddenly, there was someone behind him. 'Oi! What are you doing?'

Someone pinned his arms behind him and another man came out of a side-room and stared at him. 'Well, well. Hello, Connor. Long time, no see.' The man, much older than Connor, was wearing a smart suit. 'Come and have a seat. I could use a chat with you.' He nodded at the bouncer who promptly freed Connor's arms.

'You'll have forgotten my name, it seems. I'm Mr Rowling. Owner of GG's.' He lifted a chair and plonked it down in front of Connor.

Once Connor sat down, Mr Rowling circled him slowly. 'Liam Darby's told me all about you, Connor. You're a clean slate. You won't remember our little … agreement.'

Connor shook his head, more in bewilderment than in answer.

'That's good. But now you present me with a dilemma. Despite your … forgetfulness, you found your way to my door.

A couple of weeks back, you phoned me as well. You didn't say anything, but I did a 1471 and discovered it was you. So, I'm bound to ask myself, just how clean is the clean slate? Is there a faint trace? You see what I'm getting at? If there's a chink of light in your recall, we have to come to another agreement – or find some other way forward.'

Having completely lost track of the conversation, Connor was squinting. Changing tack, he announced, 'G's not a happy letter.'

'Pity you see it that way,' Mr Rowling said with a sly smile, 'as I've got two of them. GG Rowling. Gareth Gregor.'

Mr Rowling's voice was barely above a whisper, but it commanded respect. 'I can see the time you could have any girl you wanted has long gone. They won't be hammering down your door any more, that's for sure. You won't bring any more here. So, our relationship's got to be different, going forward. No relationship at all's the best way. What do you think?'

'Erm … Yes.'

'You're not going to talk about me or the club, are you?'

Connor shook his head, because he sensed that's what Mr Rowling wanted.

'I'll have Liam keeping an eye on you, making sure you behave.'

For a second or two, Connor carried on shaking his head, but he said, 'Yes.'

'After all, you don't want anyone to get hurt, do you? Someone like that girlfriend. Hattie, wasn't it? Or has she dumped you now? Do you have a special friend?'

'Courtney.'

'Courtney who?'

'Courtney.'

'Okay. You don't want any harm to come to her, do you?'

Connor swallowed. He didn't know what was going on, but he recognized a threat. 'No.'

'Keep your mouth shut, then. Now get out of here and don't come back. Remember, you're not old enough to come into a club like this.'

CHAPTER 13

When Connor still had a left temporal lobe, he'd got used to being cautioned.

It had been a miserable Sunday in March and Liam's first game for the team. He was lounging on the ground with the other substitutes, getting more and more itchy to come on and make an impact.

Feet planted on the goal line, Connor bent his knees. His arms were stretched out on either side of his body, making him look as wide as possible. Concentrating, he swayed slightly to the left, then to the right and back again, ready to pounce. His expression revealed confidence, while the penalty-taker looked nervous. The spot kick was the opposition's last realistic opportunity to get back into the game. Connor kept his eye on the rival striker's hips – the key to where he was going to place the ball. Connor knew that he would save the shot as soon as his opponent hesitated during his run-up. At the last moment, the striker changed his mind about his tactic. Fatal mistake for a penalty-taker. The shot was weak and chest height, ideal for a keeper. Agile as a cat, Connor dived to the left and pawed it away.

On the touch-line, Mr and Mrs Markham and the other supporters cheered. As always after one of his spectacular saves, the girls chanted his name. The coach said, 'Beautiful. We'd be lost without him.' Then he looked down at Liam. 'The game's probably safe. Get your tracksuit off and warm up. Let's see what you can do in the last ten minutes.'

Liam formed a fist and punched the air. 'Yes! Rocking.'

When the substitute jogged on to the pitch, Connor shouted, 'Come on, Liam! We need one more to be sure.'

It didn't take him long. The team's new star scored a crisp goal within four minutes of coming on.

The next game, Liam was on from the first whistle. And he made a real impact. He got two goals and, as they walked off at half time, he got into an argument with two opponents. It all got out of hand as they walked past the supporters on the line. To break up the brawl, Connor put himself between Liam and the players the striker had been baiting. The result was that Connor took a punch that was meant for someone else. Quickly, the coach and spectators dragged Liam away. In the scrum, one of the opponents took Liam's elbow in the face and ended up lying in the mud.

The referee, jogging towards the extra-curricular activity, saw only Connor pushing away an opponent. 'What's going on?' he demanded to know.

'Nothing,' the home team and supporters agreed.

'Elbow!' the boy on the ground shouted, pointing at his left cheek.

'A collision,' Connor claimed. 'Just an accident.'

The ref eyed Connor suspiciously and, making an example of him, took his name and showed him the yellow card.

'Now, don't run off this time,' Brad said from under his cagoule, wishing he'd got Connor on a lead. He knew that his mum had sewn name tags inside all of Connor's clothes, so someone could always get him home if he strayed, but it was embarrassing to keep losing him. 'Come on.' He led the way under the railway bridge.

A train rumbled overhead. Connor stood still, refusing to move, like a dog captivated by a fascinating scent.

'Come on,' Brad repeated. 'It's just a train.'

But Connor wasn't looking up at the source of the sound. He was staring at the ground where rainwater ran along the gutter and formed a puddle beside the pavement.

'Yes?' Brad prompted.

Connor pointed at the small pool of dirty water. 'Drink.'

'Well, water anyway. In case you hadn't noticed, it's raining.'

'It's not pink.'

'What is this about pink rain?'

The new Connor could turn it on just like a baby. He could look helpless, hurt, distressed, cheeky and cute, all at the same time.

'Sorry, Connor, but you're driving me mad.' Brad sighed. 'Let's get going.'

Brad's whole life had been put on hold, it seemed to him. Helping Connor had become the only thing that mattered. Before setting out on this latest mission, Brad had almost shouted at his mum, 'Connor's in the spotlight all the time. Not me. The only way you see me is if I go up close to Connor and catch a bit of his limelight.' No one came to the house and said, 'How's Brad getting on?' There was only one topic of interest. 'How's Connor? Any progress?'

Eventually, Connor followed his brother, occasionally glancing back.

Brad had been persuaded by his mum and dad to bring Connor into town, where they thought Brad might be able to stir a memory. He came to a halt outside a nightclub and announced, 'Here we are.'

Eve's was closed, boarded up. The door and window frames were scorched where, months ago, flames had fed on the paint and wood.

Connor looked around without a flicker of recognition on his face.

Brad said, 'Remember when you got arrested? It was all because of something that happened here.'

Connor seemed more interested in going back to the railway bridge.

'Come on. You must remember!' Brad exclaimed. 'No one forgets being arrested. You know, the police taking you away and locking you up. They cautioned you for underage drinking and criminal damage or something.'

'One four ... ' Connor struggled to say.

'One four? Fourteen? What's that got to do with anything?'
Connor shrugged again.

'You're really on a different planet.'

Brad hit his brother. Not hard. Not like those fights they used to have, the ones that had evaporated completely from Connor's brain. Besides, the slap wasn't really meant to harm Connor. It was more about releasing the pressure building in Brad.

Immune to the slap, Connor wore an expression of surprise and indifference.

'Pink rain and numbers! This isn't working,' Brad uttered. 'Mum and Dad are barking up the wrong tree. Jogging your memory's a waste of time. You don't really *want* to remember, do you? You don't care. You're just … as you are.'

Connor hadn't got a clue what the boy under the hood was saying and he didn't like the way water ran down the surface of his coat. He turned away.

The fixed camera opposite Eve's nightclub had not followed the action. It provided static surveillance of the scene, like a small window that allows but also restricts the view.

The young men spilled untidily on to the screen from the right-hand side. Four of their faces were hidden by hoodies. The fifth made no attempt to conceal his features and didn't seem to realize that there was a CCTV camera. His stagger suggested that he'd tanked up on alcohol.

A stone went through one window. A brick went through another. One of the men lit a hankie stuffed into a bottle, probably full of petrol. The flaming bottle followed the brick into the empty nightclub.

And that was it. A few seconds later, the gang vanished from shot. Exit left.

The brief sequence was like a snatch of a movie, a fragment of action stripped of its meaning and context. It was the middle of a story with no known beginning and no known end, but it was all played out in eerie silence because there was no soundtrack.

The young men left behind them a still street, wide and

traffic-free. It was night-time but not dark because of the street-lamps and the security lights left on in some of the deserted shops on each side of the road. After a minute, there was an extra shimmer at the window of the club as the fire gathered strength. There might have been a smoke alarm. Eight minutes later, a fire appliance arrived.

The police got a good shot of only one of the five lads. The one who seemed to be drunk. He hadn't smashed a window or committed the act of arson, but he had taken part in the crime. By hawking his picture around, the team investigating the attack eventually identified Connor Markham and tracked him down. A police officer with a number on his shoulder arrested him.

Connor could hardly remember anything about the incident except the following morning's sore head and nausea. He denied responsibility for the damage, yet he copped it anyway. After all, he'd been captured beautifully on security camera. The images were so incriminating that he had to be guilty.

But he wasn't a sneak. Even though he knew the young man who'd led the gang and the person who'd ordered the attack and plied him with alcohol, he wouldn't give their names to the police. He knew what would happen to his own house – or to Hattie's – if he grassed them up.

The police kept Connor in a cell for ages and questioned him over and over again. It was obvious that they didn't believe his plea of innocence and ignorance.

'We do know what's going on, you know. We know you lot from GG's think there's only room for one nightclub on your patch. We know Rowling doesn't like competition. He sent you to Eve's, didn't he?'

Connor shrugged.

Unable to prove anything beyond doubt, the police didn't charge him, but gave him a final warning. 'We know you didn't actually set fire to the place, so we're going to go easy on you. This time. If you ever get into trouble again … ' The officer shook his head grimly. 'Big problems.'

Yes. Connor was used to cautions.

Furtively, Hattie slipped out of school on her own. Hoping that no one was watching, she walked straight past her usual road and headed for a bus stop. She wanted a ride to the takeaway near the hospital.

Connor's parents had pleaded with her, 'Just try a few of his favourite things to see if you can jog his memory. Please, Hattie.' That was all the excuse she needed to snub her friends' advice.

Twenty minutes later, she turned up at the Institute for Memory Disorders with pizza, profiteroles and an apprehensive smile.

Hattie was pleased to see that Connor's face was not entirely vacant.

'You're … ' He made a show of sniffing.

Taken aback, Hattie said, 'What?'

'You … smell like a volcano.'

Hattie was mortified. 'A volcano? Really? That's a horrid smell.'

'Horrid?' Connor queried.

She pulled a face, crinkling her turned-up nose.

'No, it's happy.' He smelled the air again and said, 'There's another smell.'

Hattie tried to put their shaky start to the back of her mind. Opening the large thin box, she said, 'Your favourite. Spicy beef pizza followed by profiteroles. Remember?'

'What are prof … ?'

'Cake and cream and chocolate things. But you have to have the first course first.'

She pulled a piece of pizza out of the box with her fingers till the long strands of cheese snapped messily. 'Here. Try it.' She took another slice for herself, held it above her head and fed the cheese strings into her mouth and then bit into the pizza itself.

Connor followed suit.

'Good?' Hattie asked.

Connor shrugged. 'What's beef?'

'It's the meat from a cow.'

At once, Connor dropped his pizza on to the floor. 'Sprouts!'

Hattie was horrified that her best intentions were backfiring. 'What's the matter?'

'No cow,' Connor exclaimed. 'Not happy noise.'

'Okay, okay.' Hattie picked up the pizza from the floor and threw it back in the box together with her own slice. Persevering, she said, 'Let's just go for the profiteroles, then. They're the brilliant bit anyway.'

Connor watched Hattie stab a small grey round thing with a plastic toothbrush, dip it into a bath of dark brown stuff and, turning the coated ball to stop it dripping, shove it quickly into her mouth.

'Mmm.'

'No cow?'

'No,' she assured him with her mouth full.

Taking the second toothbrush, Connor tried one for himself, but he wasn't so good at avoiding the drips. His trousers and chin got splattered with brown goo. But at least the girl was right this time. He'd never tasted anything so good.

Hattie took one look at his face and, with relief, said, 'Another?'

Connor nodded eagerly and proceeded to make himself more messy.

Hattie ignored his sloppiness. She tried to tell herself that it wasn't important, but she couldn't help picturing the old Connor eating profiteroles. He was an expert. 'Do you remember … ?'

'Who are you?' Connor enquired.

'Hattie,' she said, disguising her real feelings by stuffing her mouth with another chocolate treat. When she'd finished the mouthful she asked, 'Do you want to come and see a film, or go bowling with me?' She was hoping that he'd opt for a film because in the dark there was no chance that a friend would see her with him.

Connor didn't understand what she was saying.

'A film. It's like television,' Hattie said, pointing at the box in the corner, 'only giant size.'

Connor perked up. Someone had read him stories about giants. Giants were happy. 'Do they show darts?' He imitated the throwing action.

'Er … Even better than that. They have horror films and you love them.'

'Do they have profs?'

Hattie smiled. 'We can buy some on the way.'

'Rocking.'

Hattie nodded while she cleared up the fall-out from the profiteroles. 'It's what we used to do a lot,' she said. 'We went to parties and all. I used to watch you play football as well – in all weathers.'

'Why?'

Hattie grabbed a box of tissues from a nearby table. 'You'll need to wipe yourself down.' She pointed to the corners of his mouth and chin. She was too self-conscious to do it herself, like a mother cleaning her baby after a meal. 'We hung around together because … well … we were a couple. Do you know what I mean?'

Connor nodded. He tried hard to remember some of the things that couples did. 'Did we have … ?' He look lost for a moment and then said, 'Babies.'

Hattie opened her mouth but the words didn't come straightaway. 'Er … No.'

'Did we do kissing?'

Hattie smiled at him. 'That's one thing boyfriends and girlfriends get up to.'

'Was I happy?'

'I think so. You always wanted more and all.'

He nodded mischievously. This was a bit of the past that did interest him. 'What more did we do?'

'Erm … ' Hattie hesitated. She felt a duty to tell him because anything she said might bring back a memory. Dr Nawaz and the Markhams had been very clear that they wanted Hattie to use anything that might reach Connor and the more emotionally involving it was, the better. That was the most likely way of provoking a spark of recognition or even recall. Hattie looked around to check that no one was within earshot, drew closer to Connor, then took a deep breath.

Connor was a very lot confused about love.

His mum told him she loved him, but that didn't make Mum his girlfriend. No. He loved the volcano girl with the profs. He must love her because of what she said he'd touched. Yet Mum and Dad had said something about being able to love only one person. So why did he like Courtney more than the girl he loved?

Someone said he loved that muddy ball game and the giant picture box that he couldn't remember. If love was such a big thing, why couldn't he remember? Perhaps that was it. The old Connor loved the kicking game, the big pictures, the volcano girl with the profs. The new Connor just wanted the profs. The new Connor loved Courtney, numbers, darts and music.

He became even more sure that the old Connor had gone, that the old Connor wasn't right, that he didn't want to know the old Connor. But if he wasn't the old Connor from 'before', who was he really? Who was the new Connor?

'Who am I?' he cried suddenly.

'Oh, Connor,' his mum replied, dropping whatever she was doing and giving him a hug. 'You're … ' She waved towards the photographs dotted around the living room. 'You're the boy in these pictures, the boy we're so proud of, the boy who can win a football match for his team and save lots of penalties. You're the one who hates maths, isn't keen on school, who used to go around with lots of girls and then just Hattie. You do things with Liam Darby and argue with Brad all the time.'

Connor shook his head. 'That's your … ' He sighed and muttered under his breath. 'That's your thing of who I am. It's not me … knowing what *I* am.'

'So, what sort of boy do *you* think you are?' Mr Markham asked him.

'I'm … I don't know. I'm different.'

It was like he'd been abducted to before-land where nothing was quite right. In before-land, the people had not been made properly. The ones claiming to know him were not what they appeared to be. Sometimes, Connor thought they must be fakes.

For once supporting his brother in a crisis, Brad said, 'If you're not the old Connor we know, you must be whatever you are right now. That's all there is to it.'

'But you … ' He searched the slender dictionary in his head for the right word, but it wasn't there. 'You want before-Connor.'

'That's because we think you'll be happier if you can remember your past,' his mum replied.

'*You'll* be happy, not me,' he snapped. Heading for the door, he added, 'Sprouts!'

The corridor was clear. It was safe to talk. 'How is he, Brad? Any better?'

'It's like living in the worst sort of soap opera. Connor's died and been replaced by a long-lost twin I never knew he had.'

Hattie shook her head sadly.

'And it's like living in a time warp. Sometimes, this weird twin spends an entire day listening to music and when he's finished, he thinks it's only been a few seconds. Another time, he'll get bored after a few minutes of doing something and he imagines it's been a week. Time doesn't mean anything to him any more.'

'Is he angry at the virus and all? I know I am.'

Straightaway, Brad replied, 'It hasn't occurred to him to be angry or anything else. He's just trying to get by.'

'Has he shown any sign of remembering things?'

'Not really. Even his short-term memory's up the spout sometimes. Last night, he had a shower and then he went for another one ten minutes later. We had to tell him he'd already done it. As for his long-term memory, I'm not sure it's worth … '

'Well, *I'm* still trying to help him,' Hattie said, interrupting. 'I'm taking him to a film – if he'll come.'

'It's a waste of time – like screaming in a vacuum.'

'What?'

'Sound doesn't travel in a vacuum. Space craft make a lot of noise in films but not in reality. Anyway,' Brad said, 'I don't think he wants to remember. He just wants to be what he is now. Fair enough, I reckon.'

'But … '

'He wants his own life, not the old one you tell him about all the time.'

'I don't give up so easy,' said Hattie.

'It's up to you,' Brad replied, 'but one day you'll have to decide who you're trying to help – Connor or yourself.'

CHAPTER 14

Soon would come the time for Connor to return to school.

It was early evening and Mr Markham was driving his damaged son home from the Institute of Memory Disorders when the old Connor reappeared for an instant. The traffic lights had just turned green when Connor pointed to the gates on the left and said, 'Joy.'

His dad slammed on the brakes and the car behind screeched to a halt, up against his back bumper. 'Do you recognize it? It's your school. Who's Joy? Or are you just happy?'

Connor did not respond. But he wasn't happy.

Behind them, an angry head poked out of a car window and yelled, 'Shift it!'

Connor opened the door, got out and strolled towards the school gates, while Mr Markham shouted, 'Connor, no!'

A loud and insistent car horn blared. Mr Markham twisted round, put his head out of his own window and shouted, 'Look, my son's … '

'You're in the middle of a junction. You can't stop! Bloody idiot.'

Mr Markham gave up his defence. He pulled away, desperately searching for a parking spot.

Connor strayed into the quiet school, past the cleaners in the reception and cloakroom area. He walked beyond the drama studio, down the drab corridor to the English department and turned into a classroom with tables and chairs laid out in a U-shape. Along one wall, there were large red words that he didn't understand. *SHAKESPEARE'S MACBETH*. He sat down at one particular place, elbows on the table, and wept. The tears of frustration flowed down his cheeks. He had no idea what to do in a school. He had no idea what he was doing in the school. He knew only that the old Connor had intruded on his life, kidnapped him and taken him to before-land.

Restless and confused, he got up again. There was an exit at the end of the corridor so he went back out into the open air. On the other side of the school fence, there was an adventure playground in the park. It was alien to him, but he vaulted over the barrier anyway. There was a sort of roundabout, model towers and bridges made of planks and ropes. Connor went and sat on a seat that dangled from a thing like they have at both ends of the muddy kicking field.

A little boy came up to him and said, 'My mam says you're too big to play here.'

'Am I?'

The boy nodded.

'I know here.' Connor pointed towards the school gates. 'Something happened. Not happy.'

The small boy took fright and ran off.

Then a man dashed up to him. Breathlessly, the funnybone man said, 'What's going on Connor? Come on. Let's go home.'

The strange man led him away.

It was a sort of miniature house, not made of brick. It looked as if a good kick would knock it over. It was red and its roof had feathery white stuff piled on top. Outside, there was a long line of big people and children. Connor stopped to watch.

When Hattie realized that Connor was no longer at her side, she went back for him.

He said, 'They're funny.'

'How do you mean?'

'They … er … won't all get in there.' He pointed to the small house.

Hattie smiled. 'No. They go in one at a time. That's why they're having to wait in a queue.'

'Why do they go in?'

'It's a grotto,' Hattie replied. 'They're going in to see Santa – eventually.'

Connor was baffled.

'It'll soon be Christmas,' Hattie told him. 'Three weeks to go.' She explained all about it and ended by saying, 'All these boys and girls will go in and get a present – something they want – from Santa.'

'But you said he's not … '

'Real. No. He's only pretending.'

'But the … things he gives are real.'

'That's right.' Tugging on his coat sleeve, Hattie said, 'Let's go and get those profiteroles. It's the next shop.'

Even though he was fascinated by Santa's grotto and the idea that people might pretend to be someone they're not, Connor followed Hattie keenly.

Just inside the shop, Hattie whispered to him, 'Now remember what I said you had to do.'

Connor nodded warily.

Ranji Nawaz had suggested that Connor should pay at the cinema, but Hattie thought that was a bit ambitious. Instead, she'd told him how to pay for the profiteroles.

But, at the last moment, Connor lost his nerve. He was good with numbers but he didn't know about money. He held out the cash in his hand so the shopkeeper could pick out some coins. Then he went to walk out but Hattie grabbed his arm and held him back. 'Hang on for your change,' she breathed.

Connor nodded and clung to her hand.

When the shop assistant counted out a few coins onto Connor's palm, she sneered at him. She didn't say anything, but the message was tattooed across her face. 'This boy's a good few blooms short of a bouquet. Can't handle money at his age. What do they teach 'em in schools these days?'

Embarrassed, Hattie looked round and then said, 'Come on. Let's get out of here. The film'll start soon.'

They ran across the road, through the teeming rain, to the cinema.

Connor didn't enjoy the film at all. It wasn't a new-Connor thing. Nothing like darts on the picture box. It was dark and the sound came from all around him. Sometimes he'd jump and look over his shoulder, but there were only more rows of seats. The flashing images were just too much and he couldn't understand a lot of it. He liked a bit with a man and a woman being a couple but the cars went too fast – more than thirty miles an hour, he guessed – and crashed too much. The speaking went too fast as well. To Connor's leaky memory, each new sequence was another opening scene. There were too many people he didn't recognize. He suspected that some of them were like Santa: just pretending. There was a very lot of men hitting each other with loud thuds and firing guns with loud bangs – real guns, not two eels and a thumb like Liam's gun.

Hattie wasn't really concentrating on the film. She kept taking sidelong glances at Connor, watching him cringe. 'It's all right,' she said. 'Just a special effect. The sort of thing you like.'

Connor's expression told her that the sort of thing he liked had changed.

Afterwards, when they came out into the cold night air, she said, 'You didn't like that much, did you?'

He shook his head.

Under the blazing street lights and the colourful Christmas illuminations, the spark of optimism had been extinguished. Hattie had failed. She was desperate and depressed because her boyfriend remained obstinately out of reach, because – like spicy beef pizzas and movies – she was the sort of thing Connor had once liked but not any more.

Seeing Hattie's miserable face, Connor tried to cheer her up. He said, 'The profs were happy.'

As part of the effort to acclimatize Connor to real life, Ranji took him into a local centre where the people serving in the shops were used to her visits and sympathetic with her awkward patients.

On the way, Connor pointed to a man on a moving machine and asked, 'What's that?'

Ranji said, 'A bicycle – a bike for short.'

'Can I move on one?'

'You did, yes. Your dad told me you used to go all over the place on a bike. I bet you still can. Easy.'

He looked at Ranji in disbelief.

'I know,' she said. 'You're wondering how you can ride a bike when you can't remember what it's called. It's because there are different types of remembering. There's remembering how to do things without thinking, and there's remembering what things are called. The part of your brain that allows you to do things without thinking is fine. Before you run, swim or ride a bike, you don't have to recall how to do it. Once you've learned, it's a set piece. It becomes second nature. You just get on with it because your know-how memory takes care of it. People with thirty-miles-an-hour brains remember how to cycle a long time after they've forgotten what bikes are called.'

The street through the shopping centre was wide and traffic free. It was a clear day, but last night's rain had sprinkled the pavement liberally with puddles. On the left-hand side, outside a disused club called Eve's, Connor came to a sudden halt and glanced around with a puzzled expression.

'What is it?' asked Ranji, ever hopeful that a familiar sight might make Connor's neurons fire.

'I don't know.' Connor shrugged. 'Nothing.'

Always patient, Ranji said, 'Sure?'

He nodded blankly because he didn't know why he'd stopped in the first place. Then, a number flashed into his brain. 'One four nine nine.'

'One four nine nine? What's that, Connor? A big house number? Part of a telephone number? The cost of something: fourteen pounds and ninety-nine pence?'

Connor shook his head.

'Never mind,' Ranji said, not wanting to pressure him on an outing. 'Come on. Let's go in here.' The first stop was a greengrocer. Ranji explained, 'It's called that because they sell greens – or vegetables.' She pointed to the trays, turning the trip into a lesson. 'See? This is cabbage. And there's cucumber, broccoli, sprouts.'

'Sprouts?'

'Yes,' said Ranji.

Fascinated, Connor picked one up and turned it over and over in his hand.

To move Connor on, Ranji named more vegetables, 'Lettuce, cauliflower, carrots … '

Connor stopped her as soon as she showed him the carrots. 'A green thing shouldn't have them. They're … ' Frustrated, he looked around and focused on the fruit section, pointing to the colour he wanted.

'Orange, yes,' Ranji agreed.

'Why are carrots orange?'

'Ah, now you've got me there,' Ranji admitted. 'I don't know.'

'Sprouts are happy,' Connor concluded, 'but carrots aren't.'

Outside the shop, they bumped into Liam. Suspecting that it would be difficult for Connor to identify his mate in the shopping centre, Ranji said, 'You're Connor's friend, Liam.'

Speaking to Connor, he said, 'On my ways to catch up with you and Courtney.'

Distracted, Connor sniffed the air. 'Ugh!'

Not taking offence, Liam replied, 'That's me you's nosing. I just bin to work. Ages ago, I got me a job meat-packing. Rotten smell, okay money.'

Connor felt sick. He turned away from Liam and caught sight of the abandoned nightclub. Its broken windows were boarded up and its brickwork was decorated with graffiti. Distressed, Connor looked again at Liam and abruptly vomited on the pavement.

Liam laughed. 'That's me after a few drinks, semi gone.'

Ranji said to him, 'I think you'd better … '

'I's off,' Liam replied.

The staff were good about the mess. With hardly a complaint, someone came out quickly to clean it up.

Ranji was a specialist. She could nurse a brain but not a dodgy stomach. Nausea was the stuff of Connor's normal doctor. His waiting room was a dreary place in the health centre. Two people opposite Connor kept sneezing. In between them, a man was yawning.

Turning to Ranji, Connor asked, 'Why's he got his … ' He put an eel in his mouth.

'Mouth open?'

'Yes.' Then, surprising himself, Connor's jaw tightened, his mouth opened wide and he filled his lungs with air till his ears popped pleasurably. Startled, he said, 'And why me?'

'It's called yawning and it's a behavioural thing,' Ranji began. Adjusting her language to suit Connor, she continued, 'Yawning sends an extra helping of blood to the brain, getting us ready for action or at least stopping us going to sleep. You remember what lions are? They're fierce animals that live by hunting in groups – and they yawn a lot. The leader will yawn when he decides it's time to go hunting. Because yawns are catching, all the other lions will start yawning as well, making sure they're all ready for action at the same time.'

The bell saved Ranji from Connor's next question. Instead she took him into the surgery.

After a thorough examination, the doctor gave Connor the all-clear. 'You've probably just eaten something that disagreed with you.' To Ranji, he said, 'I think it's all over, but bring him back if it persists.'

Before they left the doctor, Connor jerked his thumb towards the door. 'Everyone's going achoo.'

'They've probably got colds,' he replied.

Connor asked, 'Why do they … ' he brought his hand down like a shutter in front of his eyes, 'when they … ?' Connor imitated the noise from the stricken patients.

'Why do they shut their eyes when they sneeze? It sounds horrible but, in theory, the force of a sneeze could make your eyes pop out,' the GP explained. He added quickly, 'Don't worry. The eyelids close and muscles grip the eyeball to stop it happening.'

'Is that why you've got … ' In front of his own face, Connor drew a circle around each eye.

The doctor touched his glasses and smiled. 'No. I have these for a different reason.' He glanced meaningfully at Ranji.

Ranji took Connor's arm, saying, 'We'll let the doctor get on with his job now. I'll tell you about glasses on the way back.'

Nearing the door of the Institute, Connor stopped and pointed upwards. He announced, 'There's a lion.'

'Really?' Ranji looked up.

'There,' said Connor.

'Ah. I see what you mean. The cloud's a bit like a resting lion.'

'Why do they go dark before the drink comes down?'

'Well, I guess it's all to do with sunlight,' Ranji answered. 'It goes through thin clouds, making them look white, but when they build up into storm clouds sunlight can't get through them. So, just before they rain on us, they look black.'

'Why … ?'

Ranji put up her hands. 'Connor. I get the feeling it's time for you to take a big step forward. How do you feel about going back to school after Christmas? I think you're ready for it and you'll get answers to your questions there.'

'What's Christmas?'

CHAPTER 15

Connor wasn't sure about Santa, Jesus and God – he got them muddled – but he understood presents.

'Shopping!' Mrs Markham cried. 'He wants to go shopping?'

'Well, I don't know exactly,' Brad replied. 'He couldn't explain. But he sure wants to go into town.'

They were standing by the window keeping an eye on Connor in the garden. They'd given him a football and were watching his reaction. He was kicking it against the garden shed, but there was no enjoyment in his action. It was like watching someone doing a science experiment, exercising curiosity rather than experiencing fun.

Mrs Markham turned away and regarded her other son. 'Okay. You take him.'

'I think he needs to go ... '

'Oh, you're some sort of expert, are you?' Brad's mum retorted, guessing what Brad was going to say.

'No, but ... '

'We can't let him go out on his own. It'd be a disaster.'

Taking a deep breath, Mr Markham said, 'You know what Dr Nawaz said, love. We can't be his non-stop guardian angels. You've sewn his name and address in his clothes ... '

'Even so ... '

'I feel as worried as you, but ... '

'You're not his mother! There's no way I'm going to ... '

Brad had heard enough. 'You're ruining him!'

Immediately, his mum rounded on Brad. 'You're a fine one to talk! Over the years you've got at him at every available opportunity.'

Of course it was true. Brad had spent half of his life hating the boy he was now trying to support. At the age of fourteen years, he'd acquired a baby brother to look after. He wasn't ready for the task, he didn't feel that he was up to it, but guilt forced him into it. Was it still guilt? Brad was beginning to think that he was helping Connor because he wanted to, not because he felt responsible for the state of Connor's brain. It wasn't because he felt superior or parental. It was because he was warming to this new and simple and friendly Connor. He was trying to put up with the frustrations because he thought that he was the only one to understand Connor. Increasingly, Brad believed that, for Connor, success was to be measured not by the amount of memory recovered, but by present achievement.

'Don't speak to your mother like that,' Mr Markham snapped. But he wanted peace more than anything else, so he made a suggestion. 'Look. Why don't we all go into town but let him wander a bit on his own. We can always keep an eye on him from a distance.'

They agreed on the compromise. Nothing had really been resolved – Connor's mum and dad wanted a fully functioning brain and Brad wanted a contented Connor – but the argument had been put on hold.

In the crowds of Christmas shoppers, it was easy for Connor to be cast adrift of his family. As soon as he noticed the grotto, he pulled away from them, disappeared into the stampede and joined the queue. Q wasn't a bad letter. It was like a nought but it had an extra line, like a worm looking into a great big hole. Sometimes, it looked like a 9 with a worm clinging to its tail.

The older people in front and behind him were moaning about how long it was taking. Connor was hyped up, so he didn't notice the time that he had to wait.

The grotto was knobbly and happy and sparkly, but the old man was knobbly and weird. He was dressed head to … the kicking end in red and he had fluffy white blobs all over the place. The most extraordinary blob was the white fur, like a cat's, on his face. When he opened his mouth, it looked like a black hole in a brain scan.

Santa looked to the right, to the left, and then he peered behind Connor. 'Where's the child?' he asked.

'Child?'

'Haven't you got a youngster wanting a present?'

'Me,' said Connor innocently.

Santa's face screwed up. 'What's the matter with you, kid?'

'Nothing.'

'At your age … You don't really think I'm Santa, do you?' he whispered.

Connor smiled knowingly. This was a test that he could pass. 'No. You're not real. You're only … thinging.'

Santa wasn't sparkly. He put an eel across his black hole. 'Shush.'

In case any of the little kids outside heard this dim-witted teenager, Santa gave him a present hurriedly and pushed him out of the grotto.

Connor was delighted. It was a magic number machine. It had buttons like a talking machine. When he pressed the 6 button, the figure appeared in the strip at the top. He added more numbers to make 6690699, but this machine didn't ring or talk to him. It didn't have a banana. He shrugged and hit buttons till the first number disappeared, then he started again with another 6. He added a nought and cried, 'Sixty!' Then, oblivious to everything around him, he sat at a café table and tried to see if he could turn three sixties into 180.

Connor gathered that Christmas was supposed to be a happy thing. But it wasn't. Not really. There was a tree where it shouldn't be: inside. The lights and decorations were fun but the endless questions weren't. 'Do you remember last year when we got you those super new football boots?' 'Do you remember the time when we went away for Christmas?' 'Do you remember when you got your first bike?' 'Do you remember when you were very little and you were more interested in the wrapping paper than the presents?' 'Do you remember refusing to open a present because there were swans on the wrapping?'

Then two old people with white hair arrived from a long way away. 'This is Grandma and Grandad.'

'Grandad?' Connor smiled and nodded. 'Grandad makes pictures.'

There was an uncomfortable silence before Grandad said, 'I think you must be getting confused with someone else, Connor.'

It was everyone else who was confused. They thought Connor was someone else.

After turkey, profs, crackers and crinkly hats, they carried on with the questions and Connor switched off. He was wondering where Courtney was. He was also wondering who was with Mrs Treble Nineteen. Why hadn't they come to his house? There were two other visitors. That girlfriend – the one old-Connor loved – arrived. 'Just come to bring your present.' She handed over a small light package.

Connor had learned very quickly about unwrapping presents. He was happy at it. Inside, he discovered a stack of three green chocolate bars, all the same. With his forefinger, he traced the name on the wrapper. 'Aer … ' He got stuck.

'Mint Aero,' Hattie said. 'Remember? You used to go wild for it. I bet you still do.' In a whisper, she added, 'When you were short on cash, you used to nick a bar from the newsagents. Try it.'

Connor shook his head and put the bars down on a table. He wasn't an idiot. The chocolate wasn't a gift at all. It was another attempt to lure back the old Connor.

Liam was okay. He turned up without a present designed to jog Connor's memory. Without a present at all. 'Is you still semi … ' He waved a finger by the side of his own head. 'Gone?'

Connor guessed that Liam was talking about his damaged brain. 'Yes.'

Liam shrugged. 'No worries. Just live for today, that's what I says.' He looked at the new school bag that Connor's grandparents had given him and said, 'You's back to school next term. School's bum-numbin', man, but I guess you gotta be a trainee adult again. I's hot-footing outta here soon. Deliverin' turkey to the wrinklies today.'

Because Connor hadn't got a clue what Liam was saying, Mrs Markham replied guardedly, 'That's very ... charitable.'

'Cool.'

Brad was okay too. He'd downloaded his brother a few songs onto a memory stick. 'Not sure what you like any more,' he said to Connor. 'But these might take your fancy.'

Connor nodded in silence. He was waiting for Brad to say something about the music that old-Connor used to like, but he didn't. 'That's happy,' said Connor with a smile at his brother. Then he retreated to his room. Wired into his iPod, Connor listened to music and played with his magic number machine. Already he'd worked out by trial and error that + added numbers together and = showed the answer. $60 + 60 + 60 = 180$. But the machine was a lot slower than Connor's re-routed brain.

Downstairs, his mum apologised to the assembled guests for Connor's sudden disappearance and his dad shrugged in frustration and helplessness.

Several voices spoke at once. 'No problem.' 'Never mind.' 'It doesn't matter.' 'You're doing terrifically well under the circumstances.' 'He's rocking. I likes it.'

Mrs Dungate sat by the silent telephone and looked at the array of photographs of her family and the two Christmas cards they'd sent from that island on the other side of the world – the one they told her off for calling Australia. The one they told her was hot and sunny at Christmas. She shook her head in astonishment. 'A long, long, way away,' she murmured to herself. She reached out with a gnarled finger that trembled with the cold and stroked the image of her offspring. She wept seasonal tears.

'Close your eyes and no peeping. Are they shut tight?'

Courtney nodded.

'Okay. Here you go.'

She felt at least a couple of packages nestling on her lap. They weren't heavy enough to be the television that she wanted for her bedroom, but her mum had already made it pretty clear that she didn't approve of her watching the box upstairs. 'Can I open my eyes?'

'Uh-huh.'

Three parcels and a card. Not just a card. She ripped it open to find an iTunes token. That'd be some more downloads. The first parcel was soft. Clothes. It was the jumper she'd hankered after. Holding it to her chest she said, 'Lovely.' Then she ripped open the second. Something quite big in a box. Something that rattled. Was it … ? Yes. Something she really really wanted. A pair of super roller skates. 'Wow! Thanks!' Straightaway, she tried them on to test the fit. 'They're great. When I visit Grandad now, I can really zoom down the long corridors.'

'You'll probably *cause* an accident.'

With a broad smile, Courtney said, 'That's the right place for it – in a hospital.'

The third present – the smallest – had to be something for school. Mum never let a Christmas or a birthday go by without getting her something practical for school. The other presents were a means of softening the blow. This time it was a shiny new geometry set. Not cheap and nasty. To encourage her, Mum had got her an expensive precision set.

'Now you've started at secondary school, you'll need those,' she said.

Courtney nodded, but paid far more attention to her skates.

For no obvious reason, the old man in the corner chair, who was not taking part in the Christmas proceedings but who had a red and yellow paper hat perched jauntily on his head, cried, 'Who's there?'

Looking up from her presents, Courtney said, 'You're at home with us for Christmas, Grandad.'

There was no sign that Grandad had heard Courtney's response. He looked frightened and lost. He was missing his easel and paints. He didn't know why, but his wrinkled fingers ached to paint a young boy with a toboggan on a snowy slope.

With a frown, Hattie's mum asked, 'Where've you been, Hattie?'

'Round Alice's,' she answered, turning away.

'So, why was Alice round here looking for you?'

'Ah.'

'Well?'

Caught red-handed, and with cheeks as red as Santa's costume, Hattie had no option but to tell the truth. 'I went to Connor's,' she admitted.

'What for?'

Hattie pulled a face. 'To give him his present.'

Her mum nodded. 'How is he?' Her uppity tone suggested that she already knew the answer. After all, she was a grown-up. She knew all the answers.

Without looking into her mother's face, Hattie shrugged. 'The same.'

'It's a shame, Hattie, but you've got to think of yourself.'

Hattie plonked herself down, swallowed her tears, occupied her fingers with a ribbon that had been round one of her presents, and waited for the parental Christmas lecture.

The old man turned over the packaged turkey in his leathery hands yet again. It was a good fat bird. He looked at his wife and then at the young man who was shuffling eagerly from foot to foot on his doorstep. 'Three quarters of what's on the label, you say.' He tapped it with his finger.

'Rocking deal. No questions asked.'

'It's a bit late, but make it a fiver,' the man said, 'and we'll take it.'

The young man sniffed. 'Okay. You's on.' He held out his hand for the note. It wasn't as much as he wanted, but it was cool enough.

The turkeys were rejects from Quality Control in the meat-packing factory. They were rejects because they were underweight. And they were underweight because Liam's little finger had been under the scales, helping to prop up the pan while the computer weighed them and sounded the alarm. Because it had been the last working day before Christmas, the management had allowed staff to buy rejects at a third of cost.

There had been an unusually high number of rejects on Liam's line that day.

'Happy Christmas,' Liam said as he turned to go. 'You's can stuff youselves silly now.'

Oliver slid his forefinger under the flap and ripped open the envelope. The Christmas card wasn't signed, but it bore a signature of a kind. Inside, along with an appallingly sentimental rhyme, someone had written an appalling Christmas message. *Want a rocking New Year? Then keeps youself away from Hattie. She's taken.* Oliver wore a half smile, half frown. Liam Darby was half joke, half dangerous. When he wasn't around, everyone laughed at him. When he was, they kept their distance as much as possible. The striker spelled trouble. Actually, he'd probably misspell it.

It was the things Joy hadn't got at Christmas that provided some comfort. She'd been tested and she was free of sexually transmitted disease. By pure luck, she hadn't become pregnant either. She was free of temptation, abuse and pain.

But she was also free of edgy excitement and extravagance. She was virtually free of life.

CHAPTER 16

At school there were many reasons for being bullied or shunned: lack of interest in sport, being an asylum seeker, wanting to do well in exams, being too clever, having religious beliefs, not wanting to drink alcohol, being gay, being too small, being too big, being too shy, paying attention to teachers.

Brad ticked a few of the boxes. He wanted to get off with the opposite sex, for sure, but he was a wimp at sports and he wanted to do well in exams, so he paid attention in lessons. Some said he was too clever by half.

When he first arrived at the big school, Connor walked with him. They argued – or were completely silent – all the way. Seeing the brothers always at odds, some of the boys in Connor's year thought they'd been given free licence to have a go at Brad.

They were wrong.

Once, Brad had been surrounded in the playground. Someone had already destroyed one of his schoolbooks. By the time that Connor arrived, pushing his way through the small collection of lads, the ringleader was really getting into his stride. He was yelling at Brad, 'We've all seen you sucking up to … ' Connor didn't waste any time, he didn't hold an inquiry, didn't ask for reconciliation or retraction, he simply walloped the ringleader. He laid him out on the tarmac and walked away without a word to anyone. He did it with no more ceremony than taking a free kick after he'd been pushed in the box.

Another time, a boy who'd boasted of bullying Brad found himself flattened in the maths corridor.

'Hey!' he said to Connor, wiping his nose and checking it for blood. 'What was that for?'

'You know,' Connor retorted.

'No, I don't.'

'You've been rotten to Brad.'

'But you and him … '

'It's a brother thing.'

'So?'

'He's *my* brother, not yours. You leave him alone,' Connor demanded.

'He's a prick.'

Connor shrugged. 'Just leave him alone.'

'I don't … ' He saw white skin stretching over Connor's knuckles again and backed down. 'All right.'

The trouble was that Miss Sayell, the young maths teacher, had also seen Connor's bulging knuckles. She'd witnessed only the brief scrap, not the background to it, so Connor took the blame for threatening behaviour. Connor never mentioned that bit of brotherly protection – or the two detentions he earned from Miss Sayell – to Brad, because it might have hurt his pride to know that Connor had fixed things for him behind the scenes.

CHAPTER 17

In the New Year, Connor began big school all over again.

This time, the roles were reversed. Connor had a brother to guide him to and from school. He also had a full-time support assistant to guide him from class to class. The assistant helped him with his reading and comprehension. Most of his days in school were spent in Special Educational Needs, but he went into normal art and maths lessons. In art, he needed extra help to understand what was going on, but he coped. And he was intrigued by the teacher. He ran around with his hands at the level of his shoulders. He looked as if he was in a permanent hurry and a permanent panic. He also had a funny smell.

'Carrots!'

Hearing Connor's gasp, the good-looking girl sitting next to him whispered, 'We call him Jazz Hands. He's completely cracked.'

'Cracked?' Connor dredged something out of his memory and looked even more surprised. 'About to split into bits?'

Impatiently, the girl replied, 'No. Mad, sad, bonkers.'

'Why?'

'How should I know? It's always the art or music teacher who's off their heads. Maybe it's part of the job description.'

In maths, Connor hadn't got a clue what he was expected to do, but he was enthralled by all those numbers. And once the exercises were explained to him, he beamed because he understood. He could do it. It was just common sense. Easy. The virus had knocked the stuffing out of him, but not the common sense.

'It's really just a matter of multiplying, Connor,' said Miss Sayell with the air of a teacher who expected one additional pupil to double her workload. After all, she remembered him for fighting in the corridor and she'd been told he was a very special special-needs student.

'Multiplying?'

'Times-ing. Three times two is six. Or, if you prefer, three twos are six.'

Connor nodded. 'Three twenties are sixty. Three sixties are one hundred and eighty.'

'Very good. You can do it on your calculator.' Attempting to keep her boredom out of her voice, she showed him how. 'Try something tricky, like twenty-nine times thirty-three.'

Connor didn't bother with his magic number machine. Almost immediately, he said, 'Nine hundred and fifty-seven.'

Miss Sayell hesitated and checked the answer on his calculator. 'That's … remarkable, Connor. How about one you'd definitely need a calculator for? Three hundred and forty-four times forty-three?'

Ignoring her advice, Connor looked up at the ceiling for five seconds and then answered, 'One four seven nine two. And three hundred and forty-four is eight times forty-three.'

The maths teacher was astounded. Delighted. Here was a boy who could not learn to recognize her in an hour-long lesson, who was virtually illiterate, who had shown no interest and no talent whatever in earlier years, who she'd known as a violent boy, who now manipulated numbers mentally like no one else she had ever known. Before, if he'd ever got anything right, it would have been because a friend had whispered the answer into his ear. This attentive and willing student was a new creature altogether. An improbable, inexplicable and captivating curiosity, Connor Markham won her over at once. Miss Sayell took him under her academic wing.

Connor liked Miss Sayell. He tried very very hard to remember her name. Sayell. S is for Six. Ay is the start of eight. Ell is the start of eleven. Miss Six-Eight-Eleven. Done. Remembered. He liked Miss Six-Eight-Eleven. She gave him numbers to play with and she said she preferred the new Connor.

Hattie was still trying to get used to the idea that Connor could see her in a school corridor and walk straight past without recognizing her. On one occasion, Alice spotted Hattie's momentary look of devastation and disappointment – but not defeat. Not yet.

'Are you still hankering after Connor?' Alice asked in an uncomprehending voice.

Hattie hesitated and decided to bluff it out. 'Whatever for?' But she reddened.

Oliver was one of three friends who cried, 'You are!'

Hattie had no option. She swallowed and went for it. 'I want you lot to come bowling with … ' Surrounded by sceptics, she found it hard to utter his name and admit what was on her mind. 'I want you all to come with me and Connor – and be nice to him and all.'

There was a communal groan. Going out with a baby didn't seem like their idea of fun.

'Connor's okay,' Hattie said, trying to persuade them. 'You'll see. He's … I don't know .. cute.'

Oliver turned up his nose. 'Connor? Cute?'

Hattie sighed impatiently. 'Okay, he's like a little kid. I'll grant you that. He *is* a different person … '

Butting in, Oliver said, 'I told you so.'

'But,' Hattie continued, giving Oliver a stare, 'he's up for it.'

'Up for what?' Oliver exclaimed with a smirk.

Hattie gave him an even colder stare. 'Your brain's one-tracked. I meant, he's having a real good go at life. He's been knocked back, but he's trying.'

'And embarrassing,' Alice said.

'And hopeless,' Oliver added.

Oliver had a thing about Hattie. He'd always had a thing about Hattie. He wasn't sure why. She wasn't the looker of the school, but he still fancied her like mad. Once, he was well on his way with her but Connor muscled in. Oliver had always thought that Connor would end up with Alice but, for some reason, Connor never really hit it off with her and he took up with Hattie instead. And Oliver had never forgiven him.

Then there was bowling. Oliver had looked pretty good, he'd impressed Hattie, till she'd seen Connor play. Oliver was the stylish bowler but Connor would steal the show anyway. Connor wasn't a natural bowler: he did not so much bowl as release missiles. He did not so much knock pins down as splinter them. And somehow that got Hattie going.

Then there was football. Oliver had to admit that Connor propped up the whole team. 'He also props up every class he's in,' Oliver used to mutter.

'How do you mean?' Hattie had asked.

'He's always at the bottom.'

Yes, Oliver had outshone Connor at any school subject. He was top-streamed in everything, but that didn't turn Hattie on.

Whichever way Oliver turned, there was a brick wall called Connor Markham blocking his path. Now, with Connor out of commission, reduced to the status of a baby, the way to Hattie should have been clear. But no. According to Hattie, Connor was 'cute' now. She had built a new brick wall out of sympathy. Oliver would have to resort to being devious. He was undoubtedly more devious than Connor could ever be, so he waited for an opportunity to conspire against his rival.

Every night since their premature return from Barbados, Mr and Mrs Markham's demons had kept them awake. Connor's mum and dad felt as if they'd brought back an alien from the Caribbean. In all their attempts to put matters right, nothing seemed to have any effect. Nothing seemed capable of converting the alien creature back into their Connor. Their own prized memories of his childhood, when retold or re-enacted, made no impression on him. Everything they thought was important meant nothing to him. He was not interested in their nostalgia. On sleepless nights, they began to recognize that those memories were far more important to parents than they were to a fifteen-year-old boy.

They had been forced to admit that Connor was more likely to be stimulated by things he'd done with mates of his own age. They had to come to terms with the forgettable Christmases, the forgettable holidays, the forgettable landmarks like his first teeth, his first days at school and his first bike ride, and the forgettable player of the year award. Once they had accepted that these milestones belonged more to them than to Connor, they'd recruited Hattie and Liam in the hope that they would be able to reach him. And they encouraged Brad to talk to Connor about things they'd done together – especially those things they'd conspired to keep from their parents. But now, the letter they'd received was undermining one of those avenues.

The next day, they drew Hattie to one side. Connor's mum forced herself to appear detached and said, 'We really appreciate what you're doing to help Connor – especially this bowling night you're putting together – but … I wonder if you ought to stop now.'

Hattie's mouth opened in surprise. 'You haven't given up on him as well!'

'As well as who?'

Hattie hesitated, unwilling to throw accusations around.

'She means her mates at school – and me,' Brad put in. 'You know I think we should accept him as he is. It's not giving up, though. It's being realistic.'

'You're not his girlfriend, being pushed away and all,' said Hattie.

'Or his mum,' Mrs Markham added vehemently.

Hattie asked, 'So why are you telling me to give up when you were the ones who asked me to work on his memory? Besides, it was you who suggested taking him bowling.'

'You've been great,' Mr Markham said. 'It's a real pity, but we think it's probably time for you to get on with your own life.'

Hattie stared at them both. 'No, you don't,' she almost shouted. 'There's something else.'

Connor's parents glanced at each other. In that moment, they looked as worn and helpless as they felt. Mrs Markham sighed and admitted, 'We've had a letter from your mum and dad, Hattie.'

Interrupting Hattie cried, 'They've told you I shouldn't come round any more! It'll be something about me not wasting my time on Connor. Well, if I was Connor, I'd say "Sprouts!" to them.'

Under the circumstances, Brad could manage only a faint smile. 'Actually, he'd say "Carrots!" now.'

'Whatever,' Hattie muttered. 'Mum and Dad just make me more determined and all. You wait. I'll get everyone to take him bowling. I will. And I'll see Connor whenever I want.' She hesitated before adding, 'As long as he wants it as well, of course.'

Normally, Hattie would have avoided Liam, but she needed him. She was not yet sure whether Liam was genuine in liking the new Connor, or whether he was simply enjoying his new-found superiority over his former friend. She feared the worst.

'What about you, Liam? Do you want to come bowling with me and Connor?'

'Sure. Cool. Is Courtney in on it?'

'Who's Courtney? No. No one called Courtney.'

Hattie looked around the rest. Was Liam going to be the catalyst that she'd hoped for?

Without much spirit, Oliver said, 'I'll come as well, I suppose.'

Hattie smiled. She could almost read Oliver's mind. He was not prepared to see her go off with Connor and enjoy herself when he had the option of keeping an eye on them both.

'Okay,' Hattie said. 'That's one team of four. Who dares to take us on? Brad?'

Brad shook his head. He didn't really approve.

'Alice?'

Alice sighed. 'Oh, all right.' After all, she was a star at ten-pin bowling.

It was like getting volunteers for extra maths homework. But eventually Hattie's resolve won them over. She wasn't stupid enough to think they were giving Connor a chance. No. Her friends were doing it as a favour to her. Because Hattie was sold on the idea, reluctantly they were giving *her* a chance.

After everyone had dispersed, Oliver remained behind as always. 'Well,' he said, 'you got your way.'

Hattie nodded. 'It'll work out all right. You'll see.' She was trying to convince herself.

'I doubt it. He's mental,' Oliver replied.

Oliver was not like Connor. Hattie had to look down on him. While Connor was as tall as Hattie, Oliver was much more compact: short, stocky and muscular. And he didn't have Connor's impulsive kindness. Hattie didn't really rate Oliver. Not even as a substitute. She was even more convinced now that she wanted to win back Connor. She looked down at Oliver's hand touching hers and said, 'I know why you decided to come.' She pulled her arm away.

Oliver snapped, 'And I know why you're organizing it. But Connor's not really interested in you, is he? These days, you're not exactly walking Viagra to him.'

She whacked him across the chest. Hard. So hard that it hurt her hand. Then she stormed off.

Alcohol Abuse was in a state. His liver and his brain had been shot to pieces, pickled. He looked round at Connor and said, 'You a nurse now?'

'No. I'm ... ' Connor wanted to explain that he was merely helping with a game of bingo. When the words evaded him, he just waved at the bingo card. 'Seventeen. It's one of your numbers.'

'What's that?'

'Seventeen.' Connor leaned across Alcohol Abuse and put a line through the right number.

Next to him, Blow-To-The-Head remarked, 'Russian revolution in '17.'

A nurse was calling out the numbers and holding up show-cards for those who couldn't remember what the figures looked like. She picked another and shouted, 'Thirty-nine.'

'Thirty-nine's no good!' Stroke 3 let out a stream of short, expressive words.

'Start of World War Two was '39,' Blow-To-The-Head commented.

Before Alcohol Abuse crossed out the wrong number, Connor told him, 'You haven't got thirty-nine.'

'Haven't I? Oh.' He let out a laugh for no obvious reason. 'You're good at helping.'

'What was the number?' Alzheimer 1 asked.

'Thirty-nine.'

'Where's that man?' Grumpy was pointing to an empty place where Stroke 2 usually sat.

The nurse called, 'Twelve.'

The air turned blue again. Stroke 3 muttered, 'Someone's hiding my numbers.'

'The Titanic went down in 1912.' Blow-To-The-Head nudged his neighbour. 'Most of them died.' He seemed to remember events with lots of casualties. But he liked only the smaller numbers. If a number above eighty-two was called, he stayed silent, unable to recall anything after 1982.

'You've won,' Connor whispered enthusiastically to Alcohol Abuse. 'Twelve's your last one.'

Alcohol Abuse stood up, knocked over his bingo card and wrapped Connor in a great big friendly bear hug. 'My man's sorted for numbers. I've won!'

Connor smiled broadly.

Stroke 3 muttered, 'Bloody cheat. There was two of them doing it.'

After the game, Ranji sat with Connor. She smelled normal and she had a serious face. 'I don't know if you noticed someone wasn't at bingo today,' she began. 'You see, I'm afraid we had a death last night.'

Connor thought he understood what Ranji was saying. The way she explained it, Stroke 2 had got so poorly that his body just couldn't carry on. He wouldn't be in the Institute any more. His family thought he'd gone to a great place where he'd meet the real Santa Claus. That's what death was all about.

Connor nodded thoughtfully. Perhaps the nurses had finally made Stroke 2 swallow the poison pills they put in his drink.

'What's the last thing you see before you die?' Connor asked.

'I don't know,' Ranji answered. 'It depends, I guess. Some say it's the face of God. Some say it's a very bright light. But maybe it's just nothing: just peace and quiet and darkness. Let's hope it's someone you love.'

'But that's it? All … you know … gone?'

'Not quite. All gone as far as the body's concerned. In another way, no one dies.' Looking into his face, Ranji mentioned a few famous names. 'Amy Winehouse is still alive. No doubt about it. So is Shakespeare. Really, people don't die unless we forget them.'

Connor was puzzled. 'Who's Amy Winehouse?'

'A singer. She made music.'

'She's happy, then.'

'Yes. She'll live for ever because her music's always with us.'

'Who's Shakesp … ?' Abruptly, Connor stood up and yelled, 'Carrots!' It was Courtney. She was hurtling across the room without moving her legs. She'd fixed a set of wheels onto her kicking things. It was like she had little cars at the end of her legs.

Ranji's hand settled on Connor's arm. 'They're called roller skates. When she's finished with her grandad I'm sure she'll tell you all about them.' Then Ranji's mobile phone told her she'd got an unexpected visitor.

In Dr Nawaz's private office, Hattie Townsend fiddled with the zip of her coat and didn't look up. 'You know Connor?' she began awkwardly.

Patiently, Ranji said, 'What is it?'

'It's … I don't know … a bit of advice, I suppose.'

'Of course. What do you want to ask me?'

'Well, you know this brain thing started with a germ? I was wondering … '

Ranji completed her sentence. 'If you can catch it.'

Hattie nodded.

Dr Nawaz smiled sympathetically. 'Don't panic when I say

you've probably already got it. And me. And just about everyone else. The virus doesn't do us any harm. It's only in very rare cases it spreads to the brain. Very rare indeed. Think of it like this. We all live quite happily through storms and it's only very few of us who get struck by lightning.'

Flushed with embarrassment, Hattie said, 'So, kissing him – or anything else – won't make it happen to me?'

Ranji shook her head. 'It's more likely a plane will crash-land on you. There's nothing to worry about.'

Hattie breathed a sigh and stood up. 'Thanks.'

Before the girl left her office, Ranji enquired, 'Is he recalling anything you two did together?'

Hattie shook her head.

For a second, Dr Nawaz wondered whether she should mention Connor's fascination with a girl called Courtney, but she decided against it. Things had to run their natural course. Alerting and alarming Hattie did not serve a purpose. Connor had to learn for himself what was proper and what was not.

CHAPTER 18

Connor lived in a minefield: whichever way he turned, there was something that could blow up in his face.

'I've got to put my eels in here?' Connor cried on the night of the bowling challenge.

Hattie persevered, but Oliver and Liam both smiled. The rest of the players cringed with embarrassment. Connor had already needed an escort to the club and help with his shoe size.

'Yeah,' Hattie said. 'Like that. It's the weight you always used. Now lift it up and do what I did. Aim it more or less down the middle of the lane. Remember?'

The place was full of ants. Very busy, very noisy. Behind Connor there was a bar and, further along, a fast-food stall. They were teeming with spectators, players taking a break, people who had finished their games, and would-be players waiting for a vacant lane. In the background, the PA system was relaying music from the local radio station.

Appropriately, Connor was playing in lane 9. The nice number with a hole on the left-hand side. Connor's bowl hit the lacquered wooden lane with a loud thud and then trundled slowly towards the pins, all the time veering off to the right. In lane 10, Alice's assured bowl hurtled past and smashed full-speed into the triangular target at the end of the lane. Rumbling tentatively down lane 9, Connor's sedate bowl seemed unwilling to inflict any damage on the wedge of pins. Just before it reached the target, it toppled harmlessly into the gutter and rolled gently into the mechanism.

'Nearly,' Hattie said. 'You get another go now you've got a feel for it. Your ball's on its way back. Give it some stick this time.'

'What?'

'Do it faster. You used to fire them like rockets.'

Connor's second attempt was delivered with much more gusto but it clipped only two of the pins. In the old days, Connor's bowl would bulldoze the head-pin at the perfect angle to give him a good chance of a clean sweep.

Oliver stepped forward, saying, 'At least you've got plenty of room for improvement.' Then, with a sneer, he bowled a confident strike.

Clearly, bowling wasn't like walking, cycling and swimming. Connor's brain hadn't figured it out at an early age and locked it away as second nature. It hadn't become something he did by instinct. He would have to relearn the game – if he could be bothered.

While the others were playing their frames, Connor listened to the music and watched the computer displays above each lane. He had soon worked out the scoring system. He took more interest in that than in the game. Occasionally getting up and taking a turn at bowling was the penalty to be paid for the fun of watching the scores mount up.

The whole place was reduced to confusion when the computer crashed. The players' communal groan was audible over the din of music, rumbling bowls and loud playful voices. The screens above the lanes flashed, flickered and then settled on an obstinate blank grey.

'Now what're we going to do?' Oliver muttered. He was clearly annoyed that his opportunity to outstrip Connor was evaporating.

Hattie shouted to Connor just before he made his next delivery. 'Hang on, Connor. We've lost all the scores.'

Connor shrugged. 'I've got 35, you've got 77.' He couldn't name the other six players but he knew the score associated with each set of initials that had appeared on the monitors. Surprising

them all, Connor reeled off the information effortlessly. AF –
Alice – was in the lead with 115, then came Oliver with 94 and
Liam with 89.

'Let's get that down on paper before he forgets.' Alice spoke
to the others about Connor as if he weren't there. 'He can't keep
track of all eight scores while we're playing.'

Connor said, 'Why not?'

Alice was forced to acknowledge his presence and speak to
him directly. 'Are you saying you can?'

He nodded.

'Rocking,' Liam said with a laugh.

'No chance!' Oliver cried.

'We'll soon find out,' Alice said, picking up her bowl. It was
almost a challenge. Unlike Oliver, though, at least she seemed
willing to give Connor a chance.

While the players in the other lanes waited for the computer
to come back online or struggled over score cards, the teams in
lanes 9 and 10 carried on as normal. Every time they had a go,
they had to remind Connor of their initials so that he added the
right numbers together.

Liam plonked himself down next to Connor. 'It's cool, you
and numbers. You concentrating?'

Connor didn't know what Liam meant so he said, 'Easy.'

Liam laughed aloud. ''Mazing.'

Hattie seemed to believe that her idea of a bowling night was
beginning to pay dividends. Connor wasn't remembering the
game, but the computer error was playing into her hands. It was
bringing Connor back into her circle of friends.

'You're getting better,' she said to him.

'Couldn't get any worse,' Oliver muttered.

Connor's half-hearted bowling told them all that he had lost
interest in the sport. As the evening wore on, the old skills
showed signs of emerging, but the old enthusiasm wasn't. 'The
scores are happy,' he said. 'Better than darts.' He relished the
challenge of the complicated scoring system.

At the end of the first game, when Connor plucked the
individual scores out of his rewired brain, someone asked, 'So
which team won?'

Hattie said to Connor, 'Can you add up the scores for you, me, Liam and Oliver? That's CM, HT, LD and OB.'

Connor nodded. 'Three hundred and ninety-nine.'

'And the other four?'

'Four hundred and forty-two.'

Alice's team celebrated and they all went to buy drinks and pizzas before the second game. Hattie promised to get Connor a no-cow pizza and Liam promised to add something to his drink to give it extra zing.

'No white things!' Connor exclaimed.

Liam frowned and then shrugged. 'No white things,' he agreed. 'I's thinking of something else.'

During the second game, Hattie sat next to Connor. 'I don't know how you do it: eat pizza, play the game and keep up with eight scores, all at the same time.'

Examining his messy eels, Connor said, 'Why does the yellow go ... ?' He pointed at the fine cheese filament attached to one of his fingers, like an obstinate strand of a spider's web.

'Stringy?' Hattie and Liam looked at each other and shrugged. 'No idea.'

Whenever the players wanted to know their exact score, they had to ask Connor. Even Alice was forced to talk to him. 'I reckon I'm up to about eighty or something. Is that right?'

'Who are you?'

Looking mildly annoyed, Alice replied, 'AF.'

'You're happy. You've got ninety-one. That's biggest.'

She thanked him with a slight nod of her head.

Oliver said into her ear, 'He's not a human being, he's a human calculator. A freak.'

Alice looked at him but didn't reply. She didn't seem so sure about taking sides now.

Seeing admiration in Connor's transparent face, Hattie watched Connor watching Alice. Hattie hoped that he was admiring only her impressive bowling, because Alice was impressive in other ways as well. She wasn't as tall as Hattie and her short black hair always shone as if she was starring in a shampoo commercial. Through Hattie's eyes, Alice was as thin as a piece of paper. Her sultry looks and considerable bosom had always attracted and distracted quite a few boys.

Throughout the evening, Liam made sure that Connor was topped up with spiked drinks. After all, the boy deserved a rocking good time, what, with all those sums to do.

After Connor had announced the final team totals for the second game, he looked thoughtful.

Amid the cheering and the jeering, Hattie asked him, 'What's wrong?'

Connor said, 'My numbers were the smallest.'

'You got a strike,' she pointed out. 'It's coming back.'

'I lost.'

Hattie put a hand on his arm and, with a warm smile, said, 'No. I think you won, Connor.'

He didn't understand old-Connor's girlfriend but he didn't worry about it because he felt happy. When he stood up, he found that he was a bit wobbly. He didn't worry about that either. He felt light-headed and carefree.

While Hattie went to the toilet and the others queued for drinks, Liam drew close to Connor. 'That Alice is semi-hot. More than semi.' Taking his eyes off Alice's back, he added, 'Easy to see Hattie's still keen on you. I's looking after you's interests but … '

Puzzled, Connor scrunched up his face.

'If you's after this Courtney chick now, if I's gonna make sure she's onside as well. You gotta tell me all about her.'

'Courtney. Yes.'

'Right. Let's get outta here,' Liam said, standing up.

Connor looked unsure.

Liam took a key out of his pocket. 'Know what this is?'

Connor shook his head.

'It's a passport.'

'Passport?'

'To all sorts. D'ya want to see what I's got in mind? Want to be in the mean team? You and me?'

'The mean team.' Connor smiled drunkenly. 'Yeah.'

'Come on, then.'

They slipped away from the busy building before the others returned.

The canal was a long narrow watery dustbin. It was a depository for supermarket trolleys, polystyrene packing, Kentucky Fried Chicken and Big Mac boxes, car wheels, cans and bottles. On a dark, clear night the stagnant water looked like crude oil.

'So,' Liam asked as he strode along the towpath, 'who's Courtney?'

'She's my friend.'

'Where do you sees her?'

'At the hospital.'

'She visits you at the hospital?'

'Yes.'

'What's her other name?' Liam said.

'Courtney.'

'Forget it. Where does she live?'

Connor shrugged.

'No probs. I'll wait at the hospital.'

'Happy.'

Liam smiled and changed the subject. 'You know where I works. At GG's, doing Mr Rowling a few favours. And meat packing. That's for cash. I got a side-line. That's what the key's about. A girl called Joy gave it me. Sort of.' He turned off the towpath and whispered, 'Up here.'

The two young men walked across the playing field where a model of a dinosaur, complete with colourful graffiti, stood on sentry.

'Why have you got clouds coming out of your … ?' Connor's eels went to his mouth. 'And me.'

'Shush. No more talk. Okays?'

His lips shut tight, Connor nodded.

Liam led him up to the backs of the houses and to one particular gate. Looking warily from side to side, Liam lifted up the latch on the big wooden gate and opened it carefully and quietly. Together with Connor, he slipped into the yard.

Liam closed the gate. 'That's better. Outta sight. There's one of them yappy dogs next door,' he whispered, 'but it looks like it gets beat up if it yaps, so it don't.' Going up to the back door, he slotted the key into the lock and turned it gingerly. Almost silently, he pushed his way into the shadowy interior.

Joining his friend, Connor realized that they were in a cooking room. A tight beam of light leapt from Liam's hand, illuminating small circular segments of the room. An ancient teapot, a set of drawers, a microwave cooker.

Liam tiptoed towards the drawers, opened them in turn and rummaged around inside by torchlight. Obviously, he had lost something.

'I'll help,' Connor offered. 'I'm happy at helping.'

Liam nodded. 'Sometimes cash is stashed in here. Not now. You's can help with the living room.'

They padded down the dark hall and into the main room where the soft grey carpet deadened their footfalls. Standing near the curtains, Liam directed the spotlight into the rest of the room, away from the front window. Occasionally, the light glinted from the glossy surface of one of the many photographs that dotted the place. It also reflected from the small gold-coloured clock on the mantelpiece. The revolving pendulum sent weak flashes across the living room. Liam headed towards the dark wood of an old-fashioned bureau and tried the contents of its drawers. He still didn't find whatever it was that he was looking for.

'There.' He nodded towards the handbag left on one of the seats. 'You gives that a try.'

Connor's face was blank as he let out a noisy hiccup.

'You's looking for a purse,' Liam whispered. 'Dosh. The old dear got no plastic. Waste of time. Wrinklies can't figure out what to do with plastic.'

Liam held the light while Connor grabbed the bag. Before Liam could stop him, Connor had turned it upside down and watched everything spill out onto the floor.

'You's didn't have to do that,' Liam muttered under his breath. 'You could've just looked through, man.'

They both got down on their knees. Liam opened the purse, yanked out the paper money and tipped the coins into his palm. Then he stuffed everything else back into the handbag and put it back on the cushion of the armchair. 'That's the lot this time,' he said quietly. 'We's outta here. Come on.'

Connor was pleased that Liam had managed to find what he was searching for. Pointing to his feet, he said, 'If I had … car shoes, I could go with Courtney.'

'Shush,' Liam repeated, leading the way out.

In the hall, they heard a voice calling from upstairs. An old woman's quaky voice. 'What's … ? Who's there?'

Connor was about to reply when Liam wrapped a cold hand round his mouth. 'Let's fly,' he said.

Still unsteady on his feet, Connor followed Liam into the kitchen and out into the back yard. On a high, they scarpered through the gate and across the playing field at speed. Connor seemed always to be on the point of falling over, but he didn't. He staggered on because he didn't want to be left on his own.

Mrs Dungate looked out on the darkened playing field, the outline of the dinosaur, the hedge by the canal, and two lads running away. 'No. Surely not,' she murmured to herself. 'That's not my Colin. It can't be.'

Police Constable Knox asked again, 'Are you sure nothing's missing?'

'Well, I can't see anything … ' She shrugged but then pointed suddenly to the antique writing desk. 'I don't remember leaving that photograph there.'

'But it's not gone missing.'

'No.'

The second officer tried her luck. 'You said your purse was empty. Was it empty when you went to bed?'

'No,' Mrs Dungate replied. 'I'm sure I had … But everything's so dear these days, isn't it? A loaf of bread and that's a pound gone. My Christmas what-do-you-call-it – Christmas bonus – goes on Christmas cards. Not one under a pound now, you know. It's scandalous. And postage to Australia … I mean, New Zealand. So, perhaps I spent it all.' She hesitated and then added, 'You know, I don't think I did. Maybe I took the notes out and put them in a drawer somewhere. Now which one?' She sighed.

'You wouldn't believe how easy it is to lose things at my age. Especially money.'

The officers smiled patiently. PC Knox said, 'There's no sign of forced entry and nothing much seems to have been disturbed. Are you sure you saw two men or boys running away?'

Mrs Dungate put her hand on her hairy chin. 'Well, I thought I did.'

Hattie was frantic. The Markhams had trusted her to take Connor out, remind him of his love for ten-pin bowling, and bring him back in one piece. And what had happened? She didn't know. She'd turned her back for a few minutes and he'd gone. Standing on tiptoe at the end of lane 9, she looked round, muttering, 'Where is he?'

She sent Oliver to the men's toilet in case he'd found his own way there and then she strode up and down the place, searching everywhere for him. Her stomach rumbled nervously like the noise of the bowls rolling down the lanes. Her heart thudded as heavily as the sound of bowls hitting pins.

It was Alice who solved the mystery. 'Do a head count, girl. There's only six of us.'

'Liam's not here,' Hattie murmured.

'Exactly. Liam. Connor'll have gone off with him.'

Annoyed, Hattie said, 'Why didn't Liam tell us first?' Hands on hips, she added, 'Anyway, I'm off to Connor's house. I've got to make sure he gets back okay.'

'I thought you were his girlfriend,' Alice replied. 'How come you're turning into his mother?'

CHAPTER 19

Already promoted to big brother, Brad was expected to be Big Brother too.

That night, Hattie waited impatiently and nervously with the Markhams until Liam brought Connor home. Liam delivered him to the front door and then shot off into the night without saying anything. Of course, Connor wouldn't – or couldn't – explain what they'd done. His memories had disappeared faster than a plateful of profiteroles. Hattie guessed that Liam had been up to no good and, by going with him, Connor was asking for trouble. She wondered if she could stop it happening again.

As soon as the thought came into her head, Hattie realized that Alice had a point. Internally, she admitted that she was becoming one of Connor's guardians. But Liam had rogue written all over him and Connor needed to be protected.

Before Mr Markham gave her a lift home through the first snowfall of the winter, Hattie asked Brad to try and find out what Connor had done after the bowling.

The following day, Hattie hid her disappointment over Connor's disappearing trick. 'It wasn't so painful, was it?' an upbeat Hattie said to Alice. 'Connor was all right.'

Sympathy wasn't Alice's strong point. 'It could have been worse, I suppose,' she replied. 'More wet blanket than total dead loss.'

'He recognizes us better now.'

Alice frowned. 'Does he? Wishful thinking, girl.'

'No. But it helps him if I'm in school uniform.'

'Mmm.'

'He's talking a bit better as well.'

'Yeah. He's really motoring. If he was three, you'd be really proud.'

'Alice!'

'I'm just trying to inject some realism here.'

'What about maths? We were *lucky* he was with us last night.'

'All right, he's some sort of genius at maths,' Alice replied. 'But he's still simple. He needed you to take him to the place, he didn't know his shoe size, forgot who we were as soon as we'd turned our backs, and he was pretty grim at bowling. How do you know he doesn't need a nappy as well?'

'Alice!' Hattie cried again.

'Well, how *do* you know?'

'Because his brain's the problem. Physically, he's normal. The doctor says so.'

'Oliver's totally normal,' Alice said. 'He's smarter than Connor'll ever be. And he's panting for it.'

'Just because he's smart and panting for it doesn't make him a good deal,' Hattie retorted. 'Anyway, if you had a brother with something nasty – like Down's syndrome – would you refuse to be seen out with him?'

'That's not fair. A brother's different. A brother's family. With family, you don't get a choice. You get what you're given.'

'So, you're saying you wouldn't choose to hang around with someone disabled?'

'No. I'm not prejudiced. Don't try and make out I am. I'm just saying I'd be a mismatch with someone like that. It wouldn't work out, would it?'

'Wouldn't work out? I'm not asking you to *marry* Connor,' Hattie said. 'I just want you to be his friend. I want you to come to the youth club with us. Don't look at me like that. You don't have to dance with him and all. If you're embarrassed, you can tell everyone he's your brother.'

Since the chat at Christmas about sex, Brad had been getting on well with Connor. The storms of earlier years had subsided. Besides, Connor had completely forgotten that they hadn't got on. Now, everyone was trying to exploit Brad and his improved relationship with his brother. Hattie had asked Brad to probe the activities of the previous evening. His parents put him under the same obligation because Connor had got back so late and, anyway, they'd never been sure about Liam's suitability as a friend. Then there were the standing orders from Dr Nawaz to talk about past brotherly deeds. Misdeeds really. 'Even if you have to remind him of painful fights,' she'd say, 'that's good. Maybe you can stir him up with a particularly upsetting episode.' Everyone was trying to turn Brad into a spy and interrogator.

But it seemed to Brad that Connor had made his choice. He was going to look forward and not back. End of story.

Brad still couldn't get out of his head some of the things he'd said to Connor on Barbados. Lying in bed most nights, unable to sleep, he heard the replays. 'What do you reckon Hattie's up to, now you're not around?' 'Bet there's a load of sleep-overs back home. No idea who she'll be sleeping with.' 'No, it's about a fiver. It's priced in Barbados dollars, not US dollars, so it's about half what you think it is. You're hopeless with figures. Unless it's girls' figures.' 'With you out of the way, I bet the lads are queuing outside Hattie's house.' 'Just use your brain, Connor – if you can find it.' Then there was that wisecrack about a razor-sharp mind – and a good few more. Brad had behaved like a … like an annoying, childish little brother.

A physics teacher once told Brad about the multiverse theory. 'We all live in one of an infinite number of universes. Every time we make a decision we create another universe. We come up to a road and we have a choice. Go left or right. Let's say we go left. As soon as we make that decision, another universe opens. In that other one, we made the opposite choice. We went right. That universe follows what happens. But we went left. We made our choice and that's the universe we're in.' What Brad wanted to know is why, of all the universes, he ended up in the crappiest one. He wanted to live in the universe where his family had gone to Bangor instead of Barbados, or the one where they'd left

Connor at home, or the one where bad weather had grounded them at Heathrow for three weeks. But he didn't. He lived in the world with a damaged and derailed brother.

All he could do was help Connor. Properly help. Not help everyone else mould Connor into what they thought he should be.

Brad unwrapped the takeaway meal and, leaving both portions in their paper, pushed one in front of Connor. Connor poked the golden brown slab lying next to the chips, as if testing it for signs of life. 'What's this?'

'Fish,' Brad answered. 'Cod.'

Connor shook his head. 'No. Fish is in fizzy drink.'

'Yeah, but that's how it looks after it's been cooked.'

Connor watched suspiciously as his brother dripped red liquid all over his fish and chips until they were smothered and the colour began to seep into the paper. While Brad chomped on a mouthful, Connor reached out tentatively and dipped the tip of an eel in the red liquid. Tentatively, he placed a bit on his tongue.

Brad laughed. 'It's nice. Tomato sauce.' He could have told Connor that he used to love the stuff, but decided against.

Unconvinced, Connor tucked into his meal without splashing it with blood.

Between chewing chips, Brad said, 'You and me, we didn't get on, you know. The things I did, things I shouldn't have done, when we were younger. It's a bit late now to wish I hadn't.' Brad shook his head wistfully. 'Sometimes it was just daft things. We could fight over nothing, or anything. I don't know. I guess we just taunted each other a lot. Anyway, it wasn't a great idea because you're – you were – ten times better than me at beating up. I always came off worse. The trouble was, I was ten times better at taunting. And ten times better at being sneaky. Once, you got tickets to go to a gig with one of your girlfriends. You went on and on about how good it was going to be. Mum and Dad said I was too young to go, so your tickets disappeared – mysteriously. You never did get to that gig and you never worked out what happened.' Brad pointed guiltily at his own chest with a red and greasy finger.

Connor merely shrugged. Incident forgotten. No bad feelings.

'Anyway, where were we?' Brad murmured. 'Ah, yes. Multiplying.' He wiped his mouth. 'When you multiply a number by itself – like three times three … '

'Nine.'

'Yes. It's called squaring. Three squared is … '

'Nine.'

'Exactly. And twenty-five squared is … ?'

'Six hundred and twenty-five.'

Brad smiled and nodded. 'You're amazing.' He was about to comment that, once, Connor could hardly add two numbers together, but he curbed the impulse. Connor wouldn't want the reminder. 'Did you like ten-pin bowling?'

'What?'

'Last night.' Brad stood up, licked his greasy fingers, took a few steps and let loose an imaginary bowl. 'Strike! Ten points.'

Connor nodded. Mixing things up, he cried, 'One hundrerrrrd and eight-teeee!'

'That's a great score. Did anyone get that much?' asked Brad.

Connor shook his head and rattled off all of the scores.

'AF and OB must be pretty good,' Brad said. He knew that Connor would probably have beaten both of them last year, but there was no point dwelling on it.

'I couldn't hear music. It was a very lot … ' He put both hands over his ears and grimaced.

'Noisy,' Brad said, before he could stop himself acting like a speech therapist. Connor had made himself perfectly plain without knowing every word. 'What did you do after the bowls?'

'One hundred and eighty squared is three two four nought nought.'

'Did you go somewhere with Liam afterwards?'

'He … lost something,' Connor replied, holding up and examining a particularly long chip. 'We all forget things. I helped.'

'*You* helped someone who'd forgotten something?' Brad cried, trying to keep the grin from his face.

Connor nodded again. 'Can't remember what.'

Both of the brothers burst out laughing.

On the table, the single running shoe was mainly white with three short stripes on its side. One black, one dark blue and one light blue. Wavy stitching came round from the toe, past the stripes and up to the point where an off-white lace hung. From the sole near the back end of the trainer, another stitched seam rose towards the heel where the first three letters of the logo could be seen: *adi*. A thin dark layer at the bottom of the shoe indicated that the sole itself was black.

Connor examined his crude sketch of the trainer. He wasn't happy. Then he realized what was wrong. He added a couple of small wheels to the bottom.

The excitable tobacco-tainted teacher, his hands like restless birds fluttering around his shoulders, cried from behind Connor, 'It's drawing from observation! Sketch what you see.' He stabbed a smelly and yellowed eel at Connor's effort. 'What's that? Can you see a roller skate?' Theatrically, he stared around the art room with one hand on his brow. 'No. Not a roller skate to be observed anywhere. It's a running shoe.'

'Car shoe,' Connor mumbled.

The art teacher sighed loudly. 'No. Running shoe, roller skate. Two entirely different things!'

Behind them, Alice remarked, 'Both go on the feet.'

Jazz Hands turned on her. 'Alice Foley. Let's see how *your* trainer's coming on.' He examined it and then said spitefully, 'Tell me, how many blue stripes have you observed? Two apparently. Look again and count.'

Helpfully, Connor chipped in, 'There's two blue ones. Number three's … different. Dark.'

'You see wheels that aren't there, but you can count!'

Connor shrugged. 'I'm happy at numbers.'

'Enough,' he snapped at Connor. 'Let me tell you what's wrong with your paltry effort. Apart from the imagined wheels … '

Alice looked grateful. Connor had distracted Jazz Hands and copped the bad-tempered lecture.

Liam couldn't bear to spend much time with sick people. The old ones made him shudder. Instead, he hung around outside the Institute for Memory Disorders. Waiting. Waiting for Courtney. He breathed on his cold hands and then checked his watch. Perfect. He'd timed it perfectly to arrive just as schools closed. She could visit any time now.

He recognized her straightaway. Wasn't hard to figure it out. She was young, healthy and on roller skates. That's why Connor had mentioned car shoes and Courtney when they were raiding Joy's old house.

Liam smiled. Two birds with one stone. He'd got a fix on Courtney and he could keep Connor onside by giving him some skates. He knew Connor's shoe size from the days when they'd played footie together. The muddle over shoes before ten-pin bowling confirmed that he'd gone up one size.

Liam let Courtney roll right past. He didn't care what she did inside. He was only interested in when she came out. He would follow her home.

Rocking.

Hood up and a half-brick in his hand, Liam had decided on the direct approach. He already knew exactly where the roller skates were shelved. He already knew they'd got Connor's size. He'd checked it out earlier – when the store was open. Even if smashing the window set off an alarm, he'd need two minutes at most and his hoodie would keep his mug hidden from the internal security cameras.

Eagerly, he took a deep breath and drew back his arm.

It had been a successful and satisfying day. Liam took another swig of beer and looked up at Mr Rowling. 'She's eleven or twelve. Something like. Good-looking kid.'

GG gazed at Liam for a few seconds and then said, 'Would my clients be interested?'

'Reckon so.'

'Describe her.'

'Small, thin, tanned skin, long black hair,' Liam answered.

'Any sign of … development?'

Liam shrugged. 'Too many clothes.'

'Does she have that look of innocence?'

'A little angel.'

'She ticks all the boxes, then,' Gareth Gregor said. 'She'd be … profitable.'

'Sure thing.'

'And you know where she lives?'

'Yeah.'

Mr Rowling nodded. 'When the opportunity presents itself, we need to entice her. We haven't got Connor to help, so you do it.'

CHAPTER 20

To Connor, relationships were always going to be both very simple and very difficult.

Sitting on the wall, he lifted both legs into the air to show off his brand new car shoes.

Courtney looked at them again and said, 'They look good – a bit like mine. Where did you get them?'

'A … er … present.'

'Who from?'

'Liam.'

Courtney shrugged. 'Nice.' Making up her mind, she said, 'I'll tell you what. Let's just go round the hospital building. That's probably far enough. Dr Nawaz wouldn't want you to go any further. Okay?'

Standing up again, Connor smiled a young child's smile of delight.

As a novice, Connor took a while to get used to the car shoes. He felt wobbly, as if he was about to tumble forwards or fall backwards. He didn't feel in control of his movement, but he had enough of a knack to roll along behind Courtney. He moved at half her pace so she had to slow down for him. Even so, the world seemed to float by at twice its normal speed. Not that Connor noticed. He was just enjoying himself. Behind Courtney, Connor swept past two ambulances, several visitors, a woman in a wheelchair, parked cars, trees and shrubs, a porter who shouted, 'Careful!' at them, and a small group of staff smoking outside a fire exit.

Half way round, Courtney stopped and Connor grabbed a pillar to come to an abrupt and inelegant halt. 'All right?' she said. 'Keeping up?'

'Happy,' Connor answered excitedly. He was always happy with Courtney. 'Can we get profs here?'

'Profs?'

Connor tried to describe profiteroles but couldn't manage it. He was forced to give up. 'More car shoes?'

'All right. Let's go.'

'A hundred miles an hour.'

'We'll have to keep it down,' Courtney said with a grin. 'We're in a thirty-miles-an-hour zone.'

'Like my brain.'

Pretending she understood, Courtney nodded and changed the subject. Obviously she was used to dealing with someone who didn't make a lot of sense. 'Ready?'

About to let go of the pillar, Connor's enjoyment spilled over. Half laughing, half crying, he said, 'I'll see you when I go to Santa.'

This time, Courtney's face betrayed bemusement. Clearly, she didn't know where Connor was coming from. His perverse remark seemed to alarm her, but she managed to smile at him anyway. 'Er … Time to go back.'

Hattie had got into the habit of engineering her own name into an opening exchange with Connor. That way, she avoided the horrible tight feeling in her gut when, after all they'd done together, after all she was doing now to bring it back, he hadn't got a clue who she was.

'I'm Hattie,' she said to him, 'and I'm wondering what's in your bag.'

'Car shoes.'

'Car shoes?'

'Roller skates,' Alice explained.

Hattie glanced quizzically at her friend.

'He drew them in art.'

'Well, you can't zoom around school on them,' Hattie said. 'It's not allowed.'

'You'd have trouble with the stairs,' Oliver pointed out.

Hattie asked, 'Where did they come from, Connor?'

He shrugged.

'Who gave them to you?'

'Liam.'

'Uh-oh.'

Immediately, Alice made an assumption. 'He nicked them.'

'When I went past this morning, SprintZ had got a boarded-up window,' Oliver told them. 'They sell skates.'

Nodding knowingly, Alice said, 'Two plus two equals four.'

'Liam plus boarded-up window equals smash and grab.'

'Just don't flash them around, Connor,' said Hattie.

Oliver was sure that Connor was perfectly innocent. He didn't have the guile to rob a sports shop but, if Liam had worn a hood or avoided the cameras like a pro, maybe Oliver could get Markham into trouble anyway. Maybe he could make SprintZ think Connor Markham was responsible. Maybe Connor would get caught. And if he did, maybe that would put more distance between him and Hattie.

Oliver hadn't used a public phone before, but he didn't want the call to be traced back to his own phone. He read the instructions before picking up the receiver.

The new Duty Sergeant sighed wearily. 'You've received anonymous information about the theft of roller skates from SprintZ, you say.'

'That's right, Sarg. Well, the shop did – from a young male voice. Then they called us to say we should interview a lad called Connor Markham.'

'Tell me, what else are we working on at the moment?'

'Yes, I know,' PC Knox replied. 'Lots.'

'What do you think about the motives of the supergrass? Why tip off the shop?'

He shrugged. 'Dunno.'

'Sounds like a kid's prank to me,' the sergeant said. She looked up from her computer screen. 'Do you know what a teenager is?'

Xander Knox looked confused.

'A teenager's a machine for turning chips and chocolate into mischief,' she said with a wry grin. 'Have we got Markham on record?'

'Yes, Sarg.' Xander consulted his notes. 'He was arrested a year back by PC 1499. He's retired now. Anyway, we gave Markham a warning.'

'Why?'

'He was with a group of lads who set fire to Eve's nightclub.'

'He was with a group,' she muttered slowly. 'I detect ambiguity.'

'According to CCTV, he didn't actually do the arson.'

'That's why he wasn't charged.'

'Yes.'

'Did he name the guilty party?'

'No.'

'Was anyone inside the club at the time?'

'No.'

'So,' the sergeant said, 'it was another case of youthful … exuberance.'

Xander nodded.

'Has it been repeated?'

'No.'

The sergeant sighed again. 'All right. When resources are limited, priority's the name of the game. Did this theft of roller skates involve murder, injury, serious risk to staff, deadly weapons, or substantial sums of money?'

'No, Sarg.'

'Put it in the Pending File, then. We'll look into it once we've made the streets safe from the big boys.'

'Yes, Sarg.'

'PC Knox?'

'Yes?'

'You're really called Xander Knox, are you?'

'Yes, Sarg.'

'Doesn't that class as criminal overuse of x?'

'My mother's a Scrabble fan, I'm afraid. She likes the letter x.'

Connor looked up at the teacher. His blatant attempt to show off by recalling her name almost paid off. 'Miss Satan.'

'Sayell,' she said, correcting him with a smile. 'Miss Sayell.'

'Yes. Six Eight Eleven, not Six Eight Ten.'

Even Miss Sayell had to admit that Connor wasn't going to pass GCSE in maths – even though he was by far the most gifted mathematician she had ever taught. The mathematical concepts weren't the problem. The problem was that Connor wouldn't understand the language of exams. The phrasing of questions would leave him floundering. If he could understand the language of data handling, geometry, algebra and the rest of it, he could pass with flying colours. But he couldn't. He didn't even appreciate verbs. If a question asked him to explain, calculate or draw, he'd be stumped. For Connor, a GCSE exam was not an appropriate vehicle to prove to the world that he was a mathematical athlete.

Miss Sayell got the support assistant to work with Connor on language by exploiting his love of numbers and his natural playfulness. Together, Connor and his assistant toyed with mathematical words. They turned *ten* into *net*; *add* into *dad*, *three* into *there*, and *seven* into *evens*.

'Do car shoes,' Connor insisted.

'Car shoes?'

'Yes.'

It took a lot of shuffling of the letters to find an anagram associated with maths and numbers. The best that the support assistant could manage was *has score*. It was good enough to tickle Connor.

'What about *three*?' he said.

'We've just done it,' the assistant replied. Quickly, she added, 'But let's do it again.' This time, she turned it into *ether*.

'What's that?'

'I'm not sure. The air or atmosphere, I think.' She paused before telling him, 'I'm going to introduce you to Scrabble. A game for making words, but each letter's got a value. A's worth one, C's three and X is eight. You'd like it.'

Connor looked interested, but he was hooked on rearranging words. 'What about *Brad*?' he prompted. He shuffled the letters himself and then asked, 'Is … *drab* a word?'

'Yes. Well done. It means dull and boring.'

Connor snorted. 'That's not right.' He flung the letters from the table top. 'Words aren't happy.'

No, numbers were definitely not the problem. The problem was definitely language.

Alcohol wasn't allowed at the youth club, of course. That didn't stop a few trying to smuggle it in, but the doorman detected it and removed it with sniffer-dog efficiency and ruthlessness. Connor had refused to be separated from his skates and carried them with him almost everywhere he went. But security insisted that he'd have to leave them in the cloakroom. Reluctantly, he agreed.

Inside the club, it was noisy and roving spotlights cut through the darkness like torches in a horror film. It was dim and bright at the same time. Connor felt both intimidated and excited by the party atmosphere. And the music! It didn't just invade his ears, it pounded his whole body. It certainly had an effect on the people standing in the middle of the room. It made them wobbly on their legs. He didn't understand dancing. He'd seen Courtney jiggle about to music, but nothing as extreme as the effect in the club. The dancers were like fish in a feeding frenzy. Startled, Connor stood open-mouthed and watched. The volcano girl kept pulling on his sleeve, encouraging him to join the dancing. In fright, he shook his head.

He leaned on a table at the edge of the action. Old-Connor's girlfriend danced in a group of boys and girls but kept glancing at him. He couldn't see Courtney in the seething mass. Perhaps she wasn't there at all. Alice was wearing a skin-tight bright yellow top. Even Connor could pick her out in the crowd. She was spending a lot of time dancing with one particular boy. Connor didn't recognize him, but he was wearing a baseball cap. As Connor watched, he leaned in close and shouted something in Alice's ear. She smiled and nodded. They walked away from the dance floor. The boy went towards the bar while Alice left the room.

Connor remembered the young man when he came towards Connor's table because of the cap on his head. He sat down near Connor with a couple of dark-coloured fizzy drinks in his hands. He placed one of them on the table, put an eel across his lips, closed one eye momentarily in a strange gesture, and turned away from Connor. Intrigued, Connor bent forward to see what was happening. He saw the boy drop two white pills into the other drink thing and swirl it round, just like the nurses in the Institute for Memory Disorders used to do for Stroke 2. The boy put the drink on the table and picked up the other one for himself.

When Alice returned she stood by the table, nodded towards the lad with the baseball cap and picked up the drink that he'd bought for her.

Connor looked at Alice, about to drink, and then at the boy. Under the cap, his face was wet like a bottle with raindrops. He was itching for Alice to take a gulp.

Without warning, Connor took a swipe at the drink thing in Alice's hand. The tumbler went flying and the dark liquid splashed all over Alice's new yellow top and skirt.

Horrified, Alice screamed, 'What do you think you're doing? Look what you've done, you … '

Connor looked abashed but he defended himself. 'You'll go to Santa.'

The lad who had bought her the drink dashed away.

'You've scared him off … ' Exasperated, Alice ran out of words.

Having seen Connor's lunge, Hattie hurtled from the dance floor. She was followed by Oliver.

Alice turned towards her friend and pointed at her clothes. 'Look! Ruined.'

Hattie dug some tissues out of her bag and helped Alice mop up the worst of the damage. 'I'm sorry, Alice.'

Connor stared at the commotion like an uncomprehending child.

Oliver simply smiled to himself.

'I can't stay here,' Alice complained. 'Not like this.'

Hattie nodded. 'Let's go back to my place. Mum and Dad are away. We can patch things up there.'

Alice hesitated and then agreed. 'Okay.' Then she added angrily, 'That boy who was chatting me up was totally fit – until Connor stuck his stupid oar in.'

'Sorry,' Hattie repeated.

Connor was still standing there, gazing at the pool of liquid on the floor with a pained expression on his face.

Going up to him, Hattie said, 'What's the matter?'

'Pink.'

Into his ear, she said, 'No. It was Pepsi, I think. Anyway, come on. We'll collect your skates.'

Leaving behind the lights, warmth and noise of the youth club, the outside seemed dark, cold and quiet. Hattie walked with Connor, adrift of the rest. She asked, 'Why did you do that, Connor?' She seemed annoyed that her plan to integrate Connor had just fallen apart.

'What?'

'You know,' she snapped. 'You can't have forgotten *that* already. Spilled Alice's drink.'

Connor thought about it. He found it hard to explain. 'Alice shouldn't go to Santa with white things.'

'Go to Santa? What do you mean?'

'Be no more.'

'Die?' Hattie exclaimed.

Connor nodded.

'What are these white things?' Hattie asked.

'Boy put them in fizzy drink.' He mimed the action.

'What? The one she was dancing with? He put something in her drink?'

Connor shrugged. 'White things.' By the light of the street-lamps, he traced the tiny size on his palm.

Hattie frowned. 'Pills? You mean he put pills in her drink?'

At once, Connor's face lit up. 'Yes. Pills. That's what Courtney said.' Connor found it easier to remember things when they involved Courtney.

'Courtney? Who's … ?' Hattie shook her head. Clearly trying

to keep to the point, she said, 'So the boy who was chatting Alice up put pills in her drink and you saw? You stopped her taking them by knocking the drink out of her hand and all?'

Connor nodded.

Hattie sighed with relief. 'Okay. I'll tell Alice. She should know. It sounds like you did good.'

'Happy.'

Alice was sceptical at first. 'Really? Or are you making it up to get Connor off the hook?'

'No! I wouldn't … '

'Well, how come a total prawn remembers about drugs when he can't even remember my name?'

'Maybe it's because he's not a total prawn.'

Alice exhaled deeply, letting loose a stream of condensation.

'If you don't believe me, ask him,' said Hattie.

Alice looked into her friend's face. 'All right. I believe you.'

'Do you forgive him, then?'

'I suppose.'

'More than that. Who knows what would've happened if you'd drunk it. You should thank him.'

'We'll see.'

In the house, Hattie went to raid the fridge for drinks, Alice cleaned herself up in the bathroom, and Oliver turned on the television. 'Let's see what they've been downloading.' He fiddled with the remote control. When Hattie came back into the living room, Oliver sniggered and said, 'I hope it's not too naughty.' He sat back and the picture came to life. He cried, 'Even more embarrassing than porn. It's Countdown!'

With a groan, Hattie explained, 'That's my dad. He loves it for some reason, but he's always at work when it's on, so he records it.'

It was too late. Connor was already hooked. Rachel Riley had just plucked out six numbers and displayed the target sum.

25   4   5   7   1   9

541

Cottoning on to the idea straightaway, Connor came up with an answer in ten seconds. 'Four times seven is twenty-eight. Take away one and five. Twenty-two. Twenty-two times twenty-five is five hundred and fifty. Take away nine makes five hundred and forty-one.'

'That's incredible,' Hattie uttered, handing round the drinks. Eyebrows raised, Alice watched from the doorway.

Oliver jeered, 'Connor Markham – the next Rachel Riley!' He shook his head. 'Anyone can do it.'

'Really?' Alice responded as she dropped into a seat. 'Why don't you wait for the next one and race Connor, then?'

'Boring.' Oliver flicked around the channels until he found a horror film. 'That's better.'

Four American girls were cowering in the corner of a derelict house as someone – a faceless man with an enormous breadknife – prowled slowly, silently through the rooms.

Connor soon tired of the incomprehensible film. He didn't know why he was the only one who wanted to carry on with the counting game. The picture box thing was showing close-ups of a blade glinting in the moonlight, close-ups of terrified female faces. Connor didn't feel the tension of the scene, but the others seemed glued to it.

Eventually, old-Connor's girlfriend came to his rescue. She took him into the study and turned on the computer. 'I told Alice,' she said, waiting for the system to boot up. 'You know, about the spiked drink and all. I think she believes you. Anyway, she's feeling better about it.'

Connor wasn't listening. He was keen to see what the computer could do. Hattie left him with a numbers game and a beer.

At the end of the film, only two of the teenage girls remained alive. Bloodied but breathing. Can of lager in hand, Oliver appeared in the study to drag Connor away from the desktop. Once Hattie had finished clearing up, they set out to walk Connor home.

139

CHAPTER 21

Like any child, Connor craved independence – as long as it came with a safety net.

On the way home, between the kicking ball field and GG's, the others were absorbed in a conversation that Connor didn't understand. He lagged behind, counting the house numbers. Forty-nine, fifty-one, fifty-three, nothing house, fifty-seven. With a smile on his face, he ducked into the garden of number fifty-seven, slipping his markers again. Hidden by the tree things, he rang the bell.

It seemed to take ages for Mrs Fifty-Seven to totter to the darkened door and open it. Dressed in strange clothing, she said in surprise, 'Are you back again?'

It was, of course, an unnecessary question but Connor answered it anyway. 'Yes.'

'But … ' She glanced down at her wrist but she wasn't wearing a watch. 'It's … I don't know … midnight or later. I was in bed.'

Connor shrugged.

'Well, now you're here, you'd better come on in.' She began to walk down the hall but stopped and turned. 'Let's have a cup of tea.' Apparently, she believed that a cup of tea cured anything. Or maybe, by the time she'd drunk the tea, she would have forgotten the problem. Solved.

Mrs Dungate pointed to his left arm and asked, 'What you got there?'

Connor looked down as if he'd forgotten what he'd tucked underneath his arm. 'Car shoes,' he answered.

'Car shoes, eh? The fancy names they come up with these days! You wouldn't believe it. They were called roller skates when I was a lass, you know, and these trainer whatsits were just called pumps. Them days, you could afford a pair of pumps.'

After brewing up, Mrs Dungate took her guest into her living room. She moved aside a cluster of medals before sitting on the sofa. Noticing that Connor was looking with curiosity at the medals, she explained, 'My husband won those in the war – that was before he died. Bless his memory. I almost forgot I had them. Came across them upstairs. I expect they're quite valuable now.'

'I've got some,' Connor said. 'For kicking a ball, I think … '

Mrs Dungate smiled. She refrained from making a comparison of Connor's exploits on the football field with her husband's exploits in the battlefield. Like last time, before she took a gulp of tea she placed a little pill on her tongue.

That reminded Connor. He was suddenly proud that he could recall why he had come and what he had to say. 'I came to … thing you. You don't want pills.'

She swallowed and then said, 'Don't I? I forgot to take this one before bed. I think.'

'A lot bad. Not happy.'

Mrs Dungate sighed. 'I don't like taking them, it's true, so I stopped once but I came over all dizzy and sick and stiff. I started again straightaway, I can tell you. And my doctor told me off for stopping. They must be doing me good.'

Connor was surprised and baffled but, when he noticed Mrs Dungate's handbag nestling in the corner of an easy chair, he was distracted from the pills and medals. Puzzled, he gazed at the handbag.

'What is it, Colin?'

'I thought I … ' He shook his head, shrugged and then smiled happily. 'No. Nothing.' He stood up and announced, 'I just wanted to say about pills.' Clutching his skates and leaving his tea untouched, he left. At the front gate, he turned to the right, changed his mind, turned around, hesitated, and then shook his head.

Further along the road, a frantic Hattie cried, 'Where've you been? We lost you. Come on. Let's get you home.'

The morning after the doomed visit to the youth club, Alice called on Hattie. While Hattie was sorting out her school bag, her dad shouted, 'Hattie!' His cry was one third exclamation, one third question, and one third threat.

Venturing into the study, Hattie asked warily, 'What is it?' She found herself in front of both parents. It had to be serious. She was glad that Alice was with her for support. Besides, her mum and dad would not let fly so much when Alice was there. 'We've got to leave in a minute or we'll be late for school.'

'We want an explanation first.'

'For what?'

'Why the computer doesn't work.'

'The computer doesn't work? Why not?'

'That's what we want to know,' her dad said. 'It looks – and smells – as if someone's poured beer or something onto the keyboard.'

Hattie swallowed uncomfortably and glanced at Alice. Both of them knew that Connor was the only person to use it while they watched teenage girls being butchered.

'Er … I don't know how … '

Mr Townsend interrupted. 'You're not covering up for something that happened last night, are you?'

Her parents would never approve of her entertaining Connor in their house. 'No,' she lied.

'Only, there's a lot less booze in the fridge this morning.'

'Exaggeration. We only had one or two … '

Her mum took a guess. 'Are you covering up for *someone* who was here last night?'

'No. I … '

Alice butted in, ending Hattie's struggle. 'Yes. She is.'

Hattie stared at her friend – who was about to become an enemy. Silently, Hattie's face was saying, 'How could you, you traitor?'

'Ah, Alice,' Mrs Townsend said. 'Good. Let's hear some sense from you.'

Hattie's mum and dad had always had a soft spot for Alice Foley.

Alice said, 'Hattie's covering up for me, I'm afraid. I'm sorry. I don't know how it happened. Totally clumsy. I came in here and tripped up with a can of beer in my hand. It sloshed all over the keypad. I thought it might not do any harm. You know, when it dried out, I thought it'd be okay.' She hesitated. 'I'll pay for a new one. Sorry.' She hung her head with convincing shame.

Hattie sighed with relief.

'So, it was an accident.'

Alice nodded.

'All right,' Mr Townsend said, abruptly changing his mood. 'We all have accidents. There's no need to pay. I just wish you'd owned up straightaway. Honesty's the best policy.'

Alice nodded again. 'Yes, I know.'

Outside, Hattie whispered, 'Thanks. Thanks for … you know … keeping Connor out of it.'

Alice shrugged. 'We're quits now, me and Connor.' She'd taken the blame for the spilt beer because Connor had taken the rap in an art lesson and because he'd stopped her swallowing a drink that had been laced with some drug or other.

Later, during maths, she glanced across the room at Oliver. He was scowling at Connor. Alice nudged her friend and said quietly, 'Last night at your place. Maybe it wasn't Connor anyway. Didn't Oliver go into the study to get him?'

Hattie nodded.

'Carrying a beer, if I remember rightly,' added Alice. 'But it's no use having an inquisition. If Oliver chucked booze around, trying to get Connor into trouble, he'd deny it. If Connor did it, he'll have forgotten.' She hesitated before whispering, 'I haven't gone soft, girl. I still think Connor's a total write-off, but he shouldn't take the rap if he hasn't done anything.' She'd always hated unfairness.

There was an ominous silence in the classroom. Alice stopped talking to Hattie and looked around.

'Well?' Miss Sayell prompted.

'What?' Alice asked.

'If you'd been paying attention, you'd know the answer, Alice. It's not that difficult.'

'I was just … ' Out of the corner of her eye, Alice saw Connor holding up a piece of paper. On it, he'd written 47 in felt tip. Connor's support assistant was doing her best to wear an expression of disapproval, but a smile was showing through. Alice paused as if doing a mental calculation. 'It's … er … forty-seven,' she said to the teacher.

Miss Sayell was taken aback. 'Oh. Good. Yes, forty-seven. Well done, Alice. Despite appearances, you seem to have grasped it.'

While Miss Sayell set them all some problems to consolidate whatever principle she was trying to teach, Alice looked towards Connor for a moment. She was going to nod her gratitude but she didn't quite manage it. She could not admit to herself that she'd been saved again by a virtual moron.

By break, Alice had changed her mind about the inquisition – because she'd worked out a way of tackling Oliver. In the cloakroom, she said, 'When you went and got Connor last night, was he really on their computer?' Deliberately, she used a disparaging tone as if surprised that a brainless boy could cope with the technology.

Oliver nodded. 'Yes.'

Alice laughed cruelly. 'What was he doing? Writing, designing, surfing, gaming?'

'Guess.'

'Playing a kid's game?'

Catching Alice's infectious ridicule, he cried, 'In one. Bingo!'

Then, more subdued, Alice said, 'So, the computer was working.'

Wary of her sudden shift of mood, Oliver replied, 'Er … yes. Why?'

'Because this morning, it wasn't.'

'Connor must have done something daft to it. Surprise, surprise.'

'But you just said it was working when you went in,' Alice pointed out. 'Unless he did something daft while you were in there, it'd be down to the last person to leave the room.'

'Well, he had a beer next to the keypad. Maybe when he got up ... '

Alice interrupted. 'How come you know it was beer gumming up the works?'

Reddening, Oliver shrugged. 'Just a guess, I suppose.'

'You wouldn't happen to have tried a bit of sabotage to drive Hattie and Connor apart, would you?'

'No. Of course not.'

'*Of course not*,' she repeated cynically.

'I didn't!'

'Oh, good. Because I really don't like sneaky, nasty people. If I thought someone was being a total shit, Oliver, I'd tell Hattie what's going on. That wouldn't do their chances with her any good, would it?'

'What's got into you?' Oliver snapped. 'You don't have a good word for Connor. He's a loser, you said.'

'Oh, he's still a loser,' she replied. 'I still think Hattie should dump him, but for the right reasons, not because some dickhead's nobbled him.' She stormed away.

Alice had calmed down by the time she found Brad. Even so, she decided that plain speaking was the best policy. Besides, she guessed that Brad liked to keep things straightforward. 'Your brother's a virtual bloody moron.'

Brad was taken aback by her bluntness but he didn't deny it. 'So?'

'So, people like Hattie are trying to make him better by jogging his memory all the time. Not so much jogging as taking a sledgehammer approach. What do you think about it?'

Brad shook his head. 'Sledgehammer or gentle prod, it's a rotten idea. They ought to be helping him through today and tomorrow, not harping on about the past.'

'You're right and everyone else is wrong, then?'

'Yeah. That's what I think.'

Alice nodded in agreement. She wanted Brad to know that he had an unlikely ally.

Smiling broadly, Brad said, 'He's got to make the most of what he's got now, I reckon. Simple as that.'

The bell sounded and students began to converge on the doorways, forming impenetrable clusters in the corridors.

'Hattie's got other plans,' Alice told him.

'She's not the only one. You ought to hear my mum and dad. And his doctor's the same.'

'I can't do anything about them,' Alice said as she walked away backwards, 'but I'll see about Hattie. Don't hold your breath, though. She's pretty determined.'

The SEN assistant showed Connor the Scrabble board and tiles. 'See? Each letter's got a value – a number. The bigger the number, the better. You can put a word on the board and add up your score. You'll like this. Look. There are some special squares on the board that mean you can double or treble your score.'

Immediately hooked, Connor examined the board and said, 'Like darts. Doubles and trebles.'

His helper nodded and pointed to different squares. 'Some double or treble the value of a letter, some double or treble the value of a whole word. See?'

'Happy.'

'Okay. That's where we'll start, then.' She poked around in the collection of tiles and then handed him what he needed: H, A, P, P and Y. 'Lay them out to get the best score.'

Connor put the word down so he doubled the score for the Y and trebled the score of the whole word. 'Fifty-seven!' he cried.

'Is it? Let me check. Yes, you're right.' She hesitated and smiled. 'Well, it would be, wouldn't it? You're better at maths than me. You're not going to make a mistake.' Noticing that the nearest two tiles were U and N, she added, 'Look. You can make the word longer and get more score.' Trying to squeeze every educational drop from the game, she handed him the extra tiles and said, 'You know about 'un', don't you? If you put it in front of a word, you get the opposite. Exciting's good, unexciting's not so good. You can turn it into unhappy.'

Connor frowned but placed the tiles correctly.

'Well done,' she said. 'Six more points.'

CHAPTER 22

Somehow, Connor still intended to make Joy the last one.

He was standing with her at the entrance to GG's. They both looked too young. Connor was confident but edgy. Joy was nervous but thrilled. The bouncers gave them the once-over. The camera above the door relayed their image inside. Connor knew that Mr Rowling would be zooming in on the latest offering. Any moment now, he would deliver his verdict directly into the doormen's earpieces. Connor knew this because he'd done it before. Several times. But he'd had enough. If any of Hattie's friends saw him, they might get the wrong impression. Word might get back to Hattie about him and another girl. It would look bad. He was only doing Joy a favour. Nothing more. He wanted it to be over.

The bouncer called Ivan growled, 'Okay. You're in.' He moved aside so Connor and Joy could access the door.

Inside, Connor scanned the dimmed room for female visitors. One girl at the table on his right looked suspiciously young. Another by the bar could have been under eighteen. At a glance, the rest were probably in the club legitimately.

GG himself came out of his office to greet the new couple. Designer suit, designer shoes, designer stubble, manufactured charm.

Joy was nearly exploding with excitement. The owner himself was rolling out the red carpet for her!

'Hello, Connor. Good to see you. And this is … ?'

'Joy.'

'You're very welcome.' His voice was smooth and engaging. His smile was irresistible.

'I'm going to leave you to it,' Connor said to Joy.

'She's in excellent hands,' Mr Rowling assured him.

Joy beamed, puffed up with adult pleasure.

While Connor hesitated, GG said to her, 'We have a very sophisticated crowd here. There are a few people you ought to meet, some in the fashion and music business. See the men over there? The one on the left is a singer. The short one's got the most valuable collection of vintage cars, clothes and medals ... '

Connor interrupted. 'I just need to have a word.'

'Later, Connor. Later.'

Gareth Gregor put his hand gently on the small of Joy's back to guide her towards the bar. 'Let me treat you to a cocktail.'

Joy told herself she could recognize the seedy and avoid it. She wouldn't go with a man she didn't fancy. She wouldn't do anything without some sort of bond. Without warmth and love.

She'd got a knack of looking at boys and coming to instant decisions. Gorgeous, ugly, great body, waste of space, spotty, whatever. The men she saw in GG's wore immaculate suits and the latest styles. They were smooth, sophisticated and good-looking. They were in fashion and the music business! Beyond hot. Absolutely dazzling.

She knew people-watching worked the other way round as well. She was aware of the men giving her the once-over and coming to a decision. She reckoned she'd get ticks in the boxes for her hair, eyes, boobs, flat stomach and legs. She reckoned she was ripe.

She didn't realize seediness was more than just smelly, sick, greasy, grubby men leering at girls. Sometimes, it had glossy wrapping.

CHAPTER 23

Within minutes, Joy was captivated by the lifestyle; she was sold.

She soon found out that the men had wow-factor cars, bulging wallets, upmarket bling, neat, polished shoes, manicured hands, genuine Rolex watches and easy charm. Their world was ultra-glamorous. Sheer class.

'We could go for a drive. A cigarette, perhaps? Another drink first? Some champagne this time? What time are you due home? We'll have to get you back by your deadline. We don't want your parents to worry, do we? One of us will give you a lift.'

That first night, she came to no harm. The men made sure she had a good time. Alcohol oiled the occasion, but she was never out of control. In the company of real gentlemen, her hands stroking the BMW's real leather, she never felt so alive, so grown-up.

Meeting them a second and third time, she began to work out the group dynamics. The alpha male was Lord Williams. The one with the collection of vintage cars and neat sculpted beard. Most of the boys Joy knew couldn't cultivate more than a few stupid straggly hairs on their chins. And, yes, she was mixing with a lord! He was buying her sophisticated drinks, not rubbish cider. Lord Williams had everyone's respect. Joy could see it in the eyes of the people who congregated around him. They admired him. A real man of the world.

When they stopped for food, it wasn't a burger. They were escorted into a discreet room in a very posh restaurant. The menu listed meals Joy had never heard of. They were so expensive, the prices weren't written down. 'The cost isn't important,' Lord Williams explained. 'It's the food we're interested in. Besides, putting the price in customers' faces is so … grubby. It lowers the tone. I'm reassured that it's exorbitant.' When the courses came, one after another, they looked more like works of art than food.

The fourth evening, she got a ride in a 1916 Ford Model T Tourer. The wind blew her hair around and she felt like a film star. And she got her first spliff. It seemed right. It wasn't like it was heroin or anything. Lots of perfectly normal people smoked dope. It was recreation. It went well with the car, the wind, the drinks, the food. Mixed with alcohol, it was a way to a good time, a good giggle. It wasn't serious.

That chic lifestyle was another drug – and she was addicted already. Eager for her next fix, she returned again and again. And each time, she was introduced to another facet of the men's amazing lives. Each time, another door opened.

GG asked her into his office. There, she sat in a chair while a young man lurked behind her. 'You seem to have struck a chord with my friends.' Gareth Gregor smiled broadly. 'Excellent. You continue to … amuse them. But they expect – deserve – something in return. What do I mean? It's all about obligations. They entertain you. You entertain them. That seems fair, doesn't it?'

'Yes, I suppose.'

'You should be flattered by the attention they lavish on you.'

'I am.'

'So, you accept their generosity and you do whatever they ask. Do I make myself clear?'

'I think so.'

'You see, I wouldn't want to tell the cops about your underage drinking and the dope. That wouldn't do you any favours at all. And remember, we know where you live. My clients have given you lifts home. Liam here,' he nodded towards the young man, 'went to the bother of finding out where your mum works.'

'Oh.'

'You wouldn't want any harm to come to her or the house, or indeed to you, would you?'

'No.'

'That's fine then,' GG said. 'We understand each other. We have an agreement. Before you join the men, let's celebrate with our very best cocktail. A fantastic antidote against all that's normal and boring.'

Joy didn't know what was in the drink but it set her up for the night. She felt woozy – pleasantly out of it – almost straightaway. Her inhibitions flew out of the window.

It was a real four-poster bed. Just like in films. Dead romantic. She dived onto it, as if she were plunging into a swimming pool. The mix of alcohol, seriously yummy food, cannabis and whatever else they'd given her made her light-headed. She couldn't stop smiling and laughing.

The men – three of them this time – stood and watched.

'Take your top off.'

Joy hesitated, grinned and then stripped it off.

'And the bra.'

Her fingers fumbled and she giggled.

When she lifted it away, one of the men took a photo with his mobile.

'Now the trousers and pants.'

The smile began to fade. Did she still feel flattered? Yes, perhaps. But worried as well. Was it the right thing? She was sure these men liked her. They certainly pampered her. There was a bond between them. She removed her remaining clothes.

More photographs.

Then two of them were holding her down by her arms.

Lord Williams was on her. He was in her.

'Don't be shy of struggling,' he grunted. 'I like it when they fight back.'

Her mum wasn't home. She made straight for the bathroom. She needed to wash. She needed to cleanse herself.

She hadn't felt love. She'd felt pain. She'd felt blood running. Was that how sex was supposed to be? She didn't know what to expect. Surely not. In her mind, it shouldn't have been like that at all. When actors were having sex on the box or in films, they were always expert, acrobatic and ecstatic. It was romantic. No messing about, no mess. And they always seemed to be having perfect fun. No violence. No blood. No scratching, no hitting, no biting. At least, not like the men did to her.

At least she could easily hide her injuries. They hadn't marked her anywhere that couldn't be covered by clothing.

She scrubbed her body. Then she lay there until the steaming hot water became merely warm. She thought about those photographs and a tear rolled down her cheek.

CHAPTER 24

Unlike people, maths provided Connor with certainty and reliability.

As part of his recognition therapy, Ranji showed Connor a mathematical problem: 288 ÷ 45.

Connor had learned all about dividing, fractions and decimals from Miss Six-Eight-Eleven – and retained the information. Immediately, he said, 'Six dot four.'

Ranji smiled. 'All I was after was 'maths' or 'calculation' or something, but you've solved it as well. Brilliant.'

Ranji had researched the case notes of a nine-year-old boy who had become a genius at mechanics after a bullet took away much of his left hemisphere. She also discovered that several patients in Los Angeles had developed exceptional artistic talents after dementia had destroyed chunks of the left sides of their brains. Medical science didn't fully understand this side-effect of some brain injuries, but it had named the condition: acquired savant syndrome. Ranji was grateful that Connor had acquired an unexpected and striking skill. If all else failed, at least he had something to fill his life.

Before Ranji could continue his therapy, Connor asked, 'What are … pills?'

'Pills? People take them to make them better when they're ill.'

'But … ' Connor looked bewildered. 'They … you know … ' He pointed to the chair where Stroke 2 used to do the left half of jigsaws.

Dr Nawaz smiled wryly. 'One reason he died was because he

avoided taking his pills whenever he could, Connor. That didn't exactly help his treatment.'

Ranji took the time to explain the various types of drugs – good and bad – and Connor began to understand. Stroke 2's pills were supposed to make him better, but he'd refused to swallow them. By not taking hers, Mrs Treble Nineteen had found out that they did her good, but the man at the dance was not trying to make Alice better. It was a very lot confusing.

Hattie had heard Courtney's name twice now. First, Liam had asked if she was part of the bowling expedition. Then Connor had mentioned her when they were talking about tablets. So, Hattie guessed that she was something to do with the hospital and the Institute for Memory Disorder in particular.

It didn't take long to track her down. Dr Nawaz told Hattie all about her and then she saw the young visitor. She was expecting competition for Connor's affections, but Courtney was only a little kid. A twelve-year-old couldn't be competition. Even if she could befriend Connor, she couldn't *help* him. Courtney had no knowledge of Connor's past and, according to Dr Nawaz, she didn't have an interest in it. That couldn't help restore his memory. As the doctor said, the girl could erect extra scaffolding around the new Connor, but she couldn't cast any light on his old life. Besides, Hattie told herself, it was stupid to be jealous of a kid on roller skates.

The next day, Hattie collared Connor. 'You remember me, don't you? Hattie.' Before she got an answer that she didn't want to hear, she asked, 'Do you know how old Courtney is?'

Connor looked surprised. Time held no real meaning for him and age was just a time of life. It didn't matter.

'She's twelve,' Hattie told him. 'It's not normal for a fifteen-year-old – almost sixteen-year-old – boy to ... go around with a twelve-year-old girl.'

Unstable on his car shoes, Connor swayed and said, 'Why not?'

'Because ... it's just not. Age matters, Connor.' It was hard to explain to someone as innocent as Connor.

'Courtney's happy,' he said.

'I see you remember *her* name all right,' Hattie muttered.

Connor smiled at the compliment. 'I spy with my little eye two people beginning with C. Connor and Courtney.'

Frustrated, Hattie breathed in deeply. She was concerned that Connor might get into trouble because of his simplicity. Even if Connor was just friends with this girl, some might misconstrue the relationship. If there was more to it … Big problems. She was twelve! Hattie wished that she could figure out a new way of protecting Connor from himself, but she had only one strategy. She was even more convinced she had to carry on trying to reawaken his memory. Then, his old feelings would pour out once more. She would be his girlfriend again and the young kid would be … forgotten.

Hattie shivered, reaching under her collar to wipe away from her neck the drop of startlingly cold water that had fallen from the jagged red brick. 'Ugh!'

Alice said, 'Brad's doing a good job, isn't he? I mean, not bad for a brother anyway.'

'Brad? I suppose so, but … ' Hattie turned away from her friend and watched the rain teeming down.

'But what?'

They were standing on the canal towpath under the old bridge, sheltering from the sudden downpour. Further along, oblivious to the rain, some young boys were jumping up and down in unison on the new footbridge. If they got the frequency right, the bridge did not just wobble a bit but flexed alarmingly. Anyone using it would have to grasp the handrail and stagger as if they were on a pitching boat in a storm.

'Well,' Hattie replied, 'he was great at first, but I think he's given up. I'm not sure he wants Connor to get his memory back any more. He's not exactly falling over himself to help.'

'He's helping in his own way,' said Alice.

'What way's that?'

'I've been on Google. There are people who can't forget anything – anything at all. They remember every tiny detail:

everything they see, smell, hear, feel and taste. All the good stuff and all the bad. They go totally crazy. Information overload isn't good for us.'

'I don't think Connor's in danger of that.'

'That's not the point,' Alice responded. 'I'm just saying memory isn't everything. Forgetting's important as well, and the most important thing's not the past. It's the future.'

'How do you know what to do in the future if you don't know your past, if you don't know where you've come from?'

'With difficulty. But if someone can't remember their past, are you saying they can't have a future? "You'll stay right there, Connor Markham, and not move a muscle till you've remembered everything!" No chance. Everyone's got to move on. Connor *and* you.'

Outside the small arched bridge, the rain had eased a little. The noisy boys had got bored with the bouncing bridge and bolted.

'Ah, that's what all this is about,' Hattie exclaimed. 'You're trying to put me off Connor and all.'

'Yes, I am. I think you're going about it the wrong way. You've had a good go at stirring his memory and there's nothing there.'

'Not yet. But who knows? Maybe it'll flood back tomorrow.'

'Always tomorrow.' Alice surveyed the wet world beyond their makeshift shelter. 'Why are you still trying, Hattie?'

'It's obvious. Without a past, he's going to carry on getting lost, getting into trouble, mixing with the wrong crowd.' She would have claimed to be thinking about Liam, but really she was thinking of both Liam and Courtney.

Alice disagreed. 'You're carrying on because Connor's shown no real interest in you. The only way you're going to get your boyfriend back is if he remembers. That's why you're doing it, girl.'

Hattie's mouth opened in exasperation. 'I'm doing it because his mum and dad and the doctor want me to.'

'Yeah, sure.'

Hattie rounded on her friend. 'I know why you're saying this.'

'Oh?'

'Because you always wanted him. You want him for yourself.'

Alice shook her head and smiled. 'Don't be stupid. He's a lame duck. A dead duck.'

'You don't want him to remember he's my boyfriend because you'll miss out. That's what you're thinking.'

'I want Connor like I want a hole in the ... ' Alice stopped, clearly regretting her choice of phrase.

Hattie stared at her for a moment and then strode away down the canal-side path, not caring if she got soaked.

In the classroom, Miss Sayell said to her most eccentric, exceptional and exacting student, 'You've got to think about what you do when you leave school, Connor. You might want to consider something to do with maths.' She paused and then added with passion, 'I'll tell you something about maths. It never lets you down. Three plus three is always six. Not a bit more, not a bit less, but spot on six. It's not opinion, it's pure fact.'

'Numbers are my friends,' Connor replied. 'Six is a happy shape. Nearly perfect.'

Miss Sayell smiled. 'Mathematicians say six *is* a perfect number.'

'Why?'

'Which numbers can you divide into 6 and get a whole number – not counting six itself?'

'Two and three ... and one.'

'Exactly. One, two and three. Add them together and you get ... ?'

'Six.'

'That's what makes it perfect. All the numbers that divide into it add up to give the same number. See what I mean? What's the next-highest perfect number, Connor? Can you find it?'

Miss Sayell was only nine steps away when Connor shouted excitedly, 'Twenty-eight. It's divided by one, two, four, seven and fourteen. And they make twenty-eight!'

Miss Sayell grinned at him. 'Perfect.' She returned to his side and said, 'I'm going to get a maths expert from the university to come and talk to you about a career sometime. Perhaps he'll have some ideas.'

In the cold light of morning, the same two constables hesitated outside Mrs Dungate's house and sighed. PC Knox said, 'Here we go again. Let's go and see what's been stolen – or what she's lost – this time.'

But they were about to get a surprise. Mrs Dungate was far more precise and certain than before. No, there weren't any signs of a break-in but some things were definitely missing. Absolutely no doubt at all.

'Bless his memory, it's my husband's war medals.' Mrs Dungate hesitated while she poured the tea. 'I think some money's gone from my purse as well but I'm not so sure about that, with the cost of everything.'

'But you *are* sure about the medals?' Xander Knox was given little option but to accept the cup of tea that Mrs Dungate thrust at him.

'Certain,' she replied. 'I put them over there, on the sideboard.'

The second officer got down on her hands and knees, saying, 'I'll just check in case they've fallen down the back.' A few seconds later, she got up and shook her head. 'No, they're not there. Oh, thanks,' she added as she took the compulsory cup and saucer.

'Well,' PC Knox said, notebook in hand, 'you'd better tell me all you can about them. How many, what type of medals, and that sort of thing.'

'I've got a picture of him wearing them.'

'That's good,' Xander replied. 'Just in case, we'll get a fingerprint team to go over the place as well.'

Miss Sayell looked both tense and optimistic when she introduced Connor to the small man with the glasses. 'This is Professor Ullman. He's come to talk to you about numbers.'

'Professor?'

'Yes.' In an effort to be friendly and informal, the stranger said, 'You can call me Prof.'

Connor was amazed and bamboozled. 'But,' he objected, 'a prof's brown and … white stuff.' He indicated the size with his forefinger and thumb, and then mimicked popping it into his mouth. He smacked his lips. 'Mmm.'

For a second, Connor's visitor looked perplexed. Then he laughed. 'Got it! Profiteroles. Chocolate and cream.'

'Yes,' Connor said. 'You like them?'

'Absolute heaven – and seriously unhealthy. Can't resist them.'

Miss Sayell began to apologise for Connor's error, but Professor Ullman waved her away. Alone with Connor, Professor Ullman spelled out his position as Head of Mathematics at the university and then said, 'Your teacher tells me you have a way with numbers.'

Connor nodded. 'Numbers are happy. Nine and six are best.'

'Really? They're not my favourites because they're not prime numbers.'

'Aren't they?' Connor looked disappointed.

'Have you heard of prime numbers?'

'No.'

'Pick any number and it can be divided by itself to give one. It can also be divided by one to give itself. Follow me? You can divide nine by itself to get one, and by one to get nine. But can it be divided by a different number?'

Connor nodded. 'Two. You get four dot five.'

'That's right,' the prof replied. 'But I want you to think just about whole numbers. Okay?'

'Three,' Connor answered. 'Nine divided by three gives three.'

'Right. That means it's not a prime number. With a prime number, you can't divide it exactly by any whole numbers except one and itself.'

Connor brightened as the idea sparked in his brain. 'Like three.'

'Yes. Can you work out prime numbers going up from three?'

Connor hardly hesitated. 'Five, seven, eleven, thirteen, seventeen, nineteen, twenty-three, twenty-nine … '

The professor put up his hand. 'You're very quick. Good. I bet you could keep that up all afternoon.'

Connor nodded eagerly. He was hoping he was going to be allowed to keep it up all afternoon.

Professor Ullman asked, 'Can you think of another way of defining prime numbers?'

'What?'

'How would *you* explain prime numbers to someone who didn't know about them?'

Connor thought for a while. 'You can't make them by times-ing two smaller numbers.'

The professor seemed to be impressed. 'Yes. Good. Let's move on. Can you think of two prime numbers that add up to one hundred?'

'Yes.'

Professor Ullman smiled. 'What are they?'

'Seventeen and eighty-three.'

'Excellent. Others?'

'Forty-one and fifty-nine.'

'Not forty-three and fifty-seven?'

Connor frowned. 'No,' he said indignantly. 'Fifty-seven is three darts in nineteen.'

The man from the university nodded. 'Okay. It's time to get heavy. Very heavy. For over two hundred and fifty years, people thought that this giant's a prime number.' Professor Ullman produced a piece of paper with an immense number written on it.

147,573,952,589,676,412,927

'Some years ago, one mathematician – it was me actually – thought it might not be a prime number after all. I set out to find a smaller number that divided into it. I tried this one.' The professor jotted down another monster.

761,838,257,287

'Tell me, Connor, does this second number divide exactly into the first?'

Connor shook his head slowly. He wasn't denying it and he

wasn't refusing to try the problem, but he recognized a tough mathematical challenge when he saw one.

'It's really difficult,' the professor said. 'Unfair of me to … Don't worry if you can't…'

Taking a deep breath and holding it, Connor began to work out the digits gradually. 'One… um … nine … three … er … seven … one, no, nought.' He paused, took another breath and, staring intensely at the numbers on the paper, struggled on. 'Nought … seven … seven … er … two … one.' He stopped, let out the breath and announced, 'No prime number, that. Someone got it … you know … carrots!'

Catching Connor's excitability, the professor agreed. 'Absolutely carrots. Yes. Have you remembered the number you got or would you have to work it out again if I asked you to write it down?'

'Forget?' Connor looked shocked. 'No, I won't forget.' Faultlessly he wrote, *193,707,721*.

'Exceptional.' The prof sat back in his chair. 'Absolutely remarkable. You know, Connor, I've worked with many great and gifted mathematicians, but give them that problem and they'd all use a computer. Remove their computers and it would take them an age, even doing the long division on paper. Very few could do it in their heads. I only know one person who came remotely close to the speed and mental agility you just showed.'

Connor didn't understand every word but he thought that his visitor expected him to respond so he said, 'Oh?'

'Yes. Me – when I was much younger and I could do that sort of thing. But I was nowhere near as good as you.'

Privately, Professor Ullman told Miss Sayell that she was right about Connor. 'He can do complex calculations independent of language. He has a visual representation of maths in his head. But without GCSEs and A-levels, I can't take him onto a degree course. However …' Professor Ullman thought about it for a moment. 'There might be a way, I suppose. I have research money. I could probably use some to pay Connor as a research assistant. I do need someone studying how prime numbers are distributed and it'd be a privilege to work with him.'

Miss Sayell looked at the mathematician with her mouth open. 'But he'd need a degree for that, surely. There's no hope … '

'The university has its rules and regulations, but it's not completely inflexible. I'll have to check, of course, but I might be able to plead a special case for someone without the usual qualifications.'

'Someone without *any* qualifications?'

'Well, it'd be … unusual,' he replied. 'But prime number theory's an area ideally suited to a child prodigy. It's like chess. A few simple rules and some youngsters excel at it because they're just naturals. I need enthusiasm, an instinct for numbers, and natural talent, if not genius. Will you give him a reference to that effect?'

Miss Sayell nodded eagerly. 'Of course.'

'Then, let's not say it's impossible till I come up against an immovable wall,' said Professor Ullman.

Miss Sayell rubbed her hands together. 'Thanks. That's … great. Really great!'

Professor Ullman put up his palms to stop her gushing. 'Thanks for bringing him to my attention. A fascinating lad. But don't expect anything to happen in a hurry. I've got a lot of tricky strings to pull. And I suggest you don't mention it to Connor in case I have to let him down later.'

'Agreed.'

CHAPTER 25

Connor was becoming a local celebrity – known to everybody.

'Sarg, the computer's thrown something up.'

'That must've been messy.'

Xander felt obliged to smile at the sergeant's witticism but continued to make his point. 'You know the latest burglary at 57 Springfield Road?'

'Is that the fifth or sixth – none of which have ever been confirmed?'

'This time, it might be worth taking seriously.'

'Why?'

'We've got missing medals, two sets of dabs, and unforced entry.'

'Unforced again. Does she lock the doors?'

'Yes.'

'So,' the harassed sergeant concluded, 'if she's not imagining it, someone's got a key.'

'That's what makes it interesting,' Xander replied.

'Oh?'

'Mrs Dungate loses lots of things, but says she's never lost a key.'

'How long's she lived there? Did she change the locks when she moved in?'

'The previous owners moved out last August and, no, she didn't change anything.'

The sergeant looked up at PC Knox. 'You promised me something interesting.'

'The last owners were the Pattersons, as in Joy Patterson.'

She nodded slowly. 'I read up that case. She was one of the girls who were too terrified to say what happened.'

'Yes.'

'Okay. Give me the punch line. Who do the prints belong to?'

'One set's unknown, the other's Connor Markham.'

'Don't I know that name?'

'The case of the stolen roller skates. And we gave him that warning for criminal damage and underage drinking last April. That's why we've got his prints on file.'

'Mmm.'

'One other thing. According to records, we took him home from Mrs Dungate's near the end of October when she reported he'd been in the house. He's got learning difficulties or whatever we're supposed to call it these days.' Xander paused before asking, 'Do we fetch him in – before he becomes a one-person crime wave?'

The sergeant considered it. 'Not yet. First, go and see Mrs Dungate again. See what she knows about him. Then trace the Pattersons. Have a word with them. Did they keep a key? Is one of them sneaking back for trophies? Did they ever lose a key? And do they know Connor Markham? Is there a link between him and Joy? Because, if there is, that *would* be interesting.'

'We're going back to Springfield Road,' Xander Knox told his partner, slamming the car into gear.

'Oh, good,' she said. 'I'm thirsty.'

'What?'

'I could use a free cuppa.'

Xander smiled. 'We need to know what Mrs Dungate knows about Connor Markham – and if she's seen anyone else hanging around.'

'If she can remember.'

'We live in hope.'

Mrs Dungate thought about PC Knox's question while she

squeezed the tea bags to make the flavour flood out. 'Well,' she said, 'there's Colin. But … '

The policeman interrupted. 'Who?'

'He comes round here sometimes.' Waving a finger by the side of her head, she added, 'He's not quite right up here, you know.'

'Colin? Do you mean Connor?'

She handed out the cups and saucers. 'Yes. He carries a card with his name and address. I think the police who came to take him home found it in his pocket.'

'This was October, last year?'

Mrs Dungate shrugged. 'Don't ask me. I'm hopeless with dates. But, yes, sometime last year. Autumn, I think.'

Xander nodded and changed tack. 'Why does he visit you?'

Mrs Dungate sipped her tea while she thought about it. 'First, he was looking for someone called … Joan, was it? Or Joy. Maybe Janet.'

'Joy? Joy Patterson?'

'I don't know. I hope he finds her, though. It was bothering him.'

'Any other reason he comes?' the policewoman asked.

'He's been back a couple more times. I think he's trying to help me – or even look after me.' She grinned at the notion. 'Oh, he took an interest in my husband's medals.'

'Did he now?' Xander glanced at his partner.

'Yes.'

'And they've gone.'

Mrs Dungate cup's rattled as she put it back on its saucer with a shaky hand. 'You don't think … No. Not Colin. He wouldn't. He's a good lad, you see. Not like today's youngsters. He might have his problems, he struggles, but he *cares*.'

'He cares?'

'Yes. That's one thing I *am* sure about.'

'Does he come on his own?' asked PC Knox.

'Yes.'

'Have you seen anyone else hanging around?'

'There's always a gang of schoolchildren outside the newsagent's … '

'No, I mean, loitering outside in the road.'

'Sometimes there's a group of girls in their short skirts and make-up. They grow up too quickly these days, you know. They don't want to be children any more. It's such a shame.'

'Okay, Mrs Dungate. Thanks. That's very helpful.'

Back in the police car, Xander said, 'I think we have a classic example of a lad befriending an old lady so he can case the joint.'

His partner smirked as he drove away. 'Case the joint?'

'Yeah. I've always wanted an excuse to say that. I've never managed it before. Makes me feel like a film star. Gangster movie.'

She laughed. 'Markham isn't the only one who's soft in the head.'

'Anyway, we're getting him on a plate.'

Playfully, his partner agreed. 'It's an open-and-shut case, Holmes.'

'See? We all want to be in the movies.'

'Class!' Miss Sayell cried. 'I've got something important to say.'

For a change, they quietened quickly. It was something about her tone. 'What's she on?' Alice whispered to herself.

'I imagine several of you will want to stay on and do A-levels. And after that, some will want – will hope – to go to university when you're eighteen. Well, I'm proud – very proud – to say that this year the school's sending someone to university, not at the age of eighteen, but earlier – if he wants the honour. It's someone who's been judged so clever that he doesn't have to do A-levels first. He's going to get an offer to go straight into mathematical research – once he's sixteen.' The teacher was really on a high, building up to a calculated climax. 'It's almost unheard of and certainly the youngest person this school's ever sent to university. I think it's an achievement we should all acknowledge and I'm pleased to say the person who's done so brilliantly, brilliantly well is … Connor.'

For a moment, there was complete silence. Then there were thirty mutterings. 'Really?' 'Amazing.' 'Connor?' 'Not Connor Markham?' 'Cool.' 'Is that a joke – or a mistake?'

Miss Sayell led the applause. Hattie sat with her hands apart as if frozen. She seemed too shocked to form a single clap. Alice did clap and she even let out a little cheer. She was seeing Connor in a different light. He was not so embarrassing now. He might be a near-moron but he was a near-genius as well. Those old feelings, submerged when she got to know him and he started going out with Hattie, dead and buried when his brain went on the blink, had begun to surface again. Perhaps there was a reason to be proud of Connor after all.

Seated in Miss Sayell's classroom like three pupils anxiously awaiting exam results, Mr and Mrs Markham and Brad listened to Connor's maths teacher with increasing amazement. They were flabbergasted.

'University?' Mrs Markham muttered.

'Brad maybe, but not Connor,' said Mr Markham. 'It's not … '

'It is,' Miss Sayell assured them. 'Professor Ullman at the university thinks he's a maths prodigy. And so do I.'

'Professor?'

'Prodigy?'

'I know it's a lot to take in,' she said. 'I'll arrange for you to see Professor Ullman, but it's a year's trial and then, if all goes well, a further two-year contract. I think you should consider his offer very seriously. You see, Connor hasn't got too many avenues … '

Mr Markham butted in. 'What is there to consider?'

Miss Sayell smiled, barely able to conceal her delight. 'Exactly. It's a golden opportunity.'

Ever practical, Connor's dad said, 'The one and only, probably.'

Mrs Markham looked dazed. 'I still can't believe it,' she mumbled.

'Look, I don't want to bring you all down,' Brad put in, 'but is anyone thinking about what Connor wants? He's the important one in all this.'

Miss Sayell nodded. 'You're right, Brad. I've talked to him. I'm not sure he appreciates precisely what's on offer but, give him the opportunity to play around with numbers *and* earn money while he's doing it, what do you think he'll decide?'

'Put like that … ' said Brad. 'When does he start?'

'Tell me about Mr Dungate's medals first,' the sergeant said to her officers.

Xander's partner reported, 'There's an awful lot of medals on eBay. I looked at the recent listings, but his aren't there. Then I phoned round the usual pawn shops. No luck, I'm afraid. No sign of them.'

'Okay. What about the Pattersons?'

'They moved straight after Joy's treatment,' Xander told her. 'They needed a fresh start, they said. They settled … Sorry, but they settled in Settle. North Yorkshire. They wanted peace and quiet, well away from city life – and all its temptations.'

'I talked to Joy,' his partner said, 'but she's internalized everything. She's keeping it to herself. I couldn't get her to open up, I'm afraid.'

The sergeant nodded as if that's what she expected. 'Girls who've been through what she's been through – drugs, sex and alcohol – sometimes talk, but most don't. Some are silenced by threats and intimidation. Some keep quiet because they blame themselves. Some don't want to admit what happened to their parents.'

'I wouldn't be surprised if Joy fits all three,' Xander's partner said. Then she added, 'She reacted to Connor Markham's name, but she wouldn't fill us in.'

'So,' the sergeant replied, 'we don't have a concrete link between Joy Patterson and Markham.'

'No, but there is one thing,' PC Knox said. 'They both went to the same school.'

The sergeant thought for a moment and then decided. 'It's enough. I'm getting impatient. Bring him in.'

CHAPTER 26

Questions, questions, questions.

The Markhams told only Ranji Nawaz and Miss Sayell about Connor's arrest on suspicion of shoplifting, burglary, and sex trafficking of young girls. At once, the doctor flew to the police station to confirm Connor's unusual mental condition. She didn't tell them that he'd struck up a friendship with a twelve-year-old girl.

The Markhams' wish to keep quiet about their son's arrest was blown away by Miss Sayell. As soon as the teacher was told, she called Professor Ullman, because she thought he'd be able to help by giving the police a testimonial to Connor's good character. She thought that a professor would carry some weight and influence.

The police explained to Mr and Mrs Markham that, because Connor was a juvenile under seventeen years of age, he could be questioned only in the presence of a responsible adult – like a parent. They didn't give any of the other options in case the Markhams requested more professional legal advice for their son. Under the tension of the situation, the Markhams didn't think to ask for a solicitor.

Connor wasn't bothered. He watched the numbers displayed on the sound recorder as the interview proceeded. That was much more interesting than the questions. Stupid questions. Ridiculous questions. Impossible questions.

'Who was with you when you burgled Mrs Dungate's?'

'Why choose her house?'

'What did you take?'

'How did you get Mrs Dungate's key?'

'Why did you go there in October?'

Stupid, stupid, stupid. Carrots! There was no sense in the questions. He was amazed that the two men weren't showing him photographs as well, like Ranji and Eleanor did, and asking him to explain them.

Then one of them demanded to know, 'Where are the medals?'

At last, a question he had a hope of answering. 'In my room.'

'Your bedroom?'

Connor nodded.

Mr Markham put in, 'What medals, Connor? Are you thinking of your football medals – and the cup you won?'

'Yes.'

The two police officers sighed, not hiding their frustration.

Then they did exactly what Connor expected. They produced a photograph of an old man in military uniform, pushing out his chest laden with medals. One of them tapped the picture. 'These are the medals. Ring any bells?'

Connor's dad butted in. 'Do you recognize them, Connor? That's what he means.'

Connor shrugged. He didn't understand. He turned to the recording device instead.

'We know you know Joy Patterson. What did you do to her?'

'Fifty-seven. Pink drink. Cracked eel.'

One of the officers sat back and groaned. The other almost shouted, 'What is it with you?' Trying to keep calm, he asked, 'Where did the roller skates come from?'

Connor shrugged again. 'Er … a green thing. A greengrocer.' His answer sounded more like a question.

'That'd be a shop, I think,' his dad guessed.

'You took them from a sports shop?'

'No.'

The policeman laughed. 'You're saying it wasn't you?'

'Liam got them.'

'Are you blaming someone called Liam for stealing the roller skates?'

'Liam.'

'Liam who?'

Mr Markham asked, 'Is that Liam Darby, Connor?'

'Rocking.'

The two burly men got up. 'We'll take that as a yes.' One of them leaned on the table and said, 'We're wrapping up the interview for now to assess new information.' He quoted the time and then turned off the recorder.

When Professor Ullman turned up at the police station, he made matters worse by antagonizing the custody sergeant. He introduced himself, explained that he was Connor Markham's potential employer and testified to Connor's good character. 'I'm sure this is all a giant mistake,' he added. 'Let's be honest. This … affair could ruin his career before he even starts. The university will think again about taking him on if he's charged with something.'

The officer was not impressed. 'Going to university disqualifies someone from committing a crime, does it?' she asked.

'I'm not saying that. I'm … ' The mathematician sighed with impatience. '*If* Connor Markham's gone off the straight and narrow, you won't get him back on to it by prosecuting him. You'll do it by letting him make something of his life. He deserves that chance.'

'Take a look around,' the sergeant said. 'This is a police station, not a university lecture room. A professor doesn't trump a sergeant. Here, we play to our rules.'

Professor Ullman paused and then said, 'Okay. As I understand it, Connor's long-term memory is disabled so he can't answer questions about the past. If he doesn't answer, he's not covering something up. It's his disease. If you've been throwing leading questions at him, any answers he's given won't be valid. His short-term memory's unreliable – unless it's something to do with numbers. So, you can't trust his evidence.

His language difficulties mean he's not capable of understanding the proceedings either. And, given all that, I shouldn't think he's criminally responsible anyway.'

'Thanks for your advice. What's your subject at the university by the way?'

'Maths.'

'Really,' she said sarcastically. 'Not law?'

'No.'

'It may surprise you to learn that Connor Markham isn't the first person we've had in here with learning difficulties. We don't need a lecture on how to cope. Besides, he's got history.'

'History?'

The sergeant nodded. 'Stuff prior to his brain injury.'

No one had mentioned that to Professor Ullman. 'I'm not sure I believe … '

'You should know that one strand of our investigation is a violent, sexual crime. So, forgive me for not letting him loose on the public just yet.'

Brad was livid. According to his dad, the police seemed to think Connor had nicked his roller skates from a sports shop and broken into someone's house to steal some wartime medals. They were also linking him with someone called Joy Patterson.

'Joy Patterson?' Hattie exclaimed.

'Yeah,' said Brad.

'She was in the year below us,' Alice replied.

'The one above you,' Hattie added unnecessarily. 'And she was famous for being thrown out of a car under the railway. It was in the news. She wasn't named, but we all knew it was her.'

'She'd been drugged,' Alice explained. 'My mum covered it for the local paper. In her write-up, she didn't actually say she'd been raped. She talked about sexual abuse instead. As if that made it nicer.'

Brad put up his hands. 'Hang on! She was dumped under the railway bridge? Near that burned-out place that used to be a nightclub?'

'Yes.'

Brad nodded.

'Why?' Hattie asked.

'Because that's where Connor said something about pink rain. If she got chucked out of a car, she might've ended up bleeding. Dilute blood makes a pink puddle, I suppose.'

'Are you saying Connor was there when it happened – or had something to do with it?'

Brad shrugged.

Hattie seemed to be verging on panic. 'Sex abuse, burglary and shoplifting! And he's in prison!'

'Not prison,' Brad said, trying to quieten her. 'He's at the police station. That's all. He's only been arrested.'

'*Only*!'

'They haven't charged him yet.'

'But they think he did it?'

'I don't know. Dad reckoned it was all a bit vague.'

'What are we going to do?'

'Well, I'm not waiting for the police,' Brad replied. 'I'm going to find Liam. I don't know about Joy Patterson, but Liam's bound to be behind the other stuff. He can get Connor off.'

'How are you going to find him?'

'He works at that smelly meat-packing factory.'

'Take care,' Alice warned him.

'What about us?' Hattie said.

Alice took a deep breath and looked at her friend. 'Us? We're going to find Joy.'

Shown a way forward, Hattie calmed down at last. 'Yeah. Good idea.'

'We're going to talk to her,' Alice said, 'and find out what happened.'

Almost at once, Hattie's fluctuating mood seemed to swing back towards anguish. 'But how? She moved away, didn't she?'

'Yes,' Alice answered, 'but I've got a plan.'

CHAPTER 27

Joy didn't have the life skills to handle exploitation by men.

She clutched next door's terrier in her arms and wept. The dog put his chin on her lap and whined in sympathy. 'I haven't told anyone. Only you. I haven't asked for help, made a run for it, gone to the police. I just can't. It's like I'm under a spell.' Her hand stroked Westie by force of habit. 'You know what it's like. You're told to sit – no idea why – but you know you'll get a kicking if you don't, so you sit. That's me too. I know there'll be trouble if I don't do what I'm told. There'll be revenge. There'll be violence. There'll be photos on the internet.'

Joy swallowed back more tears. 'GG said, "You wouldn't want pictures of you in a compromising situation to go beyond our circle of friends, would you? That wouldn't be nice for you." I don't know what I saw in him. He's just threats now. I found out one girl's not with us any more. She jumped off a bridge over the M1. Horrible. But … I'm addicted to that sort of life. You know. Money, flash cars, men after me, giving me stuff. Sitting at home watching telly and doing homework just doesn't cut it any more. I can't turn time back. Can't undo things. I can't become a little kid again.'

She looked down at the scruffy off-white dog. 'Do you hate yourself when you get a beating? Do you understand what you've done to deserve it? I bet you blame yourself as well.'

Wiping her eyes, she said, 'What I get isn't really sex, you know. I don't think so anyway. It's not love. It's not even respect.

It's about them exercising power over me. But … I don't know how to get out of it. I think it's going to go on till they're fed up with me. Then what'll they do? I'll never really be out of it. They'll always have a hold over me. They know where I live, know my family and friends. Well, I used to have friends. GG's got a creepy sidekick called Liam who probably even knows about you. And those photos … '

She felt scared and ashamed.

CHAPTER 28

Apart from Connor, everybody was becoming a spy.

It wasn't a great I-spy room. Once he'd done walls, door, toilet, sink, light, ceiling, floor and bed, that was it. Not even a bottle so he could watch the clouds. If he'd been allowed to have his car shoes, there wouldn't have been enough space to use them.

Connor lounged on the bed and stagnated. He was lonely. Since waking up after his return from Barbados, he had hardly ever been left on his own. He hadn't always liked what the people around him did to him, but he always had company. He always had a game to play, a word to memorize, brain scans to admire, photographs to study and explain, an mp3 to listen to, Stroke 3's swearing and Alcohol Abuse's laughter to amuse him, a visitor with an annoying question. Now they were gone. And he didn't know why.

Left to his own devices, he began to think about his life. People told him that it must be awful to lose such a large chunk of it, but it seemed to Connor that he had plenty to fill the vacuum. There was Courtney and numbers for a start. The presence of Courtney, the sound of music, and the certainty of numbers kept him attached to the rest of humanity. Even in that bleak room, he had maths. He could happily fill his brain with prime numbers. Three thousand three hundred and eighty-nine. Three thousand three hundred and ninety-one. Three thousand four hundred and seven. Much better than trying to remember something irrelevant that had happened in before-land. Connor could no more break down the wall between himself and the old Connor than he could break out of the police cell.

Recalling the lesson with letters and numbers on tiles and the board that could double or treble the scores, the magic 'un' came to Connor's mind. It changed happy into unhappy, exciting into unexciting. He applied the same principle to his name. A lot of the questions thrown at him weren't aimed at him – Connor. They were aimed at unConnor. UnConnor from before-land. UnConnor who no longer existed.

Entice her. That's what Mr Rowling said. Liam groaned. This time last year, Connor could entice any number of girls. Not any more. So, Liam was on his own. He wasn't sure enticing was his sort of thing. He didn't do subtle. Random acts of violence were much easier. Hostility and heartlessness worked just fine for him.

GG was a cool guy. He could toggle at will between charisma and cruelty. Liam had seen it for himself, that lightning switch from polite to poisonous. Liam wasn't blessed with versatility. He had only one setting.

As he waited near Courtney's house, Liam didn't know that Brad Markham had followed him from the meat-packing factory.

'Do you remember Joy Patterson?' Alice said to her mum.

She looked up from her laptop momentarily. 'How could I forget? That picture we got. We pixelated Joy, but the puddle of blood … Tragic.'

Alice touched Hattie's arm. 'We want to go and see her.'

'Why?'

Alice had hoped that her mother wouldn't ask. As a reporter, permanently preoccupied with her latest piece, she was usually far too busy to find much time for her daughter. Alice knew that the question, hanging in the air, wouldn't blow up like a balloon. She wouldn't have to hack it for long because her mum's attention would soon switch back to whatever she was working on. 'It's not a big thing,' Alice replied. 'A boy Hattie's interested in might've had something to do with what happened to her. A quick chat would put Hattie's mind at rest – or warn her off.'

Hattie nodded in agreement.

'Well, I hope you get more out of her than I did.' Mrs Foley's concentration showed signs of wandering already. Her eyes flitted back to her screen.

'Where is she now?' Alice asked.

'She moved to North Yorkshire. Settle.'

'Settle? Have you got her address?'

'No.'

'How do you find out where someone lives?' said Alice.

'The electoral roll. If her family's registered to vote, you can get their address with an online search. Look, Alice, I've got to get on … '

'Thanks. No problem.'

Alice and Hattie consulted the electoral register, the Leeds-to-Settle train timetable and then a map of Settle. Within a couple of hours, they were on their way.

Brad wished he had an invisibility cloak. Peering cautiously round the brickwork of the end terrace house, he kept an eye on Liam. In turn, Liam was lurking behind a roadside tree, apparently keeping an eye on one particular house. Why? What was he doing? Assuming Liam was up to no good, Brad decided to wait for developments.

Few cars cruised along the street. Occasionally, a raised voice sounded. In readiness for nightfall, the street-lamps began to glow an ineffectual orange. An old man shuffled down the road with a bag of shopping, before unlocking and entering his home. A dog barked gruffly. And Liam leaned against a lime tree. In Brad's mind, the perfectly innocent scene somehow oozed menace. Perhaps Liam's potential for trouble would taint any tranquil scene.

Then it started. Hoping that no one was watching him, Brad poked his head out from the wall to get a good view. A girl –

pre-teen, long black hair – came out of the house just beyond Liam's tree. Liam jogged up to her and walked alongside. Together, they came towards Brad.

Quickly, he withdrew. To avoid being seen and recognized by Liam, he vaulted over a low wall and into someone's garden. There, he ducked down till Liam and the girl had gone past. Then he came out of his hiding place. The girl was gliding on roller skates. Liam almost trotted to keep up. He was talking casually – though Brad couldn't hear a word – and she seemed to be on edge. Her body language spoke of tension and danger. She glanced around, perhaps hoping there was someone to help if her pursuer turned frisky or frightening.

Peering out from behind a hedge, Brad realized that he couldn't follow them without making it obvious. But he had to do something. Soon, they'd be too far way to see clearly.

Unexpectedly, the girl shot ahead of Liam, turned a semi-circle so she was facing him, and came to a halt. If Liam had not been there, blocking her line of sight, she would have been staring straight at Brad. Without warning, she kicked out with her right leg.

Liam's scream was audible even to Brad.

With Liam bent double, the girl shot away at speed on her skates.

Liam tried to stagger after her but he soon came to a halt. His body language spoke of agony and annoyance.

Brad smiled.

He came out from the side-road and sauntered towards Liam as if it were pure coincidence that he was in the same area. 'Oh, hi,' he said, wondering if his feigned surprise was believable.

'What you's doing here?'

Brad decided to gamble. The girl on roller skates was now out of view but he nodded in her direction, saying, 'I came to see … what's-her-name.'

'Courtney?'

At once, Brad recalled the name. Connor had mentioned Courtney when he first came home from the hospital. Spotting his mp3 player, he'd claimed it belonged to Number 9 or Courtney. 'Yes,' he replied to Liam. 'Courtney.'

'Did you see what she did?'

Suppressing laughter, Brad nodded and winced. 'Wearing skates too. Must have been painful.'

'Bitch.'

'I bet it's not the first time you've been kicked. Don't defenders try to kick the shins out of your legs?'

'She wasn't after my shins, man. I's trying to be friendly.'

'Perhaps she didn't want to be friendly.' Brad hesitated before adding, 'Talking of friends, you know what's happened to Connor, don't you?'

'Yeah.'

'You could get him off. If you're his mate, you will. You know he hasn't done anything wrong.'

'I don't mix it with cops.'

'For Connor's sake … '

'Not for no one.'

'Do you know Joy Patterson?' Brad asked.

'Who? No.' Liam limped away with a grimace still written on his face.

Refusing to let up, Brad tagged along. 'He didn't nick those skates! You know that better than anyone.'

'So?'

'He didn't nick any medals either.'

'Dunno what you's talking about.'

'What have you done with the medals?'

Liam came to an abrupt halt. From his coat pocket, he produced a knife with an ugly curved blade. 'Don't push it. I's not in the mood.'

Brad put up his hands and backed off.

'If you's as clever as Connor used to say, drop it. Go home. Bother me some more and … ' He looked down at the knife menacingly.

Brad was strong-minded, but not suicidal. He knew when to retreat and plan a new form of attack. 'All right,' he said. 'I'm going the other way.'

At the first whiff of a sexual crime, the Connor Markham case had been assigned to a Senior Investigating Officer. The SIO asked the sergeant, 'What did we get from the Markham interview?'

'Nothing, apart from Liam Darby's name.'

'No reaction to Joy Patterson?'

The sergeant shook her head. 'He struggles with what he did minutes ago, never mind months ago.'

'I know it's tricky with mental health issues, but what's your gut reaction?'

'He's an angel,' she replied instantly.

'Really?'

'We've got statements from a Dr Nawaz, his parents, one of his teachers, Mrs Dungate, a university professor no less – all saying it as well. He doesn't even get into a sweat under questioning. That's because he doesn't really understand the trouble he's in. I think he's been led into it by his partner-in-crime. The real villain's Liam Darby.'

'But?'

'We spoke to him earlier today – where he works. He says it's the other way round. He's says he's been duped by a master-crook in the shape of Connor Markham.'

'Any evidence for that?'

'A big fat none.'

'So, is Markham denying it?'

'No. Like any angel, he's floating in the stratosphere, not defending himself at all,' the sergeant answered.

'Have we got anything on Darby that makes him the ringleader?'

'Another big fat zero. We checked his dabs. He was the other set in 57 Springfield Road all right, but that doesn't make him the boss.'

'Mmm. So, if Markham doesn't speak out, this Darby will dump him in it?'

'Big style.'

Alice couldn't remember much about Joy. There was just one thing. Her appearance had always been immaculate. Not a hair out of place. A sophisticated style, even in school uniform. Now, the girl sitting opposite Alice and Hattie clearly couldn't care less about the one thing she used to cherish the most. No glint. No make-up. No sheen. Hair all over the place. A total wreck. She seemed to have been through a wringer. It had squeezed the pleasure of life out of her. Alice almost felt guilty to be quizzing her.

'I left to get away from … to get my life back together,' she muttered. 'I didn't think it'd follow me here.' She wiped her nose with a hankie. 'I'm not saying anything.'

'Why not?'

'Because I don't want to – and I can't. I was … threatened.'

'By … ?'

Joy's expression showed contempt for the question.

'You moved to escape that, didn't you?' said Alice.

'You found me,' Joy replied. 'So did the police. That means anyone else could as well.'

'But what about Connor?' Hattie exclaimed. 'He's been arrested!'

'What's that got to do with me?'

'That's what we're here to find out,' Hattie replied. 'The police keep asking him about you.'

Joy sighed but said nothing.

Alice took a deep breath. 'Do you think he deserves to be arrested?'

'Look,' Joy said, 'What do you really want from me?'

'A few answers. That's all. Like, did he … hurt you?'

She shook her bowed head.

'Was he involved in what happened?' Alice said.

Joy didn't answer straightaway. Still staring at the carpet, she mumbled, 'Yes.'

Aghast, Hattie asked, 'What did he do?'

'Why don't you ask him?' Joy responded.

'Because his brain's damaged. He can't remember.'

'Convenient.'

It was an abrupt and facile remark yet Alice sensed some sympathy in Joy's tone.

'What did he do?' Hattie repeated.

'He had a reputation … '

'You mean, with girls?'

'Yes. He got them – and me – into a club.'

'Is that all?' said Hattie, looking relieved.

'Is that all?' Joy spluttered. 'It was like delivering lambs to a slaughterhouse.'

At once, Alice broke into the exchange. 'Did he know that? Did he know what happened to you and the others?'

Joy opened her mouth, apparently relishing the opportunity to blame Connor, but she fell silent instead.

'It's really important, Joy.'

'I don't know,' she admitted. 'But … '

'What?' Hattie prompted.

Joy gazed into Hattie's face. 'I asked him to take me. He wasn't keen because he was going out with you. Said he wasn't going to do it ever again.'

Hattie let out the breath she'd been holding.

'Did you see him afterwards?' said Alice. 'Before he went on holiday?'

Joy shook her head.

'Do you know a guy called Liam? Liam Darby.'

Joy swallowed and tried to pretend she'd never heard of him. 'No.'

'Which club did Connor take you to?'

'That's another no-go area.'

Recognizing that they'd pushed Joy as far as she'd go, Alice stood up and said, 'Thanks.'

Barbados minus thirty-six hours. Connor didn't really want to go, but his mum and dad would never forgive him if he got himself into so much trouble that they had to abandon their precious holiday in the sun. It was the holiday that they'd been looking forward to for months, the most expensive one they'd ever been on, and it was going to be absolutely fantastic. The holiday of a lifetime.

Connor knew that he was standing on the edge of an abyss. If he ruined Mum and Dad's mega-holiday, they'd push him over for sure. His life wouldn't be worth living.

GG was prowling back and forth in front of him. Then he stopped and stared into Connor's face. 'I appreciated you bringing Joy – and so did she. But … '

'What?'

'Things just got out of hand. That's all. One of my clients got a bit too … enthusiastic.'

Connor held up his smart phone, showing a page from the local newspaper's website. 'It says here a girl was thrown out of a car. It's obvious it was Joy. She was drugged and all sorts. Look at the puddle. It's blood.'

Mr Rowling sighed, still cool and calm. 'As I said, a friend got overexcited. You know how it is. In the heat of the moment, a defender overreaches himself and hacks an opponent's legs. He gets booked or sent off. Maybe there's a penalty. Then everyone forgets it and gets on with the game. I've shown someone a yellow card. Any more and he's off.'

'This,' Connor replied, waving his mobile, 'is more than a booking.'

'It's never wise to argue a ref's decision.'

Connor began to object, 'But it's more serious than … '

That insolence triggered GG's sudden switch from serene to surly. He grabbed Connor's phone, dropped it on the floor and stamped on it. 'No more!'

He nodded to one of the heavies behind the chair and a knife appeared in front of Connor's face. Another nod. Ivan's knife sliced through the air. Too quick for Connor to avoid the slash. Immediately, his right forefinger stung. 'Ow!' Blood flowed freely down Connor's finger, across his palm and dripped onto the floor.

Shocked, Connor opened his mouth, about to protest, but he fell silent instead.

'Next time,' GG told him, 'it won't be a finger. I'll leave that to your imagination.' Then the switch operated again. With a grin, Mr Rowling said, 'You're about to go on holiday, aren't you? A fancy holiday. Go off. Have a good time. Enjoy yourself. Think about things. All right? Come back in a more cooperative, relaxed frame of mind.'

To Connor, it seemed like running away. No, not running. Flying. To Connor, it seemed that guilt was making him fly away, as if an aeroplane could outpace blame.

As a parting shot, Gareth Gregor said, 'And Connor?'

'What?'

He pointed at the bloodied finger. 'Get that stitched up before I send you the bill for carpet cleaning.' He smiled sweetly.

CHAPTER 29

Apart from Connor and Liam, everybody seemed to be assisting the police.

It was Brad's turn to try his luck at the police station. After his encounter with Liam, he couldn't sit at home and do nothing. He had to do his bit for his absent brother. He wasn't beyond a bit of grovelling and a lot of anger when the occasion arose.

'Can't you understand?' Brad cried at the custody sergeant. 'Dr Nawaz'll tell you. He's got a hole in his head. He doesn't know an eel from a finger. And roller skates aren't exactly big time, are they?'

'It's still theft.'

'Okay, they matched a pair that were nicked. But what makes you so sure they're the same ones? How can you tell? Even if they are, he could have just bought them in good faith from whoever pinched them.'

'There was a phone call. A tip-off.'

'What?' Brad was outraged. 'Who from?'

'It was anonymous.'

'Ah.' With a sneer, Brad said, 'That'd be whoever really stole them, trying to blame Connor. My money's on Liam Darby.'

'Do you have anything to back that up?' she asked immediately.

Brad admitted that he hadn't. 'But have you found Mrs Dungate's house key or war medals on Connor? No. His fingerprints are in her house because they're friends. Strange but true.'

'What am I listening to? Another lecture?' The officer's smile was brief and humourless. She did not change her aggressive tone. 'Have you got anything specific to say or, like the others, are you just telling us he's a boy with a medical problem who wouldn't harm a fly? Because, if it is, we've already got that message. But we've also got a witness who says Connor's behind the theft from Mrs Dungate's, the shoplifting and … maybe other things.'

'Another witness? The same one? Who?'

'I can't tell you that, but I'd be interested if you had any definite information about Liam Darby.'

Brad nodded knowingly. 'I see. You can't seriously believe anything *he* says.'

The sergeant looked into Brad's face. 'We don't have any facts to the contrary.'

Brad shook his head sadly. 'Out of the two of them, who do you see as Mr Big? Who's the mastermind – and bully?'

'My opinion's not fact,' she retorted.

'How about this?' said Brad. 'I saw Liam trying to chat up a young girl – and when I tackled him about it, he pulled a knife on me.'

'What? Hang on. One thing at a time. How young was this girl?'

Brad shrugged. 'Ten, eleven, twelve.'

'Where and when?'

Brad gave her the details and then said, 'She talked to him for a bit, but she looked jittery to me. She kicked him where it hurts and ran off. Actually, she rolled off. On roller skates.'

'Do you know who she was?'

'Courtney.'

'Courtney who?'

Brad shrugged again. 'But I know where she lives.'

'Can you take us?'

'Sure.'

'And you say Darby was carrying a knife? He threatened you with it?'

'Yes.'

The custody sergeant smiled wryly. 'Thank you. Now that is … helpful to our inquiries.'

Courtney and her mother sat on the sofa. Opposite them, the senior investigating officer sat upright and stiff like a soldier. Brad and a policewoman stood to one side.

'I put up with him for a few minutes,' Courtney explained, 'because he said he was Connor's friend. Is that true?'

'Sort of,' Brad answered.

'I know he gave Connor a pair of skates.'

'How?' the SIO asked.

'Because Connor said so.'

'I see,' the SIO replied. 'What did Liam say to you? Brad told us you gave him a good kicking so he must have said something you didn't like.'

'He started talking about Connor and football. If you call what comes out his mouth as talking. Anyway, that was okay. But then … he asked me out. Pervert.'

Courtney's mum sucked air through her teeth.

'Where did he invite you to?'

'He didn't get that far. After what I did to him, he couldn't speak.'

The policewoman sniggered. 'I didn't say this, but … well done.' Then, glancing at the SIO, she looked embarrassed.

'Seconded,' Courtney's mum added with a proud grin.

Only Brad and the SIO looked disappointed. They'd been denied a fresh lead.

'Did he produce any sort of weapon?'

Courtney shook her head. 'No.'

'Did he try to force you to do anything you weren't comfortable with?'

'I got the feeling he might,' Courtney answered. 'That's why he got a skate between the legs.'

It was obvious, even to an amateur like Brad, that the interview was going nowhere. The police were not gathering truckloads of evidence that would free Connor and convict Liam

Darby. It was more likely, he thought, that Courtney could be charged with assault. Except that Liam would never complain to the cops.

The SIO did not look happy. 'Why did Joy Patterson speak to you and not to us?'

Alice almost snorted. 'You're the police and we're girls. You like catching people and putting them away. We're just after the truth. And fairness for Connor.'

'Well,' the SIO replied, 'there's not a lot I can do if a witness won't speak on the record, but what did she say?'

It was Hattie who answered. 'Connor only took her to a club. That's all. He didn't hurt her.'

'Club? Which club?'

Hattie shrugged. 'She wouldn't say. She was told to keep quiet – or else.'

Alice said, 'I'll guarantee you this. She knows Liam Darby. She pretended she didn't – but she did. She almost gasped when I mentioned his name.'

'Yes, well,' the officer replied, 'I have other information – from a reliable and quotable source – suggesting Darby might … have an interest in girls. I'm keen to have a word with him, but he's gone off the radar. Nowhere to be found.' He paused before adding, 'And we've been talking – discreetly – to girls at your school, but no other victims have come to light.'

Alice did snort this time. 'They wouldn't, would they? They're going to keep totally quiet in case their mums and dads find out. Especially if they've been scared into silence.'

Miss Sayell had been keen to shout news of Connor from the rooftops. Not any more. Now, when the students asked her where he was, she clammed up. She wouldn't answer their questions. 'Has he gone to the university already?' 'Has he gone back into hospital?' 'Is his brain playing him up again?' But Miss Sayell wanted to talk only about homework.

Hattie and Alice weren't saying much either.

Oliver didn't ask a question about Connor. He didn't need to. He kept his head down to hide his wide smile of satisfaction. His telephone tip-off had finally done the business. With Connor out of action in a police cell, Hattie had to rejoin the ranks of the unattached.

Privately, Ranji Nawaz and Hattie had both begun to fear that reconstructing Connor's fractured memory was beyond their grasp. Neither would admit it, though. Not even to each other as they plotted one particular tactic.

Once again, Hattie stood nervously in front of the same SIO and custody sergeant. 'If you really want to know what happened,' she said, 'why not sort-of reconstruct it? Yes? We all want to know where Connor took Joy and what happened. If you put him in the same situation again – with someone who looks like Joy – it might jog his memory. Dr Nawaz said it might work.'

The officers were nodding. Clearly, they liked the idea of a reconstruction. They would certainly get a better picture of the important crime – sex trafficking of girls – if the prime suspect could recollect what he'd done with the latest victim.

'Have you consulted Markham's parents?'

'I mentioned it to them, yes. They seemed to think it was a good idea. Anything to get Connor's memory back.' Hattie hadn't mentioned it to the other Markham. Brad wouldn't be happy with anything that forced Connor to go backwards rather than forwards. He was out of step with his own mum and dad, Dr Nawaz, Hattie, and now with the police.

CHAPTER 30

The reconstruction was supposed to be a shortcut – a time-tunnel – to the events of last April.

Joy's look-alike was actually a police officer's daughter and her name was nothing like Joy. But, for the next hour or so, she would be Joy Patterson. Hattie had helped with her appearance. Immaculate. Not a hair out of place. A sophisticated look. Elegant make-up. A little too adult for her age. The new Joy had been briefed and she was waiting for the new Connor inside 57 Springfield Road.

She wasn't the only one. Hattie, Dr Nawaz, the SIO and Mr Markham were all on hand. Mrs Dungate had given the go-ahead for the reconstruction, but she was bewildered by the bizarre bunch of visitors. Fussing over them, she muttered, 'This is a rum do. My teapot's not big enough.'

'It's all right,' Connor's dad replied. 'I don't think we're in the mood for drinking.'

Flanked by PC Xander Knox and the look-alike's mother, Connor was guided to what had been Joy Patterson's house. It was late afternoon. Street-lamps and twilight. When the group halted by the hedge, Connor's face lit up. 'Treble nineteen.' On the path up to the front door, he hesitated, gazing at the palm tree with long pointed crimson leaves like a frozen gush of blood. 'Cracked,' he said.

'Cracked?'

Connor nodded.

'Well,' Xander said, 'you're here. Press the bell.'

Connor expected an old lady, but instead a girl opened the door. Behind her stood a woman whose peel was a funny colour, just like Courtney's. 'Hello, Connor. I'm Ranji Nawaz and you weren't expecting me here, but I want you to play a new sort of game.' She put her hand on the girl's shoulder and continued, 'I want you to pretend this is Joy Patterson. You remember Joy Patterson? She spoke to you at school last year. I want you to go with this Joy. Don't worry about it. Just take her where your instinct tells you. Okay?'

Connor glanced down at Pretend Joy's footwear. Confused, he said, 'No car shoes.' He looked like a little boy who had just been told that his pet had died.

'No,' Ranji replied. 'But, if you do this, I'll see if I can get the police to give you your roller skates back.'

Connor's immediate smile faded almost as quickly as it had appeared.

Guessing what was going through her patient's troubled head, Ranji added, 'Courtney wants you to take her where you took Joy.'

Connor sighed. 'All right.'

He walked down the path and the girl followed him.

Unknown to Connor, the two police officers in tow were in constant radio contact with their SIO. Pretend Joy Patterson was also wired for sound.

Connor didn't really know what was going on, but he was pleased to escape the cramped unhappy room and breathe cold, crisp air. He was pleased to see mini-clouds coming out of his mouth.

Straightaway, Pretend Joy asked, 'Does this remind you of anything?'

Connor moaned. 'No.'

At the gate, he turned left along Springfield Road. Underfoot, the sludge couldn't make up its mind whether it was snow, ice or water.

Moment-by-moment, night settled on the area and the

193

street-lights seemed to get brighter and brighter. Yet Connor was unable to cast any light on the past. He was devoid of answers. They had all been swallowed by the black hole in his brain.

Four thousand five hundred and forty-nine. Four thousand five hundred and sixty-one.

Interrupting Connor's generation of prime numbers, Pretend Joy announced, 'I want you to take me to the club.'

At once, Connor stopped and cried, 'Carrots!' He stared into her face for a few seconds and then asked, 'Are you sure?'

'Yeah,' she replied. 'I want some fun.'

'But … ' Connor carried on walking down the darkening road. 'I'm not happy. I don't want Courtney to find out.'

Trying to hide an expression of surprise, Pretend Joy replied, 'I won't tell her.' She paused before adding, 'I suppose you don't want to be seen with me because you're going out with Hattie.'

Connor ignored her remark. 'Courtney's rocking. She's three squared.'

Connor liked the letter C a lot. It was one of the few letters he could remember. It didn't have a dead end like an unhappy G. It needed only a bit of filling in to become a nought. And a downward line on the right made it into his favourite number: 9. That's how he remembered it. The number 9 was a shortcut to Courtney's name.

Four thousand six hundred and twenty-one.

Pretend Joy Patterson did not give up easily. 'What sort of a club are you taking me to, Connor?'

'Joy knows.'

'I've forgotten. What's it called?'

Connor had no desire to revisit the past, and no obvious way of doing it, but sometimes he experienced uncomfortable feelings and painful pictures he wanted to purge from his brain. Suddenly downcast, he muttered, 'Pink Drink.'

'Is that its name?' she asked.

Connor shook his head.

Four thousand six hundred and thirty-seven.

'Are we going the right way, though?'

Connor looked around. They were walking past a gym and

on the other side of the road was a greengrocer. He pointed at the fruit shop. 'Yes. Green … '

'Grocer.'

He nodded. Grappling with the language, he said, 'Yes. GG. Horrible letter.'

Pretend Joy looked bewildered and discouraged. She probably thought that she was failing. There was no one to tell her she'd scored a spectacular success.

The police officers were within sight but a long way back, presumably to make the reconstruction more realistic. They would be listening in, no doubt, but maybe even they didn't grasp the significance of Connor's words.

But none of them had long to wait before they understood.

At the end of the road was a building unlike all the others. It was bigger, more colourful, with signs up outside. *GG's Nightclub*. Connor stopped and stared at it. Yes, the place was horrible, but it also drew him in. He couldn't resist the attraction any more than a piece of iron could refuse the pull of a magnet.

'What? Is this it?' said Pretend Joy. 'Oh, I get it. GG. GG's Nightclub.'

'Yes.' Mesmerized, Connor walked forwards. 'You're going to see a man with … ' He stroked his own chin. 'Hair.'

'A beard?'

'Yes. He's got a collection of cars, clothes and medals.' Connor seemed to be reciting what someone else had said rather than understanding the words he'd uttered.

The club had not yet come to life. It was still too early for this evening's pack of party animals.

Pretend Joy grabbed Connor's coat. 'I don't think we should … ' She glanced back over her shoulder, probably trying to spot her mum.

Connor had forgotten he was leading two police officers as well as Pretend Joy to GG's. He ignored the tugging on his sleeve. UnConnor was taking unJoy for a good time.

CHAPTER 31

More lambs to the slaughter.

The SIO was running towards his car. The two police officers were running towards GG's. Connor and Pretend Joy were at the door of the nightclub. A bouncer's body was blocking the entrance.

'We're not open and you're too young.'

Breathless, Xander Knox and Pretend Joy's mother dashed up to the young couple. 'There's been a … misunderstanding,' Xander said. 'They weren't trying to gate-crash … Anyway, we'll leave you to it.'

While the policewoman led her daughter and Connor away, there were two more arrivals, both best known by initials. The SIO screeched to a halt in his car and GG appeared behind the bouncer.

Gareth Gregor peered at the retreating youngsters and said, 'What's going on?'

The SIO replied, 'Never mind that. I've got some questions for you.'

'About?'

'Can we come in?'

'Of course,' GG answered with a welcoming smile. 'I've got nothing to hide.' He stood to one side and Ivan the bouncer did the same.

The place was empty apart from a member of staff tidying the area behind the bar, preparing for the evening's onslaught.

Cool and confident, Gareth Gregor Rowling sat in one of the metallic chairs and leaned back with his hands clasped behind his head. 'Can I offer you a non-alcoholic drink?'

'No, thanks,' the SIO replied, taking the chair opposite him. PC Knox stood to one side of the table.

'What can I do for you?'

'Have you heard of Connor Markham?'

Rowling took a breath as he thought about the name. 'No, I don't think so. But … ' He shrugged. 'I see and meet a lot of people in this business. I can't remember every name.'

'How about Joy Patterson?'

GG shook his head. 'No. Wait. Yes. I don't know. It's familiar for some reason.'

'She was in the news, nearly a year back.'

'That'll be it, then. Why?' GG said innocently.

The SIO ignored the question. 'Have you come across Liam Darby?'

GG smiled wryly. 'Yes. Quite a character. Not the most … savoury one, either.'

'Why do you say that?' the SIO asked.

'Because I've noticed him taking an unhealthy interest in certain girls. Young ones.'

'You allow underage girls in?'

'No. I value my licence. But Liam Darby's been abusing my hospitality for years. I tried to do something about it. Barred him. But that didn't help. He does his business outside. When my doormen turn the underage ones away, he trots after them. Sadly, I can't protect them when they're not on my patch.'

'You could have reported him to us.'

'With all due respect, I don't think people like you take people like me seriously. There's not a great deal of love lost between you and the nightclubs, is there? We operate in very different worlds. And I confess I didn't want to draw attention to GG's. I don't want my club getting a bad name.' He laughed gently before adding, 'Some say GG's is a terrible name already.'

Gareth Gregor Rowling was like a purring cat that, in a flash, might bare its claws. But not yet. His claws would show only after the interview.

The SIO remembered something that the look-alike's microphone had picked up as Connor made for the club. He asked, 'Do you know a bearded man who comes here? He collects cars, clothes and medals.'

'As I said, I've got a lot of clients. Too many to get that chummy with. I know a couple who are musicians but, other than that, I don't get up close and personal.'

In a quiet corner of the cloakroom, where Hattie normally confided in Alice, she talked instead to Brad.

'There was a tip-off about the roller skates,' Brad told her. 'Someone phoned to say Connor nicked them. You won't need many guesses before you come up with Liam, trying to blame it all on Connor. That's usually the way it goes.'

They both knew that Connor had a proven ability to take the blame.

'What are we going to do?' Hattie cried.

Brad shrugged.

'You don't care!'

Brad looked into her face and said, 'You're wrong. I just don't know what to do for best. That's all. I could have another go at Liam, but he's likely to go one step further this time and murder me.'

'No one knows where he is anyway. He's gone off the radar, according to the police.'

'So, what do *you* think we should do?'

'It was me who thought of the reconstruction,' Hattie replied. 'It was a good idea. It jogged his memory.'

'Sort of,' Brad muttered. 'It didn't clear him.'

'No, but … '

'Connor's brain's kaput. There's no magic wand, no drug, no operation. He's got a hole and that's it. The idea is to work out a way of living with it, not to keep shovelling rubbish into it.'

'You always look on the black side.'

Failing to keep a lid on his simmering bitterness, Brad said, 'Did your reconstruction make Connor happier? No. Maybe it's made you and the police happier. And Mum and Dad. But not Connor. So, don't tell me it was a good idea.' He strode away.

Flouncing across the quad, Brad bumped into Alice.

'Are you okay?' she asked him. 'You're … fuming.'

'I've just been having a chat with your mate, Hattie.'

'About Connor?'

'Yeah.'

'That explains it.'

'The cops still don't know anything,' Brad said. 'They reckon Connor might've led Liam!'

'That's total role reversal if ever I heard it,' Alice exclaimed.

'Connor's not denying it.'

'He wouldn't, would he?' she replied. 'He probably hasn't got a clue.'

'It's all going carrot-shaped for him.'

'What?'

'It's putting his job at uni on the line.'

Alice nodded. 'I suppose so. That'll please Hattie.'

'Will it?'

'I guess. She won't want him out of her clutches.'

'She won't want him in prison either.'

'Well, there is that,' Alice replied. 'She won't have anything come between her and her precious relationship.'

'You two really aren't on the same wavelength any more when it comes to Connor, are you?'

'She's on a nostalgia trip and I'm not.'

Brad nodded his approval.

'What was so good about the old Connor?' Alice continued. 'Sorry, Brad, but that's just the way it is.'

'I know. He's changed.'

'Yeah. Nine point nine on the Richter scale. The new Connor's … ' Alice struggled to find the right word and failed. Instead, she said, 'He's surprised me.'

Brad scrutinized her face. Taken aback, he realized that Alice was complimenting his brother.

'I heard about Connor being arrested,' Oliver said softly. 'I'm sorry.'

'Are you?' Hattie retorted. 'Why?'

Oliver shrugged. Perhaps his opening line hadn't been a good idea after all. He hadn't expected Hattie to query it. She was supposed to accept it and say, 'Thanks.' Now, Oliver was struggling to think of a response. Why should he be sorry? He'd got what he wanted: a clear path to Hattie. 'Well, because it must be rotten with his brain problem.'

'You've got a nerve. You've been dying to get rid of him and all. I still think it was you who chucked beer over my dad's keyboard!'

'Me?' A look of tortured innocence appeared on his face.

Her accusation seemed to needle him so Hattie dropped the subject.

'I'm sorry about Connor,' Oliver continued, 'because it bugs you.'

'I just wish I could do something … '

'You can,' Oliver replied at once.

'What?'

'I told you. Forget him. Alice told you as well. He's a loser.'

Hattie muttered, 'I think Alice has changed her mind.'

'Really?' Oliver tried not to show his pleasure. Perhaps Alice would take Connor off Hattie's hands after all.

'It's just that she wants … ' Hattie looked annoyed. 'She's like Brad. They want Connor like he is now. They don't want him to get his memory back.'

'Well … '

'Don't say another word,' Hattie growled.

Between school and home, Brad suddenly realized that someone was close behind him. Following him, perhaps. Looking over his shoulder, he saw Liam Darby looming large. Heart pounding, he stopped and faced Connor's sort-of friend.

'The filth's after me,' Liam said. 'Is that you's blabbing?'

'Me?' Brad replied. 'What would I tell them?'

'Medals, roller skates … '

'No use me telling them what I think. They'd want some sort of proof.'

Liam eyed him suspiciously.

Brad was hopelessly outgunned if it came to a scrap, but he tried to put it out of his mind. Taking his role as big brother seriously, he said, 'I thought you were Connor's mate.'

'Yeah.'

Connor's brain disease was teaching Brad who Connor's friends really were. And Liam wasn't one of them. Brad was amazed to find Alice, Miss Sayell and himself gracing the list of goodies. As far as Brad was concerned, they were the only goodies.

'So why are you getting him involved in stuff?'

'Stuff?'

'Like nicking cash from old ladies.'

'We's just having fun. Connor doesn't need draggin'. He likes it.'

Brad took a deep breath. 'Talking about the police, why did you tip them off about Connor's skates? That's not having fun. That's blaming him for something he didn't do.'

'What?' Liam looked genuinely surprised. 'Someone grassed Connor? Is that what you's saying?'

'Exactly.'

Liam puffed out his chest like a dominant male facing a challenge. 'It wasn't me. And I don't like being … '

Interrupting him, Brad asked, 'Who, then?'

Liam grabbed Brad by his school jumper and said in a low threatening voice, 'Dunno, but it wasn't me. You thinks about it. Am I goin' to go blabbing to the filth? I wouldn't speak to them about nothing and no one.'

'All right.' Strangely, Brad believed Liam.

'If you's weren't Connor's brother, you'd be flat on the floor by now.' Liam let go of the fistful of jumper and pushed Brad backwards.

Trying to hang on to the remains of his courage, Brad demanded, 'Just leave Connor alone.'

Liam laughed. 'One more thing outta you and you's gonna see the insides of a life support machine, real close up.'

Liam strutted down a side-street, disappearing as quickly as he'd come.

Four thousand seven hundred and three.

Connor sat on the floor, back propped against the bed, in that bare grey room and toyed with numbers in his head, until something else pushed the digits aside. He didn't want to be distracted but the decision wasn't his. After the reconstruction, neurons fired in his wounded brain, frantically fumbling for a piece of the jigsaw, imposing an uninvited image on him. Eyes closed, he saw a short man with a beard, drinking at a bar. He saw a girl like Pretend Joy by his side. He saw a smart man wearing a sharp suit in front of him.

Then his broken brain merged separate fragments into a faulty whole. He saw a burning building, a red stain trickling down his forefinger, spreading over his palm and plopping into a pink puddle by the kerb. He was a very lot confused. He felt scared, perhaps ashamed, and deep within him was a fear of blame.

Connor opened his eyes, clambered on to the bed, curled up defensively and banished the ugly images. He hated before-land. It wasn't a happy place. He didn't want anything to do with it. All he wanted was Courtney, but … Where was she?

Four thousand seven hundred and twenty-one.

The custody sergeant reviewed her notes of the Markham case and quickly came to the conclusion that she no longer had sufficient reason to hold him. Given that Connor Markham was a welcome visitor at 57 Springfield Road, there was no valid fingerprint evidence against him. There were no eyewitnesses and neither the keys to the house nor the missing war medals had turned up somewhere incriminating. On top of that, Mrs Dungate spoke highly of Markham.

There was no certain connection between Markham and the

break-in at SprintZ. The CCTV footage of the hooded looter was ambiguous, the tip-off was unusably anonymous, and Markham had told friends that the roller skates were a gift from Liam Darby.

As for serious crime, the reconstruction hadn't dragged Markham deeper into the mire of a sexual offence. There was an obvious link, but no proven intention.

Charging him with anything was out of the question. It would be easier to make a charge stick against Darby – if his whereabouts were known. He couldn't explain why his dabs were inside 57 Springfield Road and a magistrate would never believe his claims that Markham had coerced him into crime. But, to make sure, she really needed the Dungate medals in his hands or at least plastered with his prints and DNA. Until then, her grip on both Darby and Markham was slippery. It was time for Connor Markham to go home.

Her job required a firm and frosty front but, inwardly, she was pleased to sign his release papers. What was the point of holding him any longer? He wouldn't or couldn't even answer questions. Once he was free, though, she feared what the big cruel world would do to such a simple boy.

CHAPTER 32

Truth has a heavy price tag.

When Connor and his support assistant walked into the art room, late for the lesson, there was a buzz that threatened to escalate into a cheer – until Jazz Hands, the cranky teacher, called for quiet and concentration.

Afterwards, out in the quad, Hattie said to Connor, 'I'm really glad you're back.'

Connor sniffed. It was the volcano girl, but her name escaped him. He looked at the other girl – the nice-looking one – and something stirred. Emotional engagement was kicking in. Grinning, he said, 'AF. Big number at … ' He stopped, stumped for a word.

Alice smiled. It was the first time that he had got close to remembering her name. She nodded. 'That's right. Alice. Demon bowler.'

Hattie glared at Alice and invaded their cosy chat. 'What did they ask you, the police?'

Connor looked blank and bewildered. He shrugged.

When Brad joined them, Hattie ignored him. She continued to quiz Connor. 'What happened, Connor? What's this about pinching roller skates, breaking into houses, girls and all?' She talked more like his mother every day.

Connor's expression hardly changed.

'What do you remember?'

Battered by demands for buried information, Connor's

brain gave up. He snapped, 'Remembering's not happy. Carrots!'

Pulling the plug on Hattie's inquisition, Alice told Connor, 'At least it'll be over soon. You'll get away from Liam by going to uni.'

Hattie made a face, but did not say anything until Connor's support assistant came to take him away to Special Educational Needs. Then, in a mood, she muttered, 'It's not right.'

'What's not?' Alice asked.

'The whole university thing. He'll be way out of his depth and he won't exactly be mixing with people like himself, will he? He won't get on with them.'

Brad butted in. 'You never know. The students might take to him *because* of his problems. They might respect his … whatever it is. His ability.'

'You saw the reaction in maths when Miss Sayell announced his job,' Alice said to Hattie. 'Everyone wants him to make a go of it – even if it's just to get him out of school. You're the only exception. And you're the one who called him cute! The people he mixes with at uni might think cute's enough. They might love him for it.'

Hattie scowled in reply.

Alice continued, 'You don't want him to go because he'll get away from you.'

'That's … cruel.'

Alice shrugged. 'That's the truth for you.'

Indignant, Hattie said, 'It's not that. It's nothing to do with me. I'm only thinking of Connor.'

'Come off it! You've got to learn to back off, girl. Oliver's a scheming twat but he's right about one thing. Your Connor's gone. The one that went bowling, played football, went to see horror films, he's totally dead and buried. Like it or not, this Connor's got the hots for maths and a twelve-year-old kid called Courtney. Right, Brad?'

'Right.'

Hattie shook her head angrily. She was about to storm away when she stopped herself. 'Having the hots for a kid isn't a good place to be right now.'

'The thing is,' Alice said, 'he's always going to be under suspicion until the cops find out who did what.'

Brad agreed. 'Liam knows the answers.'

'But he's going to lie like crazy when the police catch him,' said Hattie.

Alice nodded. 'Maybe we're better placed to squeeze the truth out of him.'

'How do you mean?'

'We did better with Joy Patterson.'

Hattie snorted. 'Liam Darby isn't Joy Patterson. Nothing like.'

'So,' Alice replied, 'we use a different tactic.'

'Like?'

'I'm thinking about it.' Alice hesitated before adding, 'How difficult can it be to out-think Liam?'

Brad smiled but he said, 'It's not the thinking I'm worried about. His talent for hurting people will be harder to handle.'

Ivan was too big for the seat. He overhung it on both sides. He wasn't fat. He was pure beef, like a heavyweight boxer. He spoke with an eastern European accent. 'The windows are boarded up,' he told the SIO. 'The door's padlocked. I don't know what's happening. I turn up for work and ... No club. No Mr Rowling. GG's closed.'

'Did Mr Rowling say anything to you about it last night?'

'No. Nothing.' The out-of-work bouncer was plainly disgruntled.

'So, why have you come here?'

'How do you say? To blow the whistle?'

'What do you want to tell me?' the SIO asked.

'You should know about the girls. Young girls. It's not right.'

The police officer kept his excitement under wraps. Casually, he said, 'Okay. Let's hear it.'

'I had instructions. No underage boys and no groups of underage girls.'

Straightaway, the SIO interrupted. 'You mean, you wouldn't let them into GG's nightclub?'

'Yes,' Ivan replied in his gruff voice. 'But young girls on their own who were desperate to get in … That was different. I guess they were more …'

'Vulnerable?'

'Yes.'

At last, the SIO thought. A break. Of course, the doorman could have reported the club much earlier but, while it gave him a job, he'd chosen to keep quiet. The SIO decided not to comment on the bouncer's motives and morals. He wanted to exploit his resentment first. 'How did these girls arrive?'

'A boy brought them.'

'Who?'

Ivan shrugged.

'Connor Markham?'

'Connor, yes.'

To be sure, the SIO produced a photograph of Markham from his case notes and slid it across the surface of the table. 'Him?'

'Yes. That's the one.'

'Right. Just to be clear, who gave you these instructions about letting vulnerable girls into GG's?'

'Mr Rowling himself.'

'Are you sure about that?'

'Yes.'

'Do you know where he is now?'

'No.'

'Tell me what happened to the girls.'

Ivan shrugged again. 'They mixed with the punters.'

'Were they given drinks? Alcohol, I mean.'

'Most of the time I was outside but, yes, I saw some with drinks. Some looked drunk.'

'What was Liam Darby's role in all this?'

'Liam? He was a regular at GG's. That's all.'

'Did you ever see him taking an interest in underage girls?'

'No. He just did favours for Mr Rowling.'

'All right,' the SIO said. 'I have a lot more questions, but right now I need to take a break.'

Emotions no longer in check, the SIO hit the incident room like a tornado. 'Listen up,' he shouted. 'Good news. We've got a whistle-blower bad-mouthing GG Rowling. We can get him for grooming. Bad news. He's taken fright – it must've been the reconstruction. He's done a runner. Find him for me. Top priority.' He was about to leave when he paused. 'Someone tell me, are we getting anywhere with that car collector who goes to GG's?'

'There's a Lord Williams who's got a big posh place in Harewood and a well-known collection of vintage cars, medals and fashion items. Some of it's open to the public. We're checking him out.'

'A lord, eh? Be careful. He's probably got friends in high places.'

'Right,' Alice said. 'Here's the plan. We tell Liam Connor's been back to the old lady's place in Springfield Road and found out she's won a whole heap of cash.'

'That'd grab his attention,' said Brad. 'Then what?'

'We camp out in her front room with a camera phone. If Liam's got a key ... '

Brad put up his hands. 'Hang on ... '

Hattie butted in straightaway. 'It'd work. We could tell Mrs Dungate we're doing another reconstruction. She wouldn't know any better. She'd go for it.'

'I wasn't thinking of that,' Brad said. 'Liam would smell a rat if one of us told him Connor had seen a lorry-load of tenners. He'd only believe it straight from Connor. Which means we'd have to train Connor to tell Liam she's got a wodge of money. That's somewhere between tricky and impossible.'

'Good point,' Alice said. 'But maybe there's a way. We could get help. I think we should recruit Courtney. I bet he'd do it for her.'

Brad nodded. 'Maybe.'

Hattie muttered to herself.

After school, at the Institute for Memory Disorders, Brad said to Courtney, 'Remember me? Connor's brother.'

'Yes.' She looked askance at him and the two girls beside him.

'These,' he said, waving a hand towards Alice and Hattie, 'are his friends. Real friends. Not like Liam.'

'The one you kicked in the nuts,' Alice added delicately.

'So … ?' the kid prompted.

'We need your help. Connor needs your help.'

'To do what?'

'Put Liam away.'

Courtney broke out into a smile. 'I'm all yours.'

The police hadn't cottoned on to Liam's love of football because they weren't waiting on the touchline with a pair of handcuffs.

The game in the park meant nothing to Connor. He watched for a while but kicking a ball up and down seemed pointless. It didn't spark a memory or an emotional jolt or even an interest. He was attracted more to the nearby house with funny tree things outside.

Courtney whispered, 'Have you got it, Connor? Today, you went to 57 Springfield Road … '

'I don't think I did.'

'No, but this is a pretend thing. Okay? You went to 57 Springfield Road and saw the woman who lives there. You know her. She's old. You saw her stuffing a lot of money into her purse.'

'Money.'

'Yes. That's what I want you to tell Liam.' Discreetly, she pointed at the striker who'd just fouled a defender. 'It'd be great if you'd do that for me. Will you?'

He nodded. 'Mrs Treble Nineteen has got … '

Courtney completed his sentence. 'Money.'

'It's hard to remember, isn't it?' Brad said. 'Let's make it easier. Let's put a figure on it. You saw her with one hundred and fourteen pounds.'

Connor's face lit up. 'One hundred and fourteen. Double fifty-seven. Happy.'

'So, what are you going to tell Liam?' Courtney asked.

'Mrs Treble Nineteen has got one hundred and fourteen money.'

'Close enough,' Brad and Courtney agreed.

At the final whistle, Courtney and Brad melted away as Liam made straight for Connor. 'You's out,' Liam said. 'They still looking for me, but they's too busy catching bad guys.' He nodded towards the pitch and added, 'You not gonna reclaim you's place in the team just yet, eh? Maybes later.'

Concentrating like crazy – like Courtney requested – Connor said, 'Mrs Treble Nineteen's got one hundred and fourteen money.'

'What you's talking about? Mrs Treble Nineteen?'

Connor pointed towards Springfield Road. 'Number fifty-seven.'

'Oh. Yeah. I knows it.' He let out a laugh and thumped Connor playfully on the arm. 'You and me – the mean team – went together. What's this about money?'

'One hundred and fourteen … '

'Quid?'

Connor looked puzzled.

Liam tried again. 'Pounds?'

'Yes,' Connor replied with a grin.

'You know she's got a hundred and fourteen pounds?'

'Yes.'

Smirking, Liam nodded. 'Sounds like I gotta pay her a visit – before she spends it. Tonight's a good night.'

'Happy.'

A moment later, Hattie and Alice rushed up and, pretending to be as concerned as overprotective parents, dragged Connor away from a bad influence.

Job done. Seed planted. They took Connor away before he said something that ruined the plan.

Connor knew he was going out with Brad and the two girls to meet Liam. Tonight, the mean team would not be two people but five. Mrs Treble Nineteen would make six. Perfect.

Connor looked at the girl walking alongside him, hesitated, and then said, 'AF. Er … Alice.'

She nodded. 'Spot on. Again.'

Connor smiled, proud of himself for once.

The boy was the brother who lived with him in the same house. His name was Brad. He wasn't so sure about the second girl. He turned to her and said, 'You … smell like a volcano.'

She winced and turned her face away.

'It's all right,' Brad explained. 'A volcano's a flower.'

'Oh. Well, that's … nice.' Rearranging her face, the girl beamed happily at Connor and touched his upper arm. 'I don't mind being like a volcano now. My name's Hattie.'

Connor nodded and murmured, 'Hattie.'

Brad seemed to be nervous, but he was covering it up with playfulness. As they walked past the kicking field, he said, 'Mobile fully charged? Check. Movie mode working? Check. Stab-proof vest? Ah. Forgot it.'

'Get movies of Liam breaking in,' Alice replied, 'and you won't need the stab-proof vest.'

'Really?'

'Totally.'

'How's that going to work, then?' said Brad.

'I've got another plan. But I need to see the house first.'

Mrs Dungate opened the door, glanced at Connor and smiled. 'Oh. Hello, Colin. And your friends.'

'Hello,' they all chimed.

'Have you come for a party?' the old lady asked. 'I'm not having one.'

'A party?' Brad replied. 'No.' Having watched a lot of TV cops, he knew what to say. 'We have reason to believe you're going to be burgled tonight.'

'What? Me? Tonight?'

'Yes.'

'We're here to stop it,' Hattie chipped in.

'If you'll let us,' Alice added.

'Is this right, Colin … I mean, Connor?'

Connor nodded.

'You'd better come in. I'll put the kettle on.'

Over compulsory tea, they asked about her habits. When

did she go to bed? Did she lock up? Did she switch the lights off?

Alice finished her tea and said, 'Do you know how the robber got in last time?'

'Well, the two of them went out the back. I'm sure I saw them running towards the canal. I suppose they came in the same way.'

'Okay.' Alice went out through the kitchen to reconnoitre.

'Are you sure this is all above-board?' Mrs Dungate said anxiously.

'Yes,' Brad replied. 'Look at it this way. If we spot him tonight, it'll be the last time. We'll hand him over to the police and you won't have any more break-ins. We might even get your medals back.'

'Really? That would be nice.'

'Just leave it to us. All you've got to do is act normally.'

The sun had set at about half past four but Brad didn't expect Liam to strike until much later. He'd surely wait for Mrs Dungate to turn off the downstairs lamps when she went to bed. She did that after the ten o'clock news. So, they organized themselves by ten-thirty. Brad, Connor and Hattie in the unlit front room. Alice shivering outside. When a restless Mrs Dungate went upstairs, everything was in place.

The trap was primed.

Just for a moment, a shaft of light originating from the towpath lit up the dinosaur that stood between the canal and the back of Springfield Road. The beam swung from side to side across the playing field and then homed in on number 57.

The house was pitch-black. The old dear had gone to bed. Noiselessly, Liam lifted up the latch on the wooden gate. Opening it carefully and quietly, he slipped into the backyard. He closed the gate and, by the light of his torch, tiptoed to the back door. Shining the light on the lock, he slotted in the key and turned it gently.

It clicked. He was nearing that stash of money. He turned the handle, pushed and then froze.

Mrs Dungate's phone rang.

The stair light came on and Mrs Dungate fumbled her way down to the living room. Brad, Connor and Hattie blinked in the sudden brightness when she switched on the lamp. Picking up the landline receiver, she muttered, 'Hello?'

There was a gap while she listened to the voice on the other end of the line. Her face evolved from worried frown to child-like glee.

'Oh, thank you! I thought you might have forgotten ... You're busy, after all.'

Brad and the others couldn't help but hear half of the conversation.

'So, you're about to go to work. I can't get used to you having day in our night. And summer in our winter.'

'Yes. I'm having ... an interesting day. I can't tell you what's been going on here recently. It's all about things disappearing like your dad's medals. I've had the police round, doing a crime reconstruction. There's something happening now, would you believe? Not the police. It's a sort-of set-up.'

'No, there's no need to be worried about me. It's quite exciting actually. We're going to catch a burglar red-handed.'

'Yes. Tonight. Connor's set a trap.'

'Well, you know me and my memory but, yes, this is going to be a birthday to remember.'

Brad glanced at Hattie and grimaced with embarrassment. He should have noticed the two birthday cards earlier. They were standing on the mantelpiece, either side of the clock with the revolving pendulum. Now, he understood why she'd mentioned a party. A birthday party. Together with Alice, Connor and Hattie, he'd invaded her special day. Their reckless scheme had put her in danger on her birthday.

When she put the phone down, Brad mumbled, 'Sorry. We didn't know ... Happy birthday.'

'Thank you, young man. I won't forget this one in a hurry.'

'You might,' Connor said.

She laughed. 'Well, when you get to my age, birthdays come

and go really fast. They don't mean so much. They're just a number. But … '

Connor interrupted. 'Numbers are happy.'

Mrs Dungate nodded. 'I'm happy as well now. I'm going to bed.'

On her way out, she shrouded her visitors in darkness once more.

From the kitchen doorway, Liam didn't hear every word but he heard the bit about a set-up. He heard it wasn't the police. He heard that Connor had set a trap.

He had two options. He could run. Get outta there. Or he could vent his fury. Get his own back.

Seething, he chose the latter.

Brad had barely got settled back into his position, squatting down by the couch with his mobile at the ready, when the door opened again. Torchlight danced crazily over the opposite wall and then fell, illuminating the grey carpet. There was a stifled cry like someone being strangled. And the lamp flooded the room with light again.

Hattie and Connor both stood, mouths gaping. Brad tried to keep his nerve. He hoped the smart phone in his right hand would go unnoticed.

Liam was standing behind Mrs Dungate, gripping her tightly and holding a knife to her shrivelled throat.

CHAPTER 33

Honesty's not always the best policy.

Mrs Dungate was pale at the best of times. Now, her crumpled skin was bloodless, virtually white. Her skinny legs had become rigid, locked at the knees. There was terror in her eyes and a stain on the front of her nightdress.

Liam must have grabbed her in the hall – before she'd set foot on the stairs. Never far from aggression, he seemed to be treating her as disposable. An antique at the end of its lifetime. He appeared to have one final use for her – as a means of exacting revenge on the people who had lured him to the house.

First, he glared at Connor. 'What's this crazy stuff? I thought we's mates.'

'Strange kind of mates,' Brad mumbled. At once, he regretted it because he didn't want to draw attention to himself, to the phone in his palm. His arm hung limply but his hand, by his thigh, was angled upwards in Liam's direction.

'I've warned you before,' Liam barked at him. He stared at them all from behind Mrs Dungate's shoulder. 'Why you done this?'

Hattie blurted out, 'To prove you're guilty and Connor's innocent.'

'Proof? What you says isn't proof,' he sniggered. 'Cops want evidence. So, where is it?'

Hattie didn't answer.

Brad wished she'd kept quiet in the first place.

To Liam, Hattie's honesty was a weakness to be insulted and exploited, yet his brain didn't figure it out straightaway. After a few seconds, though, he guessed. He looked Hattie up and down then shifted his gaze to Brad. Glancing down at his right hand, he said, 'You's filmin' this!' He almost laughed with derision. 'Give me it or she's dead meat.'

Brad sighed. Fearing for Mrs Dungate, he didn't see an alternative. He threw the phone towards Liam.

For a moment, Liam let go of his petrified victim and caught it. Like an impish child, he pulled a face directly into its lens. Then he smashed it with his knife. Laughing, he threw the mobile angrily across the room. It crashed into the small golden clock perched on the mantelpiece. The delicate mechanism didn't stand a chance against Liam's temper. Its glass case shattered and its revolving pendulum came to a standstill like an ailing heart inside a broken body.

'If any of yous double-cross me again, the wrinkly's dead. Got that? She's semi-dead already. Wouldn't take much to finish the job. That's what happens when you screw me around.'

Knowing that Mrs Dungate was now incapable of attempting an escape, Liam delved into his pocket with one hand while still threatening her with the knife in the other. He plucked out the backdoor key and threw it towards Connor.

Brad shouted, 'Don't touch … '

He was too late. Connor stepped forward and caught the key.

Liam smiled. 'There. Yous prints and DNA on it now.'

Brad groaned. The whole scheme was going carrot-shaped.

'This is what you's gonna do – if you want the old dear alive … '

'Actually,' Alice said from behind him, 'I'm going to tell *you* what to do.'

'You!'

'You didn't see me lurking in the yard, did you? But you used your torch. Very handy. Just enough light to take the edge off the darkness. I got better pictures that way. I filmed you fiddling with the lock and key, and coming in.'

Liam manoeuvred Mrs Dungate so Alice could come in and join the others. Still triumphant, he grinned at her. 'Hand it over!' he snarled. 'Or … '

'That's where I'm ahead of you,' she replied. 'Because I haven't got it. It's somewhere you won't find it. You could murder us all and you're still totally nicked.'

'I'll tear this place apart! I'll find where you've left it.'

Standing between Brad and Connor, Alice smiled. 'No, you won't. Because I gave it to my accomplice – that's what the police say, isn't it? An accomplice. She'll be half way home by now. She might even have called the cops already.'

'You's lying.'

Brad didn't know anything about an accomplice. He agreed with Liam. He guessed that Alice had still got her mobile or she'd hidden it in the backyard. He held his breath.

'Go on, then,' she said. 'Call my bluff.'

For a while, Liam was as dumbfounded as Mrs Dungate.

'Take your time,' Alice said, apparently calmly. 'The longer you wait, the more likely the police will arrive. But I might be able to stop my friend ringing them if you do a couple of things for us.'

'Like?'

With a glance at Connor, she said, 'Tell us if Connor knew what he was doing when he took girls like Joy to GG's.'

'Yeah. 'Course he knew.'

'So, he knew what happened to them? He knew about the sex and drugs?'

Liam shrugged. 'Maybe not. Brains were never his best bit. He didn't do nothing … '

It wasn't a clear-cut answer, but Brad suspected it was the best that Alice would get.

'Second thing,' she continued. 'You go to the police and tell them the truth. Connor didn't steal anything.'

'Me? Go to the filth? What planet are yous on?'

Alice shrugged. 'No deal, then. My mobile goes to the cops.'

Liam stared at her for several seconds, probably trying to decide if she was bluffing or not. 'I'll take my chance.'

'Better let Mrs Dungate go and run like mad, then.'

There were a few more moments of silence until, outside, a car roared past. The noise seemed to galvanise Liam. He pushed Mrs Dungate violently away. Then, unencumbered, he squared up to Alice. Well within striking distance, he thrust his knife at her neck.

Hattie caught Mrs Dungate as if she were some priceless and fragile statue.

Aghast and transfixed, Brad watched helplessly as the knife flashed past him, towards Alice's throat.

Before it found its target, though, Connor's powerful arm came up and deflected the lunge. The force of Connor's unexpected strike sent the knife looping through the air. When it landed on the carpet, Brad slammed his shoe down on it.

Deprived of his weapon of choice, Liam went to grab Alice. But Connor immediately imposed himself between them. Confronting Liam, Connor gazed quizzically at him and demanded to know, 'Why did you do that to Mrs Treble Nineteen – and … Alice?'

'Because they makes me mad.'

Connor shook his head. 'I make people mad as well.'

'Yeah,' Liam replied, 'but you's got an excuse. You's got a mad brain.'

Connor thought about it for an instant. Finally delivering a verdict on Liam, he stated, 'You're not happy. We're not the mean team.'

Liam had not yet exhausted his armoury. He drew back his head on his muscular neck and then thrust it forward, aiming at Connor's nose. But Connor was too quick. He lurched to the left, dodging the head-butt. Even angrier, Liam clenched his hand into a heavy fist and pulled back his right arm like a trigger.

But the blow never materialized.

Surprising everyone, Alice sprang forward. With both ferocity and glee, she punched Liam hard in the face before his knuckles found her friend.

Stunned, Liam dropped at once. His head hit the sideboard and he slumped inert onto the carpet.

Mrs Dungate was shaken but unhurt. At least, she was physically unhurt. 'Well, I never,' she mumbled, as if waking up from a deep sleep, not yet making sense of the world. Then, she shook her head and the shock hit home. She cried, 'My clock! It was a wedding present.'

Brad was more concerned about what would happen when Liam regained consciousness. 'Someone call 999,' he said.

Alice took out her mobile.

Brad nodded. 'You were bluffing. You had your phone all along.'

For the second time, Alice said, 'How difficult can it be to out-think Liam?' Then she returned Brad's smile.

'Bluffing and boxing. Good work.'

Hattie helped Mrs Dungate back onto her feet. The old lady said, 'If those policemen are coming back, I'd better get the kettle on. They can't do anything without a cup of tea.'

It had been in April. For months, Connor had been doing girls a favour. He was so popular with them that, whenever one wanted a good time, she'd get Connor to take her to GG's nightclub. There, they would be introduced to men, given drinks, given anything they wanted. Lots of attention. Lots of rewards. Where was the harm in that? The girls were grateful.

But things had changed for Connor. He'd taken up with Hattie. He went to GG's to tell Mr Rowling why he didn't want to bring any more girls to the club.

GG shook his head. 'This sudden reluctance to cooperate, going forward,' he said. 'It's because of a girlfriend, you say.'

'Hattie.'

Gareth Gregor nodded. 'Hattie.' He handed Connor a small glass containing an almost colourless liquid. 'Drink this. It's for you.'

'I don't want to be seen with other girls.' The drink smelled powerful. Highly alcoholic. But Connor didn't want to push his luck by refusing. He threw it back and then winced at the burning in his throat.

GG smiled. 'Hey. You knocked that back like a pro. You'll want another.'

Liam poured a second drink and readied a third.

'Honestly,' Mr Rowling continued, 'I understand what you're saying. You don't want to upset Hattie. But it's not like you're dating these girls or anything. You're bringing them here for fun, not going out with them.'

'I don't want to give the wrong impression.'

'That's not going to happen, is it? Have another drink. You've got obligations to me, not just to Hattie.'

The alcohol seemed strong enough to strip the lining of his throat. Connor would not have been surprised if it had also begun to dissolve the glass. 'But … '

Mr Rowling interrupted. 'Look. Why don't you go with Liam and a few others tonight? In fact, I insist. It'll be … educational for you. They're going to Eve's. Frankly, we don't want or need another nightclub round here, so they're going to encourage this one to shut down. You'll see how it's done. A little fuel and fire goes a long way. Then,' GG said, leaning very close, 'think about Hattie's house. You wouldn't want her to get the same treatment, would you? No. Think about it while you're out with Liam. Think about what would happen if Hattie was inside at the time.'

Liam pushed another glass of vodka in front of him.

'Now,' Mr Rowling said, 'be a good boy and … nothing bad will happen. We'll just carry on as we are. We'll all be fine. You, me *and* Hattie.'

CHAPTER 34

At last, everyone had to admit that there was only one direction for Connor: forward.

It was like going back to the early days of Connor's disease. His mum, dad and brother sat in Dr Nawaz's office, awaiting her prognosis. This time, though, it felt final, like GCSE results or an end-of-year report.

Ranji explained, 'Older patients who've damaged the same part of the brain as Connor sometimes recall distant memories – childhood events and that sort of thing – but nothing recent. It's probably because the older the memory, the more likely they've revisited it over the years. The brain's so well-rehearsed at retrieving deep-seated memories that it doesn't need a temporal lobe to do it. No instructions necessary. That's why my grandma – she's not brain-damaged, just getting on a bit – remembers every detail of taking me on holiday when I was six but can't remember me taking her shopping last Tuesday. But Connor's too young to have firmed up memories like that. Fifteen-year-olds don't go in for a lot of nostalgia. Apart from the numbers, he hasn't shown any sign of recalling long-term memory, I'm afraid. We succeeded with some recollections of a general nature – like where he lives and that he enjoys certain foods and music. Actual episodes, like a particular meal or a specific song, have vanished. And so have his memories of relationships.'

'For good?' Mrs Markham checked. She already knew the answer, though.

Ranji nodded sadly. 'Almost certainly. As you know, I've always been hopeful, but his brain's sustained too much damage.'

'We've got to build a new relationship with him,' said Mr Markham. 'And we have to accept him as he is now.'

Quickly, Brad put in, 'Is that so bad? I say that's a pretty good deal. Connor's all right.'

Ranji smiled. 'Yes. He *is* all right, isn't he?'

The whole story of girls, GG's nightclub and sexual exploitation seemed to Connor to be just that: a story. It was some distant event like a legend. He accepted that it was real, that he had a part in it, but he couldn't persuade himself that he owned that slice of life because he couldn't remember it himself. It was someone else's experience, someone else's truth. It was old-Connor's. UnConnor's. Then there were the old photographs around his house. He featured in many of them so they must reflect things that had happened to him but, because the recollections weren't locked into his own brain, he could never fully believe in them. He hated those snapshots of unConnor in before-land.

At morning break, Oliver asked, 'How's it going? How's the maths?'

Connor smiled. 'Numbers are happy.'

Brad explained, 'Next month, he's sixteen. He's okay to start uni. We got it in writing yesterday, subject to him not being charged by the police.'

'No problem,' said Alice. 'Liam's in the firing line, not Connor.'

Brad turned to his brother. 'You're going to work with numbers all the time, aren't you, Connor?'

Eagerness and excitement etched on his face, Connor answered, 'Yes. I'm the prime number ... '

'Expert,' Brad told him.

'Yes, that.' He looked as if he'd just won the national lottery.

'By the way,' Alice said to Oliver, 'I worked it out.'

'What?'

'Liam Darby doesn't leak anything to the police. Not about roller skates, not about anything. So it was you who grassed up Connor.'

Oliver shook his head, but his reddening cheeks gave him away.

'You've blown it,' Alice said. 'Blown it with Connor, blown it with Hattie. She's not as touchy about fairness as me, but I bet she still won't forgive you. It's your own fault for being such a jerk.'

It was a still night, so quiet that it was eerie. At two o'clock, Mr Markham was wide awake, propped up against the headboard. His wife was lying down but he could tell from her breathing that she was not asleep. 'You know where we've been going wrong, don't you?' he said in a whisper that sounded like a yell.

'Yes.'

Silence.

'It's like a death in the family,' Mr Markham added. 'We mourn, but there comes a point where we have to get over it and get on with our lives.' He turned his head towards his wife but he couldn't see her face in the darkness. 'You know how we should deal with this?'

'I think so. What do you think?'

'We've got to tell ourselves we've got a new son with the same name as the other one. We should be grateful. It's like having a new member of the family: a third boy.'

Mrs Markham let out a long breath. 'Yes.'

'Tomorrow, I'll put the old photographs away. Tomorrow, we start again. All right?'

Quietly, Mrs Markham replied, 'I guess it's for the best.'

The police had interviewed everybody. They'd had tests carried out by forensics. They'd reached their conclusions. They'd separated the good guys from the bad. But they hadn't got their hands on the baddest.

First up: Alice Foley.

'What's your relationship with Connor Markham?' the SIO asked.

'Relationship?' Alice hesitated for a moment and then said, 'Just a friend, I suppose.'

'What's your relationship with Liam Darby?'

'Totally not a friend. An acquaintance through Connor.'

Together, Alice and the officer established what happened at Mrs Dungate's house, aided by Alice's photographic evidence. Her account matched what the others said as well.

Next up: Liam Darby.

He was clearly livid with Alice Foley, Connor's brother, Hattie Townsend and Mrs Dungate. 'Alice Foley,' he snapped. 'Hot chick on the outside but inside ... Bitch!' He also seemed angry with himself. He'd walked straight into a trap like an innocent little kid. He probably thought he was too slick and streetwise to be overhauled by the likes of Brad and Alice. 'Fuck 'em.' Presumably recognizing that he was batting on a bowler's wicket, he muttered, 'I's saying nothing till I gets me a solicitor.'

'Fair enough,' the SIO replied with a smile. 'You're going to need one. Might as well be now.'

Lord Williams was a short, bearded antique collector. He lacked the stature implied by his title. He denied everything. When a search of his collection revealed Mr Dungate's wartime medals, he claimed he'd bought them in good faith from Liam Darby at GG's. When he was shown a picture of Joy Patterson, he denied knowing her, seeing her, having anything to do with her.

'So,' the SIO continued, 'you won't mind supplying us with a sample of DNA.'

'What on earth for?' Lord Williams asked, plainly startled.

'We kept certain items of Miss Patterson's clothing and they contain DNA of an unknown origin. If you didn't meet her, it can't possibly be yours, so you wouldn't mind us running a check. You'd have nothing to fear.'

'No. That's ... ridiculous. I ... My lawyer will have something to say ... '

'This isn't about receiving stolen goods any more,' the police officer said. 'We're way more serious. I'm having that DNA.'

When Lord Williams' DNA matched the samples on Joy's clothes, he was charged with child sexual abuse. Then he dished the dirt on everyone else.

Assured that the abusers were behind bars, three girls agreed to make statements. Their accounts followed the same pattern. 'They got me doing things with them I didn't want to do. You know. They were nice at first. Bought me all sorts. Designer stuff, drinks, weed, anything really. Then it got out of control. They gave me other stuff I didn't want to take. I don't know what it was, but it made me do anything.'

The SIO now had a direct connection between Liam Darby, the Dungate medals, GG's nightclub and Joy Patterson's abusers. But Rowling was nowhere to be found. The SIO put out an alert to every airport and other point of exit from the country, but Gareth Gregor Rowling eluded the lot. Exasperated, the SIO said, 'He's looked after his own skin and abandoned everyone else – from a doorman to a lord.'

'And Liam Darby in between,' the custody sergeant added.

The SIO nodded and sighed. 'They're going to take the rap while the ringleader's sunning himself on some foreign beach.'

'Or setting up another club somewhere,' she replied ominously.

Connor had become a star again. He was setting some sort of record for going to university early. He'd escaped the law's clutches. He could do gymnastics with gigantic numbers in his brain. Best of all, he'd tackled a thug with a knife using his bare hands. He'd stopped Alice getting stabbed.

When Brad and Alice went up to him after lessons, he was surrounded by a crowd that included Hattie. Brad had come to take him home and Alice had come to console her friend who was always left distraught.

'Okay,' Alice cried. 'Break it up. We're out of here.'

The crowd shuffled slowly away. After all, they were mostly boys and boys mostly let Alice have whatever she wanted.

Watching the Markham brothers leaving through the school gates, Hattie said, 'I don't know if it's going to work out for him and all. I really don't.'

'What'll happen will happen.'

'I still don't know exactly what he was doing with those girls, taking them to GG's.'

'No,' Alice replied. 'Face it. You never will.'

'But ... '

'Look. He was never a deep thinker. Maybe he didn't think it through. Either you have faith he didn't get them into trouble on purpose or you don't. You're not sure, you don't have faith, so de-friend him.'

'What about you?' Hattie asked.

'Me? I have faith.'

'Really?'

'Really,' Alice replied.

On their way home, Brad said to his brother, 'We're taking a detour down Springfield Road. Try to remember what you've got to say and do. Remember what the police gave you.'

Connor looked tense.

'Don't worry if you forget,' said Brad. 'I'll help.'

They turned and walked up to Mrs Dungate's house.

More nervous about visitors than she used to be, the old woman peered at them through a narrow gap. Then she undid the chain lock and flung the door wide open, saying, 'Colin! And ... your brother.'

Connor glanced helplessly at Brad, as if to say, 'I told you she's got a dreadful memory.'

Mrs Dungate invited them in, sat them down, disappeared for a few minutes and then reappeared with a tray that she placed on the table.

'It's nice of you two to come and see me again,' she said as she poured three cups of tea and offered round the plate of slightly soggy biscuits.

'Are you all right now?' Brad asked.

'I must be made of stern stuff.'

Brad nodded. 'You've had your locks changed? Not that there's anyone trying to get in any more.'

'A nice man did it, but he said he didn't drink tea.' She shook her head in amazement. 'I'm just struggling to work out which key's which. It's a bit … confusing.'

'The police told you how it all turned out, didn't they?'

'Yes, I think so.'

'Connor's got some good news about your medals, haven't you, Connor?'

'Have I?'

Surrounded by bungling brains, Brad's warm smile showed through. 'Yes. The police said you could return them to their rightful owner.'

'Oh, yes.'

Connor yanked a row of medals out of his schoolbag and held them out to Mrs Treble Nineteen.

Her gnarled hand grasped her husband's wartime trophies and tears came to her face. 'Oh. That's lovely. Really lovely. After everything that's happened, it's marvellous to … ' Overcome, she ran out of words. She stroked the display of medals fondly as if it were her husband's long-lost hand.

At the Institute, Courtney had finished another one-way chat with her grandad and, out of habit, looked around for Connor. His usual place was empty.

Ranji noticed Courtney's reaction and smiled. 'Yes. It's strange without him.'

Courtney nodded. 'Has he stopped coming altogether now?'

'Officially, yes. Sometimes he wanders back in – a reflex action, really – but he won't show up much from now on. His family's come to terms with the fact that Connor lives for today and tomorrow. All his yesterdays are still lost in fog.'

'That's not so bad. It's all about the future, isn't it? He's got much more of that than … most of the people in here.' Courtney's measured gaze lingered on her senile grandfather.

Ranji agreed. 'He's young, lively and he's got a real talent. Connor will be fine.'

In a solemn voice, Courtney added, 'In a way, I'll miss him not being here to talk to, though.'

'I know.'

'He could say some funny things – and do some funny things – but … I liked him.'

Dr Nawaz was looking on the bright side. She had failed to repair Connor's memory but at least her unit had given him a key to the future. She had given him the gift of numbers. Ranji touched Courtney's arm affectionately. 'Thanks for your help with him. You really made a difference.' Inwardly, Ranji was grateful that one cloud on the horizon had not developed into a storm. Connor had been weaned away from Courtney not only by maths but also by attraction to a girl of a more suitable age.

When her phone rang, Hattie Townsend snapped it up straightaway. 'Yes?' But it was only Oliver. Again. Again, she refused to meet him in town. Again, she refused to have anything to do with him. After all, she agreed with Alice that it must have been Oliver who had tried to get Connor put away by tipping off the police. She accused him of being cruel, hard-hearted, treacherous and all. Again, she rejected him and hung up.

Alone, she waited for endless hours for a call she knew Connor would never make.

CHAPTER 35

Connor's second life took off at the age of 16 years.

It was the university's open day and Connor was on show. Of course, Connor did not appreciate the veiled messages that his new employer was sharing with the public. By exhibiting Connor, the university was encouraging young people into maths, proving that it didn't discriminate against the disabled, and flaunting its ability to spot a rising star. Connor was just enjoying himself. He'd forgotten how good it was to be the centre of attention, but now he was lapping it up. If he could have remembered, he would have likened it to facing a penalty kick and the crowd chanting his name once he'd made another stunning save.

Right now, the last of the ten people seated in a semicircle in front of him selected a number between one and a hundred and said it aloud. Connor filed the number in his brain, along with the other nine, and nodded. Starting again at the first person, he regurgitated all ten numbers without a single error. Very quickly, he summed the ten numbers and gave the answer. It took more effort and more time to multiply them all together, but he did it. The student operating the laptop that displayed all the answers on a screen out of Connor's sight could hardly keep up with him.

Freed from unwanted images of a pink puddle and demands to remember before-land, Connor was able to devote his brain entirely to maths. Two at a time, volunteers stood up and Connor added, subtracted, divided and multiplied their two numbers. He called out the answers almost immediately. His figures always agreed with the numbers on the display screen behind him, but sometimes Connor got there first.

There were occasional outbursts of applause and rumblings from the onlookers. 'How does he do it?' 'Amazing.' 'They say he's only sixteen.' 'Never seen anything like that.' 'Rachel Riley's a dunce compared to this boy.'

There was one visitor who looked particularly pleased and impressed. When the session came to an end, she approached Connor and said, 'That was brilliant.'

'Alice.' Connor was proud of his ability to fascinate an audience, but he was even more proud to remember this girl's name. He was also delighted that he'd paraded his skills in front of her.

'Totally cool.'

Connor shrugged it off. 'Easy.' He was not being modest, just honest. For him it came naturally. 'It's like doing the scores in … ' Remembering the name for ten-pin bowling was far more difficult than maths, so he mimed the action instead.

Alice smiled and nodded. 'I always knew you were a show-off.' Referring to the retreating audience, she said, 'They loved it. You had them totally hooked. My mum's coming into the next session. She wants to do a report on it for the local press.'

Unsure, Connor nodded.

'Is there a limit to the number of sums you can do?'

'A what?'

'A limit. Just how many sums can you do?'

Connor didn't know. 'My brain's a sort of infinity,' he said flaunting a mathematical word he'd already learned and retained at university. 'It's got a big hole where most things go. Numbers don't, though.'

'How do you manage getting into work every day?'

'A man called … ' He began to struggle.

Alice guessed. 'Someone who works here gives you a lift and takes you home?'

Connor nodded.

'How come you remember me, Connor? You know my name these days.'

'I remember things by giving them numbers. Like Miss Sayell. She's Six Eight Eleven.'

Alice smiled again. 'To you, am I a number as well, then?'

Connor nodded as if it were something to be ashamed about.

'What number?'

'Six.'

'Just six? Is that all? Why six?'

'Because … er … ' Reddening, Connor said, 'Six is a perfect number.'

Alice looked away for a moment and composed herself. 'Hey. When you've finished, do you want to come for profiteroles, then down the youth club?'

Connor looked at her, grabbed her arm and beamed. 'Yeah. Happy.' Profs and a girl like Alice. He could feel the tears of joy beginning to form.

Coming up behind them, the laptop-student slapped Connor on his back. 'That was awesome. You slayed 'em. If we get enough volunteers in the next batch, do you want to try with fifteen numbers?'

'Er … yes.'

Once Connor's helper had gone to find more chairs, Alice asked, 'How do you get on with the students?'

'They're happy with me. Very happy.'

'Are you happy with them?'

'Yes.'

'And what do you actually do?' Before Connor could ask her what she meant, she added, 'What's your job here?'

Delighted to be able to show off another university word, he replied, 'I'm checking a formula for all prime numbers.'

'No regrets, then?' Alice said.

Connor didn't understand.

'You're still pleased you got the job?'

Connor thought about it for a second. Sullenly, he answered, 'No. I don't like it.'

Shocked, Alice muttered, 'Really?'

Connor's expression changed. He grinned at her like a small tickled child. 'No. That was a … '

'Joke?'

'Yes.'

Alice sighed and smiled. Clearly, she expected that sort of banter from someone normal but not from Connor. In mock rebuke, she said, 'You're picking up too many bad habits, Connor Markham. You'll be like everyone else soon.' Smiling widely, she turned and walked away.

Returning with extra chairs, the student said, 'Did I hear that girl asking you on a date?'

'A date?' Connor queried.

'She was asking you to go to a club with her, wasn't she?'

'Yes.'

Distributing the chairs, the helper shook his head. 'Some people get all the luck. Never happens to me – not with ones that look like her anyway. Gorgeous.' He gazed at the larger layout and then said, 'Tell you what, Connor. Let's get this last one over with quickly, then you can go after her. When you get an offer like that, you don't want to miss out – not even for the noble art of entertaining the public with maths.'

At the youth club, Connor gazed at Alice, standing in front of him, holding a drink. She was truly dazzling. He didn't work out carefully what to do next, he didn't plan his move. He reacted to an impulse. He didn't question the urge any more than he questioned how to do maths. He just did it. Yet he was better at maths than anything else. Unannounced, he flung his arms round her.

She let out a shriek of surprise and the glass in her hand went tumbling, spilling her drink all down her clothes.

Connor jumped back in dismay.

Alice looked at him and said, 'Hey, not so fast! I'm not sure I'm ready … '

In despair, Connor interrupted. 'You're unhappy with me.'

'No, I'm not.' As soon as she said it, Alice had a sudden revelation. 'I'm really not.' Genuinely, she surprised herself. She looked down at her best black dress and then shrugged. 'It's all right. It's only a dress and it hardly shows.' She stepped up to Connor and whispered into his ear, 'Forget it.'

With a huge grin, Connor replied, 'Yes, I can do that.'

By the same author

THE OUTER REACHES

A world inhabited by two distinct and non-interbreeding humanoid species: **majors** *(the majority) and* **outers**. *The two races are outwardly similar, but they have different talents, different genetics and different body chemistry.*

In this world, meet major Troy Goodhart and outer Lexi Iona Four. They form an amazing crime-fighting partnership.

BODY HARVEST

When the body of an outer is discovered in the woods, young detective Troy Goodhart and forensic specialist Lexi Iona Four are partnered on the case. Then two more bodies are discovered, and all three corpses are found to have body parts missing. Somebody is killing with a purpose. As major Troy and outer Lexi unpick the case, they enter a complex, dark world of deception, where one false move will mean death.

234

LETHAL OUTBREAK

Three scientists wearing airtight protective suits are found dead in a sealed, high-security laboratory. They had been studying an unknown substance brought to Earth by the recently returned Mars probe. Was this substance responsible for their deaths? Was it an accident – or could it be murder?

FATAL CONNECTION

Is it a coincidence when four people die at the same time with the horrible symptoms of mercury poisoning? Especially when all four lived in different parts of the country and didn't seem to have anything in common. Is there a connection between the victims? Can Troy Goodhart and forensic specialist Lexi Iona Four stay alive long enough to solve this mysterious crime?

BLOOD AND BONE

A van is found crashed and abandoned, with a cargo of brains, bones, blood and eyeballs still on board. Inspection of the ghastly collection soon identifies it as animal rather than human. Most are from endangered tigers and rhinos. Who or what could justify slaughtering animals on such a scale?

Malcolm Rose is an established, award-winning author, noted for his gripping crime/thriller stories – all with a solid scientific basis.

Before becoming a full-time writer, Malcolm was a university lecturer and researcher in chemistry.

He says that chemistry and writing are not so different. *'In one life, I mix chemicals, stew them for a while and observe the reaction. In the other, I mix characters, stir in a bit of conflict and, again, observe the outcome.'*